MW00718873

# TWO BENT TREES

*An American Revolutionary War Novel*

## DAVID G. TIPPENS

First edition 2016

Published in the USA by *thewordverve inc.* (**www.thewordverve.com**)

eBook ISBN:        978-1-941251-59-1
Paperback ISBN:    978-1-941251-60-7
Hardback ISBN:     978-1-941251-67-6

Library of Congress Control Number: 2016933458

~~~~~

**Two Bent Trees**
A Book with Verve by *thewordverve inc.*

*Cover artwork by Rick Sanders*
http://www.strangetimesbysanders.com

*Full cover design by Robin Krauss*
http://www.bookformatters.com

*Interior book design by Bob Houston*
http://facebook.com/eBookFormatting/info

# Chapter One
## BENT AND BATTERED

T he young man reloaded his musket and thought, *Farm work doesn't seem quite so bad right now.* Most anything would be more pleasant than the sights and sounds he had already witnessed this day. But the day and the task before him weren't over yet.

Still, it had been a marvelous June afternoon in this year of 1775, on Breed's Hill just across the Charles River from Boston, Massachusetts. Young Robert Loxley Glynne and his comrades-in-arms had repulsed the British army's attempts to drive them out of their fortifications on Charlestown peninsula. What made this so marvelous was that the finest, toughest, most disciplined army in the world had been stymied by a ragtag bunch of farmers and shopkeepers . . . patriots who were standing up for what they believed.

From early morning, it had been a noisy, dirty, smoky day of war as the British warships bombarded the fortifications and set the town of Charlestown ablaze. The cannon fire and musketry had become so commonplace that the citizen soldiers in the fortifications had ceased to flinch when shots hit nearby. They had all stood fiercely and bravely when the British regulars tried to overrun them. Each time, they held their fire until directed by the officers to shoot nearly point-blank into the red faces of the enemy. Each time, the red-coated ranks seemed to crumple and melt and flow back in the opposite direction. The fortifications remained intact and out of British hands, at least for now.

Young Robert Glynne had been right in the thick of things. Firing his rifle and reloading repeatedly, concentrating on hitting the target and listening for the commands of the officers. He was hardly aware that his rifle had grown hot from being fired so many times. He was also unaware of some of the men around him falling, unaware of the blood, screams, and explosions.

It was relatively quieter and calmer right now as the citizen soldiers from the surrounding areas continued to work on the fortifications and to watch the British preparing for yet another assault. They meant business this time, for the red-coated soldiers were removing their heavy packs for this attempt. They had underestimated the resolve of those holding the earthworks before. Not so this time.

Robert watched with the others as the British prepared for the next attack. He had killed Redcoats before today, and though he felt a horrible gut-wrenching feeling of repugnance, he held stronger feelings of a just cause—that it was necessary and vital for his own survival. It was kill or be killed, and he had no intention of letting the British kill him as long as he was able to do anything about it.

The chatter of the drums suddenly changed to signal the columns of infantry to move forward. Robert and his comrades watched the impressive, spellbinding sight of the red-coated soldiers, properly dressed, in their orderly lines. The defenders quickly looked to their weapons, checking to make sure they were loaded and primed. Some anxiously looked over the parapet with ashen faces and taut lips. Others sat with their heads down, awaiting orders and thinking of loved ones and memories of home. Officers paced back and forth behind their respective commands.

Robert looked to his right at his young friend, Verdin Girard. Simultaneously and wordlessly, they extended their right hands and grasped them in a firm handshake, their eye contact strong and steady. They had met on board ship when they served on the HMS *Hawke*. Neither of them had any real close friends at the time. But the trials of the past few months and especially of this day had forged a bond of friendship that would endure the rest of their lives. They quickly smiled at each other as a reminder that they would face this ordeal as close friends and could be depended upon as such.

Shells from the British warships rose from the flame-belching mouths of the cannon to fall screaming, shrieking, and bursting. They were hitting mainly on and in front of the earthworks. Pieces of dirt, rock, and shards of metal filled the air, along with lots of black powder smoke that made it seem like a cloudy day, although it wasn't. Time seemed to stand still to the defenders as the bursting shells, smoke, explosions, confusion, and anxiety all worked to numb the senses.

Suddenly the officers began bellowing orders to stand and take aim. Every defender capable of obeying complied, standing at the ready, weapons aimed and cocked to fire. At the command to fire, the defenders added a roar and wall of flame to the noise, confusion, and sights of war. The volley again thinned the British ranks, but this time those standing kept coming in numbers greater than the defenders could stop. Without wavering, the Redcoats plowed forward, not stopping at the bottom of the sloping earthworks. They swarmed up the sides of the fortifications, some firing at defenders as they came on. Some stopped on top of the parapet and reorganized into ranks to fire down into the defenders struggling to reload and fire, and fight hand-to-hand with bayonet-yielding British soldiers.

Robert had fired his rifle at the command to fire and, without looking to see if he hit the target, dropped to one knee to quickly reload. He had just cocked the piece to fire again when a British soldier appeared on the redoubt above him, weapon poised to fire. Robert fell back to a sitting position and fired at point-blank range. The Redcoat recoiled as though kicked in the teeth, and fell backward out of Robert's sight.

Dropping his rifle, Robert unslung the English longbow from his back and in one swift, graceful movement, pulled an arrow from the scabbard, notched it, and let it fly. The target was a British officer standing on the parapet. Struck in the neck, he fell on his face before Robert, blood gushing from his mouth and the arrow protruding from both sides of his neck. Again, Robert fitted an arrow and fired at another soldier who was coming at him with bayonet extended. The arrow struck the soldier right where the shoulder straps crossed over his heart, and he too fell at Robert's feet.

Whirling from side to side, arrow notched and ready to fire, Robert looked for his friend, Verdin. He saw him a few feet away locked in a fierce struggle with a British soldier trying to bayonet him. Robert slung his longbow over his shoulder and grabbed the British soldier's musket from behind him, twisting it out of his grip. He then rammed it into the man's chest. Pulling the bayonet free of the dead soldier, Robert quickly stuck his hand out to help Verdin to his feet.

Together, they backed toward the rear of the redoubt, calling for other comrades to do the same, as it was apparent the British were in and around them in overwhelming numbers and intent on killing and capturing as many as they could. By now, the rebel Americans had begun to slowly and orderly evacuate their Breed's Hill fortification and make their way toward those on Bunker Hill. Suddenly a group of Redcoats standing on top of the earthen wall let go a volley.

Robert and Verdin both turned to fire, but had no chance. Two musket balls struck Robert: one passing clean through his left thigh, the other glancing off the left side of his skull. A ball struck Verdin in the shoulder, spinning him around, and lodged there. Robert was knocked unconscious instantly, but his body refused to accept that state of affairs. Both of his arms dropped slowly to his sides, and he stood there staring blankly for several seconds.

In those few seconds, Verdin, who was now facing Robert, saw the wound in Robert's thigh, and then looked up to see the bloody wound to the side of his head and blank, unseeing eyes. Not yet feeling pain from his own wound, Verdin instantly stooped and lifted Robert across his back. Without stopping to look around, he ran with his burden while the British troops on the parapet reloaded. *Keep moving, keep moving.* Verdin stayed focused on getting his friend to safety.

In just a few moments, they were relatively safe with other refugees hidden from sight of the British by the uneven terrain and undergrowth. Keeping to the west side of Bunker Hill, it was quite a while before Verdin stopped to carefully lay the injured man on his back; the sound of gunfire could still be heard in the distance. Verdin looked around quickly while he got his breath. The path he had somehow taken had led him away from the greatest number of American soldiers streaming to the rear for safety. Every now and then he would see people hurrying along— sometimes small groups of civilians, sometimes entire American families who felt compelled to abandon their homes to the British.

He quickly assessed the situation and realized he needed to get help, not only for Robert, but for himself as well. Their wounds were going to need some attention, and they would need a place to eat and rest until they could heal. He pulled the unconscious Robert to a sitting position, then stooped to sling him over his back. In that fashion, he headed west, about a mile and a half from the battlefield onto the road going to Lexington.

With head down, blood streaming from the both of them, Verdin trudged up the road down which the harried British regulars had come after their disastrous march to Lexington and Concord. He swelled with pride every time he thought of those events of just two months ago. The British had certainly taken a licking that day, and they had been severely handled today too. Not something they would be forgetting for a long, long time, Verdin figured.

People were coming and going on the road to Lexington, with some walking wounded and others carrying bloody, sometimes lifeless forms. No one could help Verdin as he walked, head down, a determined purpose to his gait. He never really gave anyone any time to assist him as he trudged on toward Lexington. Civilians trying to help the wounded would glance at them every now and then, but Verdin kept pressing on toward Lexington.

Verdin stopped several times to rest his weary body for a few minutes. Then he would continue on his way. It was still daylight, late in the evening of this long June day, when he finally stopped near a mill.

He was now in pitiful shape himself from loss of blood and exhaustion. He laid his friend under some trees next to the millstream. Tearing a strip of cloth from his own shirt, he wet it in the stream, then set about cleaning their wounds. Robert was still unconscious, but the wounds were not bleeding so badly now. Verdin's own wound had grown steadily more painful as the day and his efforts wore on. It hurt severely to move his left arm, and he was beginning to feel the effects of loss of blood more and more.

Just out of sight of the road among the trees and next to the millstream, Verdin lay next to his friend for a few minutes' rest. He closed his eyes and listened to the sound of voices passing on the road, the rush of horses' hooves, and the clatter of wagons and coaches. Verdin heard his friend moan and move slightly in his sleep before returning to deep, regular breathing of slumber.

It was just breaking light in the east when Verdin awoke. He sat up slowly, taking in everything around him, his memory and recollection coming at once to this moment in time. He looked over at Robert, who seemed to be sleeping peacefully. As soon as he'd cleared his mind of sleep, Verdin winced at the pain in his shoulder—it now hurt with a vengeance. Upon trying to stand, he found he was dizzy and lightheaded. He gained his feet, but carrying someone else was out of the question in his condition. He was feeling feverish as well. They needed help if they were to survive this situation.

He winced, holding back the urge to yell from the pain, as he took off his bloody coat and tucked it around his unconscious friend. He then straightened up and cleared his head to determine the best course of action.

Without knowing why, he decided to follow the stream instead of going to the road to look for help. He had gone about a hundred yards downstream when he came to a rock wall that ended at the stream but ran in a perpendicular direction away from it, disappearing through the trees. Verdin crossed the wall, gingerly holding his left arm across his body with his right hand.

Shortly, he came to a small spring that had been dug out to provide a small rock-lined pool of clear, cold water. The water ran from the pool and tumbled gently down a deep-cut trough into the millstream. Not far away were the house and barns of a small farm. The house, though not very large, was well kept, as were the barns and other outbuildings. Verdin knelt down and drank from the spring for several seconds before walking toward the barn in back of the house.

As he neared the barn, Verdin began to see what he thought were flashing lights in the sky. He also began to notice that the early morning sky—still gray as daylight struggled to make an appearance—was turning upside down. He thought how foolish for him to be able to see the sky and tree line between the upturned toes of his boots. Then just before completely losing consciousness, he realized that he had fallen to the ground and the effort to remain upright was no longer required. He smiled in tremendous relief as he succumbed to the darkness.

***

Wilbraham Medford was more than a farmer. He was something of a local veterinarian to his neighbors. He had helped many a poor, sick animal during the last thirty years. Along with that came the responsibility of putting his skills to work occasionally on human beings in need of a doctor's care. He had treated wounds, set bones, sewed up cuts, removed splinters, and nursed many other ailments. So it was no great shock to him to see a man with a gunpowder-blackened face, wearing torn, dirty, and bloody clothes, lying on the ground outside his barn. He correctly assumed "wounded soldier" and went into action to help the injured man.

SCALE:
½ Mile

# Battle of Bunker's (Breed's) Hill

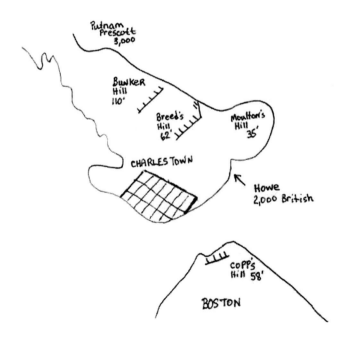

Putnam
Prescott
3,000

BUNKER
Hill
110'

Breed's
Hill
62'

Moulton's
Hill
35'

CHARLES TOWN

Howe
2,000 British

COPP'S
Hill 58'

BOSTON

# Chapter Two
## UNTANGLING THE PAST

When Verdin Girard became aware of what was going on again, a day had passed during which the musket ball had been removed, his dirt- and gunpowder-begrimed body thoroughly washed, his clothes mended and washed, and warm broth poured down his throat. He was unconscious through the whole ordeal, which Wilbraham explained to him later was a blessing.

When he opened his eyes, he was staring up at the ceiling of an attic bedroom. He had no idea where he was, and it took a little time for him to remember everything up to when things went black. He moved his eyes around and surveyed the neat little room with a window visible several feet from the foot of his bed through which he could see the darkening horizon.

To his surprise, on a small single bed just like his own, his friend, Robert Glynne, was lying just to his right. Robert's head was bandaged, and his left thigh was bandaged and propped up on sheets and quilts. The rest of him was covered in clean, white bed linen. Red spots could be seen on both bandages as blood seeped through from the wounds. Robert was still unconscious, lying motionless, eyes closed, breathing deeply.

Verdin wearily sank back down on his own clean linen and listened to the sounds around him. He could not hear any cannon fire. What had happened in Boston? He could hear birds in the trees outside the window. He could hear the *clip clop* of horses' hooves faintly. He could hear sheep or goats bleating not too far away and something that sounded like a cowbell. He could hear voices, both male and female, from somewhere in or near the house.

He could smell the wood of the house, a wood fire, the clean bedclothes, and a faint medicine smell, like some sort of liniment. His stomach growled, and that was when he also smelled the food. He could sure use some of that.

In a few minutes, Verdin heard a swishing noise, then steps on the staircase. The lady of the house appeared at a small doorway just to the right of the window. The swishing noise had been her full skirts brushing the sides of the narrow staircase. She held a cloth in her hand and smiled a gentle smile when she saw that Verdin's eyes were open and full of questions.

"I see you have slept enough to be wondering where you are and what has happened," she said, as she stopped at the foot of the beds. Verdin gathered himself a moment and then addressed the slender, attractive older woman who looked down at him with warm, dark blue eyes.

"Yes, ma'am," he said, "I feel much better and rested, and I sure need to thank you and whoever else is responsible for all your kind help." As he spoke, he tried to move to a sitting position by propping on one elbow. The motion immediately sent searing pain through his wounded shoulder. Holding back a cry of pain, he grimaced and sank back in the bed.

"There, there now!" exclaimed the kindly lady, with a look of concern on her face. "Don't be doing injury to yourself. Just lie back and let yourself have the time to heal," she said in the crisp New England dialect of the day.

Verdin sank back to his position on the pillows and closed his eyes until the pain subsided to the bearable throb it had been before his hasty move. He then looked into the kindly blue eyes while she fed him spoonsful of mouth-watering, steamy clam chowder. She spoke in a soft voice barely above a whisper while she patiently fed him, telling him that her name was Mayanne Medford, and that "Mayanne" was one name, not a first and second name. Her mother had not given her a middle name. She told him how her husband had found him lying on the ground and how he had roused himself long enough to tell her husband about his injured friend. Wilbraham had immediately enlisted the help of the other family members and soon had both of them in the house, where their wounds had been attended to.

Verdin turned his head to look at Robert, who remained unconscious. "Mrs. Medford, how is my friend doing?" he asked, as he slowly turned back to look at her eyes.

She dropped her eyes from his and shook her head slowly before looking back up at him. "We've done all we know to do for him," she said. "Now it's up to the Good Lord and time . . . and the strength of your friend. Only time will tell."

The chowder was good and warm and, when followed with a drink of cool water, brought about a state of sleepiness and a feeling of comfort and security. Soon Verdin sank into a deep, peaceful sleep in spite of his throbbing shoulder.

*** 

Meanwhile, the unconscious Robert Glynne was totally unaware of his current situation or location. His mind was off on a trip of its own, released from the bonds of his body by the sudden blow of the musket ball glancing off his skull. In his mind's eye, his body immediately embarked on a journey back into the mists of time from which he came. It was as if his body had taken flight, slowly at first, then gathering momentum until he was zipping along above the trees and houses, smoke, shells, and running soldiers. Over the terrain of Charlestown Peninsula. Over the gray, misty waters of the Atlantic Ocean. Then he could see the green fields and forests of England speeding past him, and suddenly his childhood home appeared. It was almost as if he'd fallen out of the sky and landed on his feet on the path to the small rock barn that stood behind the small rock house, which stood two miles from the small village of Claysdale and next to a small stream that bordered Bowland Forest. Morecambe Bay was only ten or twelve miles northwest.

In his mind's eye, young Robert went about his chores, cleaning the stalls, putting out fresh hay, and checking the hen's nests for eggs. He went about his tasks happily, whistling softly, barely audible to anyone but himself. He remembered his mother and younger brother and sister were in the warm small house, where he had just left them after a hot meal of beef stew and coarse bread. Not fancy eating by any stretch of the imagination, but tasty, hot, and filling.

His mind wandered, thinking of his father, who was away at sea. He was first mate of the merchant vessel owned by Lord Burntthorne whose estate was nearby. The captain was their neighbor, landlord, and young Robert's uncle: his mother's older brother, Jonathan Loxley. Jonathan had taken Robert Christopher Glynne, young Robert's father, under his wing even before he had married Robert's young, beautiful, strong-willed sister.

The Loxley family were descendants of the famous outlaw of Nottingham and Sherwood Forest of nearly two hundred years ago, who allegedly robbed from the rich to give to the poor. Most people now believed that to be just a bunch of tall tales, but the Loxley family members knew from written family history and oral tradition that it was more than just a myth.

Another part of the family tradition that had been handed down through the generations was the mastery of the English longbow. Captain Jonathan was an expert longbowman and had begun teaching and training his nephew, young Robert, at an early age. By the time of his thirteenth birthday, Robert, known by his friends and close family as Rob, had attained a level of skill and expertise with the longbow that many grown men would have been proud to have. Rob practiced every day, and not only learned to shoot the weapon but mastered the art of making the bows and arrows as well.

Rob's mind continued to wander over his recent past and family history. The Loxley family, of more modest means in recent years than they had enjoyed under King Richard the Lionheart, valued education and enlightenment probably more than most families. Rob's mother had received a sound education for women of her day and, during her teen years, worked as a teacher for some of the nearby families who had the means to hire a teacher for their children. Young Robert and his siblings, of course, received the same tutelage and, as a result, were well read and better educated than most children of their social standing.

Rob's father had been lucky enough to receive a better-than-average education due to Lady Burntthorne's efforts to help educate the children of their community. While she was alive, she hired well-qualified teachers to educate not only her children but the neighboring children as well, at her own expense. This had been against the wishes of her husband, the dour, humorless Lord Burntthorne, but she had gone against his will and done it anyway.

So it was that the farm boy, Robert Christopher Glynne, received his early years of education alongside that of the youngest son of the Burntthornes, Edward Burson Burntthorne. Some of the brightest teachers of the time were their instructors. Of course, young Burson's formal education continued after the death of his mother, which brought young Glynne's education to a screeching halt, along with that of the other children of nearby families. Lady Burntthorne became quite ill one night after she had retired to her bedchamber, and died two days later from a high fever. Robert Glynne, Rob's father, always held her in great admiration for making it possible for him to receive a much higher than average education for his day. He also was grateful to her for making it possible for him to meet the future Mrs. Glynne, who was also a pupil at the Burntthorne School.

Rob's mother, Faith was thirteen years old when she came to school for what turned out to be the last year of the Burntthorne School. She was two years younger than the handsome fifteen-year-old farm boy, but they hit it off at once. He, with his long, straight, brown hair and green eyes, and she, with her long, straight, auburn hair and green eyes, became fast friends. He met her older brother Jonathan within a few days of her starting school. They, too, became good friends while Jonathan was home on leave from the sea. Faith and Robert's friendship blossomed into a courtship, and they were wed five years later.

Robert had returned to the farm and worked there for three months. He spent his spare time with Faith, Jonathan, and other Loxley family members. Jonathan would fill him with tales of sailing on the seas and the ports of the world, including those of the English colonies in the New World. It was just a matter of time before the influence of the older man and the call of excitement, adventure, and sights of the world lured young Robert Glynne away from the farm.

Fourteen months after their wedding, Robert and Faith welcomed into the world their firstborn, a son born July 4, 1758. They named him Robert Loxley Glynne, after his father and maiden name of his mother. He was cheerful and lively from the first, walking before he was a year old, and always a curious fellow. Young Robert's parents were again blessed with a healthy child two years later, a daughter they named Hope. Their last child was born a year later, whom they named Christopher Jonathan Glynne. The three children grew up on the little farm on the northwest coast of England not far from the sea. They were unusually close to each other—went to church together, played together, studied together, and were taught by their well-educated parents.

When he was twelve years old, young Robert first went to sea with his father and Uncle Jonathan. After acquiring his "sea legs" and getting over the severe bouts of seasickness, the boy learned fast and became rather adept at climbing the rigging, furling and unfurling the large canvas sails. He adapted to the rigid discipline of the sailor's life and became accustomed to the confines of their cramped living quarters.

He loved the smells, sights, and beauty of the sea—and the time spent with his father and uncle. He continued his studies while at sea and even began to unravel the mysteries of navigation, and map and chart reading. Even more important to him, he learned to handle a cutlass, pistols, and rifles, becoming an excellent marksman by hitting empty casks thrown in the water as targets while the ship was underway. He even learned to load and fire the smoothbore cannon (two were left on board the merchant ship after the war with the French in the 1760s).

His father and Uncle Jonathan also shared with him their knowledge on the use of the English longbow. He spent hours, both at sea and at home, perfecting his abilities by shooting at all types of targets.

Young Robert's mind continued its journey of reminiscing: following those four and a half years of two or three months at a time at sea, and the intervening periods at home on the farm. Although he loved the sea, his heart and soul were more at home on the farm, fields, and forest areas nearby. His father had grown up on the family farm not many miles away and had passed on his love of the land, animals, and nature to all of his children, with Robert taking it most to heart.

Robert's mind swirled from event to event, remembering the smallest of details right down to the day that his world had been wrenched away. He was now in the care and confines of the Medford family, but as yet, his body was unable to get a grasp on his wandering mind, which was off on a journey of its own.

It had been midmorning on a Wednesday of that hot July nearly a year ago. His father and Uncle Jonathan were away preparing for the next voyage of the *Cardinal*, one of the merchant vessels belonging to Lord Burntthorne. They were due back in a day or two and would be home for a week before leaving. Young Robert was going to stay home this time in order to help with the fall harvest.

As with any farm, there was always something to do, and young Robert busied himself with various tasks. Pausing only a few minutes for the noonday meal, Robert continued his labors until the peak heat of the afternoon. He quickly slipped up the stepladder to his sleeping loft and gathered up his longbow, a sheath of arrows, and a hunting knife made from an old cutlass. He slung the bow and arrows over his shoulder and strapped the scabbard of leather with the knife around his waist so that the knife hung on his left side. Uncle Jonathan had given him the knife, which was handmade from a ground down cutlass. A wooden handle was fastened around the upper part of the shaft, which was sandwiched between two pieces of thin, dark, oak wood, rudely yet carefully shaped and crafted to fit a man's hand perfectly.

The old curved hilt of the cutlass had been modified into a simple hilt crosspiece that gave the knife the appearance of an elongated cross. The razor sharp edge rounded to form a point at the upper, thick edge of the knife, making it an efficient tool and hunting knife, as well as a formidable weapon.

Armed thusly, Rob headed toward the small stream that ran northwesterly beyond the barn. The dark and mysterious Forest of Bowland lay along the east side. Rob merrily splashed through the water, crossed a narrow strip of grass, and then plunged into the dark cool confines of the forest. He kept in a northerly direction, the stream to his left, for nearly a mile. A small meadow clearing on a slight knoll offered a view of the creek as it broadened into a small pond for the mill. In the distance above the roof of the mill building, the Burntthorne Manor House could be seen, its dark gray stone walls somberly overlooking the grassy fields and the tended crops in the valley.

Rob stood gazing at the tranquil scene as he often did when he had a chance. Suddenly, his hair pricked on the back of his neck and he instinctively crouched in the high grass, staying as motionless as possible. He had a feeling of being watched. He slowly turned his head to carefully look around him. He saw nothing. Not a soul was stirring in the vicinity, at least that he could see. *Probably just a silly boyish intuition.* Still he couldn't shake the feeling, and for several minutes he sat absolutely still, peering through the grass blades.

Finally, he rose to his feet and, staying stooped so as not to be visible above the grass, moved off to his right and into the forest shade. For the next hour or so, he roamed the forest. He peered at the small animals that scampered away, twice startling deer on their way to drink from the stream. Stealthily, he prowled the area between the two millstreams, the two meeting just before flowing into the millpond. The V-shaped area formed by the two babbling brooks was a paradise of sights, sounds, and smells, and he tirelessly roamed the area that he knew so well. He knew intimately about nine or ten square miles of the forest area, all lying to the northeast of his farm home, and the unnamed brook that began as a bubbling spring on the small rocky hill behind his home.

Hot and sweaty from running about and exploring during the heat of the day, young Rob found himself back near the millpond. He hastily decided to enjoy the refreshing waters of the pond and cool off a bit before starting home.

As he had often done before, either by himself, with his father, uncle, or some of the boys from the little village farther downstream, Rob quickly took off his weapons and clothes, except underwear, and walked out into the chilly water at the confluence of the two small streams. Cattails, reeds, and other water lilies grew along the shoreline and into the shallow water. Their abundance and height made it possible to wade and swim here completely undetected by anyone down at the mill.

Rob slowly sank down in the water and for several minutes let his body revel in the soothing water. Here, just above the ebb flow, the water was cooler than it was on down in the millpond. The water was only three- to eight-feet deep just about anywhere in the pond, except at the rock dam where it was considerably deeper.

This was one of the places where his Uncle Jonathan had taught him to swim and to float on his back. Young Rob stretched himself out flat on his back and anchored his heels in the soft dirt of the bank. For quite some time, he laid there, half submerged, gazing up at the blue sky and white clouds.

The position of the sun indicated that it was nearly midafternoon. He should start home soon. His mother would be looking for him. She was used to his wandering in the woodland and his quest for solitude at times. He didn't want to cause her undue worry though.

He decided to ease away from the bank a bit and float on down into the warmer waters of the pond before going home. With arms straight out from his sides, Rob gently nudged free of the bank with his toes and taking a deep breath, he floated slowly through the reeds on the slow current. Eyes closed, the warm sun and water enveloping his body, he drifted in paradise. Slowly turning with the current, his stretched out body actually turned a complete circle before seeming to settle on a headfirst course. Opening his eyes briefly, he saw he was safely out of sight, hidden by the reeds on both banks. Closing his eyes, he continued to float along, hardly moving at all, head pointed to the center of the pond.

Suddenly, his head softly bumped into an object, perhaps some reeds, or a floating tree branch. He had just opened his eyes and was turning his head to see what it was, when suddenly the world around him erupted into an explosion of water and ear-splitting shrieks. Totally unprepared for anything like this on the usually calm, tranquil visits to the pond, Rob instantly vied for a position in which to defend himself. Feet went down and instantly contacted the soft bottom of the pond. He straightened his knees and let forth a roar as he shot straight up out of the water, fists formed and ready to land a blow. His feet momentarily lost touch with the muddy bottom, and when they did settle back down, he scrambled to regain his balance and to find a stance better suited for defense. As he was scrambling and splashing about, water flying and splashing in his eyes, he continued to roar at the top of his lungs, half out of fright, half out of trying to scare away his attacker.

Meanwhile, his attacker was involved in an equally earnest attempt to regain balance and scare away the intruder. Both parties, blinded by the splashing water, hearing nearly deafened by the loud screams and roaring, simultaneously lowered heads to spring away from the perceived threat. However, instead of springing away from one another, both disoriented parties lunged toward each other. The resulting forehead-to-forehead collision and recoil caused both parties to grab their pained heads and stagger backward a step or two. They held their heads in their hands for several seconds, wiped the water from their eyes and, in a knocked-half-senseless manner, peered through their own fingers to behold what or who it was that had perpetrated this attack upon their persons!

The screaming and loud bellowing had ceased with the collision. Now there was only silence, except for the sound of water dripping from arms and shoulders, the sound of the water wheel and machinery of the mill about a hundred fifty yards away, and two hearts beating double-time.

Rob held his throbbing head, eyes blurred, half-seeing, and after a few seconds tried to focus on the figure before him. He shook his head, brushed his long hair back, and slowly dropped his arms to his sides.

What he saw took his breath away. His mouth fell open and his eyes nearly popped out of his head. It . . . she was the most beautiful creature he had ever seen.

Standing in mid-thigh-deep water was a young woman, hands still clasped to her head and a startled expression in her deep blue eyes. Her hair that she had quickly swept back out of her eyes and face was golden red with blond streaks. Her skin was a healthy glow of peach complexion that only comes from fair, freckled skin. Rob's eyes began darting quickly from one part of her to another as he vainly tried to take in all her beauty. She was tall, slender, and perfectly proportioned.

As he looked her over, he noticed that she was doing her own inspection, her gaze flitting across his body. He was immediately grateful for his toned physique, and he knew he was a decent-looking fellow. At least, she didn't seem put off.

They were breathless as they gazed at each other. Finally, as if by mutual consent, their eyes met and locked. Simultaneously, they let go a slight gasp . . . then silence again as they looked into each other's eyes. This lasted for several seconds, and then without further ado, they began slowly bending their knees to submerge their bodies, eventually sitting down to allow the water to cover them almost to their necks.

Sitting there in the warm water of the millpond, they stared into each other's eyes for several more seconds, still trying to catch their breaths. The geese down near the mill began an angry uproar about something, then the quiet sounds of the afternoon returned.

Rob finally lifted his chin and opened his mouth as if to speak. The

young woman instantly raised her white, delicate hand out of the water
and pressed her fingers slightly against his lips. Their eyes still locked.

She ever so slowly and gracefully withdrew her hand from his lips
and allowed a half smile to touch her lips, lighting up her face. Then a
sound that could only be described as a giggle came from within her as
she quickly stood in a flash of light and splashing water. She turned as
her body came out of the water and began walking and splashing noisily
toward the reed-covered bank only a few feet away. The prettiest
backside in all of England was thus turned in the direction of Robert's
staring, disbelieving eyes, and he watched as she quickly gained the
shore and dry footing. Once there, the fair maiden paused to toss her
head and fling her long, red tresses expertly in place down her back.

She raised her arms to allow her hands to brush back loose strands
around her face and ears. He hungrily took in every little movement she
made. She had turned sideways to him, and for a brief moment, he saw
her perfect silhouette: elbows up, head tilted slightly skyward, back
slightly arched as she stood on tiptoe for just a second.

Then she reached down and retrieved a pile of clothing that had been
lying on some bent reeds. Holding the bundle in her hands, she gathered
it over her chest and stomach, and turned briefly toward him. She stared
a moment, smiled, and then was gone into the reeds and trees beyond.

He had been so mesmerized, so completely lost in her breathtaking
beauty, that he just sat there for a moment as if the scene would replay
itself. Finally, he stood up, heart pounding, mouth half-open, water
glistening on his muscles, arms slightly extended toward her—or at least
where she had been—his palms upward. She did not return.

Unwittingly, he let out a slow groan and allowed his body to slowly
topple backward into the pond. He couldn't believe what had just
happened. It had the makings of a fairy tale. He splashed around briefly
before resting on his knees in the water up to his neck.

He had lost all track of time. Although everything that had transpired
from the time he had entered the water only took ten minutes or so, he
could not discern that. He suddenly wondered how long he had been

gone from home. He quickly waded back upstream to the rest of his clothes. He threw them on his frame haphazardly, grabbed his weapons, and headed home at a brisk walk. This time he crossed the farm brook, stomped through the reeds, weeds, and grass to the road leading to the farm.

He glanced about quickly once he had gained the road, taking a final look behind him toward the pond. Sighing, he then took off at a trot and didn't stop until he reached their barn. Once there, he quickly ascended into the hayloft and plopped down to relive that episode at the millpond. His face flushed red as his mind replayed the events of that afternoon. Questions came rushing out of his innards. Who was she? What was her name? Where did she come from?

In a little while, he came down and began his chores. By the time he crawled into his bed that night, he was exhausted from thinking about the young woman. Soon he was sound asleep, dreaming about floating on the water at the millpond.

\*\*\*

Rob's sleep would not have been so peaceful and his dreams so blissful had he seen the figure watching them at the millpond. Unknown to him at that time, another young man had followed the fair maiden discreetly that afternoon. She had taken a carriage ride from the Burntthorne house. Besides the driver was the kindly old governess for the Burntthornes. While the driver and governess took care of business at the mill, the girl told them she would take a short walk, returning in a few minutes. She walked among the trees and into the reeds along the bank on the north side of the pond. Once there, she quickly decided to cool off in the pond as she and her sisters often did at their home near Nottingham.

That was how she came to be in the water and how she came to meet Robert face-to-face, so to speak. But neither of them saw the other young man lead his horse into the trees and leave the animal tied there, so he could follow stealthily on foot. He was able to work his way down to the pond's edge and peer through the reeds where he had witnessed the whole episode. Twice he had agitated some of the geese feeding right near his hiding place and winced at their vocal displeasure.

After they had both left the scene, the young man remained concealed. He heard her moving through the reeds and then stop to dress. He then watched Robert make his way to the road and begin his trot homeward. All the while, he was red-faced from anger.

The young man had forced himself to calm down, stoop over, and tiptoe his way back to the trees north of the pond. He quickly retrieved his horse and, leading it, made his way back to the mill. He stood there a few moments and saw her through the trees, approaching the mill, her hair and clothing disheveled and damp. A smile on her face and a dreamy, absent-minded look in her eyes. She didn't even seem to notice him and his horse. Instead, she casually brushed some wisps of hair away from her face and walked to one side to go around him. The young man glared at her as she passed by, but she seemed unaware of his displeasure. She climbed into the carriage just as her companions came out of the mill.

Oden Furston Burntthorne, youngest son of Lord Burson Burntthorne, was the young man that eventful summer day. He was six years older than Robert, and though they had seen each other a few times during their youth, they really didn't know one another. Odie, as he was fondly called by his parents, led a life of privilege, adept at an early age at getting what he wanted . . . and he was madly infatuated with his niece, Hannah.

*** 

Of course, Robert had no inkling of this. He went about his merry way, wondering who the beautiful, dreamy vision of a girl was. She, too, wondered who the handsome young man was. Neither of them knew who to approach to inquire about the other. After all, as far as they knew, no one else had seen their brief meeting. Neither of them wished to explain their encounter to anyone else in order to obtain information about the other, for obvious reasons. So only the three people knew what had happened that day, with Robert and the young girl believing they were the only ones.

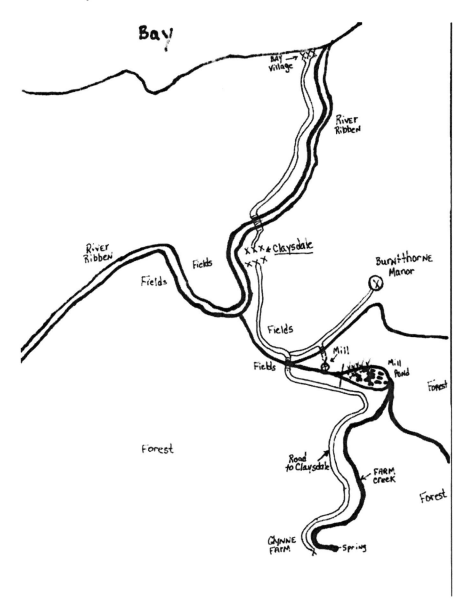

# Chapter Three
## "BURN IT!"

The next day, young Rob's father and Uncle Jonathan came home. The day was filled with talk of the upcoming voyage and final preparations to attend to. It was a day of excitement and sadness. Faith and her children would miss the older Robert, her husband and their father. He and Faith's brother, Jonathan, were both cheerful, fun loving, energetic, and passionate in their beliefs. They attended church each Sunday with their families. They prayed often and read the scriptures. They quietly voiced their opinions to each other and their families about God and religion and political matters.

Uncle Jonathan and Robert both had business contacts, friends, and even relatives among the colonists of America. So, it wasn't unusual for them to have sympathy, and even support for the colonies in their recent disagreements with the Crown. In fact, more than once, the two men had voiced a desire to uproot and move to the New World.

So it was that on Saturday afternoon, the whole family went into Claysdale Village. There, a few last minute purchases were made for the two seagoers. Faith and Jonathan's wife, Mary, went around to the shops, booths, and stalls. Saturdays were always festive days in comparison to the others. The local farmers came to town to sell, buy, and socialize. Music, laughing, and merriment were heard. The young people roamed about, talking excitedly and satisfying their curiosity.

Young women remained close to their mothers, which sometimes became small groups of moms and daughters. Quite often, young men or several young men could be seen shadowing these groups of single, available young women. Following along, many of them engaged in subtle flirtations with the girls. Some of the older ones would openly speak to one another. All of this was okay and proper, chaperoned as they were by their mothers, aunts, or cousins.

Young Rob had been trailing along with his mother, sister, Aunt Mary, and two little girls they had taken in to raise. Suddenly a hush came over the crowd around him, and eyes—all eyes—turned to view the occupants of an open carriage slowly going by on the street.

Lord Burson Burntthorne sat in the backseat with his daughter, Sarah Elaina. Facing him was a beautiful young lady that had not been seen around town before. Rob instantly recognized her as the girl from the pond. The carriage passed him standing there stupidly with his mouth open. He could clearly see her in the gorgeous dress and matching hat that sat atop her lovely hair, pulled back and braided away from her face. She was smiling and talking to Sarah Elaina, twirling her parasol absentmindedly, totally unconscious of those outside the carriage.

Robert stood and stared after her as the carriage went on down the dusty street. He became conscious of people whispering amongst themselves. "Who is that pretty lady?" "Where did she come from?" And so on. A lady spoke up and said she believed it was Lord Burntthorne's niece. She didn't know her name.

Suddenly realizing he could move, and thus keep the girl and carriage in closer proximity to himself, Rob began jogging to keep up. As he approached the carriage, he saw her eyes come up and . . . he could tell she recognized him. He was nearly even with the rear wheels of the carriage. Their eyes locked then, and she blushed crimson red. At the same time, a merry twinkle came to her eyes and a smile played upon her lips. One gloved hand immediately went to her lips as though to hide the smile.

Just at that moment, the driver began to make a left turn at the only cross street in the little village. The carriage turned directly in front of Robert and almost remained motionless for a second as the horses made their turn and then pulled the slack out of the traces. Running, head up, eyes still locked with hers, Rob was unaware of the turn. He ran into the side of the carriage just behind the door. At the sound of the loud thump, the horses startled, jumped forward, and began to prance and jump, trying to run. Rob was fortunate that he was not in front of the rear wheel of the carriage, but instead in the little space allowed by the curve of the carriage body. The rear axle swept him off his feet. His foot wedged between the axle and suspension brace, and his limp, semi-conscious body was dragged by the carriage and skittish horses.

After about twenty feet, the driver was able to bring the carriage to a halt. Jumping quickly from his seat, he ran to the head of the team to calm the horses further. Everyone in the carriage had heard the loud thump of the collision, along with many people on the street. A collective "Oh" had gone up, which was heard all over the little village. This had been followed by an awesome silence when the crowd witnessed Rob being swept over by the rear axle and dragged by one foot.

When the horses calmed down, Rob's foot became untangled on its own. He lay there in the street on his back, arms stretched out above his head. Blood was streaming from his nose and his eyes were slightly crossed, staring unblinkingly.

At the moment of impact, the young lass had moaned "OH" with everyone else and clutched both hands tightly together at her neck. She had tossed her parasol into the air, which then proceeded to bounce off Lord Burntthorne's hat, then off the side of the carriage before careening directly toward the hapless victim lying on the ground. Comically, the upside down parasol came to rest right between Rob's outstretched legs.

When the carriage had come to a stop, the girl from the pond, muttering a little cry, stood up and looked down to see the young man on the ground. Instantly she opened the carriage door and was on the ground by his side, hands lifting his bruised head off the ground and turning him so she could look him in the eyes. "Sir? Sir? Are you all right? Can you hear me? Sir?"

She used her gloved hand to wipe away some of the blood from Rob's bleeding nose. She then moved closer to cradle his head on her knee. Someone had the presence of mind to bring her a wet cloth. She immediately cleaned his face, brushed back his hair, and continued to ask softly "Are you all right, sir?"

After only a few seconds, Rob moaned loudly and began to turn his head slowly from side to side, though still staring with obviously unfocused eyes. In a bit, he shook his head and stared straight up at the little patch of sky he could see with everyone staring down at him.

He slowly looked around at all the concerned faces. Then he immediately focused on the tear-stained, worried face of the girl from the pond. For a few brief seconds, their eyes locked again and a smile flitted across both faces. Rob was just beginning to say something and try to sit up, when a torrent of water hit him right in the face.

***

Oden Burntthorne had been on horseback just a few paces behind the family carriage. He had seen the whole thing, including every little expression on Hannah's beautiful face and lips. He sat motionless at first, watching the scene. He then slid from the saddle and told one of the townsfolk to get a bucket of water. When the bucket arrived, he carried it, leading his horse, and stood near Rob's bruised head. Then unceremoniously, he dumped the whole contents on Rob's upturned face and let the empty wooden bucket drop onto the lad's stomach.

Rob immediately rose to a sitting position, spluttering and gurgling water. The young lady too was soaked by the water, her skirts becoming soiled by the mud instantly formed by the water and dusty street. She sprang to her feet and glared at her cousin who had done the deed.

Oden ignored her glare; instead, he snarled at Rob and nudged him with a boot toe. "Get up, you lazy lout! You've delayed His Lordship enough with your clumsiness!" He then walked to the carriage door and offered his arm to the red-faced Hannah. She ignored his arm as he said, "My Lady," and slightly bowed his head mockingly, with a snarling look of contempt on his face. She mounted the carriage step, whirled around to angrily sit in her seat, head turned away from Oden. He slammed the carriage door shut and bellowed, "Driver!"

The carriage parted the crowd and left the scene with poor Rob sitting in the mud in the middle of the street with water running down his blood-streaked face. He clutched the empty bucket on his lap, the parasol still between his legs, and looked around him, bewildered.

Oden Burntthorne expertly swung back into the saddle. Without another word or even a glance, he rode his prancing gelding on toward the manor.

*** 

Quickly, friends of Rob rushed to help him to his feet, inquiring as to his state of health. They brushed him off and brought him his tri-corner hat, which had gone flying upon contact with the carriage. Once he'd been cleaned up, the laughter started. Menfolk slapped him on the back, telling him how funny it all had been. They had to fill him in on the details because he couldn't remember most of it.

Out of all the babble and talk, of which Rob was mostly a listener, his ears pricked up at one line of discussion in particular. "Lady Hannah Burntthorne" was one thing he heard. "From Nottinghamshire" was another. "Lord Burntthorne's niece" clarified things further—she was Oden's first cousin! Then . . . "Oden's helplessly in love with her, but she won't have anything to do with him."

Slowly, Rob recovered his composure and sense of humor. He talked and carried on with his friends, laughing and retelling the story as everyone wandered into the Village Pub and capped off the merriment with a few pints.

Eventually, Rob's father and Uncle Jonathan motioned for him from the doorway of the pub. Rob walked to the door, calling goodbye to his friends as he went out. His father and uncle had not witnessed the incident, so Rob gave them a brief accounting, leaving out the girl entirely.

The family joined together at the little cart pulled by Rob's horse. The ladies got into the cart with their purchases, and they turned homeward, which was about three miles from town. Jonathan and his wife would travel another two miles to their farmhouse.

Robert and Faith and their children worked together to finish the afternoon and evening chores before eating the final meal of the day. Once the table was cleared, dishes washed, and food put away, the family sat around the big solid oak dining table, with benches on either side, made by Robert shortly after he and Faith had married seventeen years earlier. The after-meal conversation covered various topics, including the problem King George was having with the colonies.

Eventually, as darkness fell, Robert bade his children goodnight and goodbye. Jonathan would be back just before daylight to join Robert in journeying to their ship, the *Cardinal*, now awaiting them at the port on Morecambe Bay. If all went well, they would take the favorable outgoing tide to sea later in the morning. Young Rob shook his father's hand like a man and wished him a safe voyage. Then the two hugged affectionately. There was a strong bond between the two. They had been together at sea and on the farm, and had grown to respect each other not only as kin but also as men.

The family slept soundly until morning, awakening with Uncle Jonathan's merry holler and loud pounding on the door. Young Rob slid down from his loft bed, quickly dressed, and then let his uncle inside.

Jonathan and Robert planned to use the farm horse to pack their belongings. Young Rob would go with them to the ship, and then return with the horse. So while a hurried cold breakfast was put together for the departing ones by Faith, Rob went quickly to the barn to get the horse.

In the pale light offered by the moon and a faint glow in the east, Robert expertly found the horse in the barn; he put the bridle on and then the saddle. Finished, he quickly turned to go to the house when out of nowhere, a fist smashed into his face—twice—and he lost consciousness.

When he came to a few minutes later, his hands were tied behind his back and his feet bound. He had been thrown to the ground just outside the front door of their home. He tried to roll and sit up, but a rough boot in his back shoved him back down. He watched as his father and uncle were brought from the house—bleeding and roughed up, hands and feet bound as his were—and dumped on the ground by him. His mother, sister, and brother were trundled into the back of their wagon, which had been hitched to the horse Rob had gone to the barn to get when he was viciously attacked. Helplessly, Rob, his father, and uncle watched the wagon disappear down the road toward the village.

As they watched and listened, the three bound men realized that these men were in military uniforms and carried on as men obeying an officer's orders. They were able to make out that somewhere between twenty and twenty-five men surrounded the area at the moment. Suddenly a torch was lit, then another, and the flickering lights disappeared into the farmhouse. They could hear their home being ransacked. Belongings were snatched up and thrown into another wagon, which had been waiting down the road a ways. Then someone barked, "Burn it!" And the men with torches ran in again to set fire to the interior.

The old wooden house quickly caught fire, and in just a few minutes, the fire had spread to the roof. In the fire's glow, they could plainly see their captors now. Jonathan yelled, "Why are you doing this?" He yelled it several times as the home invaders paused to watch the flames.

Two figures who had been keeping back a ways on horseback, slowly walked their horses up to the bound men. Immediately, they recognized Oden Burntthorne as one of the figures. He wore a contemptuous snarl on his face, now plainly visible in the light from the burning house.

"Major, shall you tell them?" Oden asked the young officer next to him. Without answering him, the major stated loudly, "Sir, you and your companions are charged with treason against the Crown of England . . . for plotting to use a ship owned by a faithful, loyal subject of the king, in illegal trade with His Majesty's colonies, and to willfully participate in smuggling goods into England. Your homes and property therein and attached thereto, are hereby confiscated as retribution. Your wife and children shall perform services for the damaged ship owner for a period of seven years as indentured servants on his properties as he sees fit. Furthermore, the three of you are to serve no less than seven years with the Royal Navy, in a capacity to be determined by officers in your command. Your service will be without compensation of any kind, or reward. So it is commanded by a duly commissioned officer of the Royal Marines of His Majesty the King." He paused for a moment then added, "Sergeant! Put these men in the wagon and let's move out. Quickly!"

Three large linen bags were produced and put over the three hapless, stunned victims' heads. They were lifted and thrown into the wagon with their household belongings. The Royal Marines smartly formed abreast into two lines behind the wagon, and they started down the road.

Behind them, the house was fully engulfed now, crackling and popping in the smoldering dawn.

# Chapter Four
## MEETING OF FRIENDS

Young Rob, his father, and his uncle were thus taken from their homes, lives, and property, solely on the evil whim of one man. They were transported unseen through the village of Claysdale to the port on Morecambe Bay, where Lord Burntthorne's merchant vessel, the *Cardinal*, was at anchor. Also there was the frigate HMS *Hawke* 28 guns, now ordered to the Caribbean to protect British shipping there.

The three were literally thrown into the brig in chains by the Royal Marines. Their personal belongings were divvied out to any of the Marines who wanted them. Within two hours of their arrival aboard, they were underway.

For three days and nights, the men were chained in the brig and fed twice a day from regular rations of the crew. When their chains were finally removed, they were escorted topside into the bright sunshine on deck.

They were immediately washed down with buckets of seawater thrown on them by the young sailors, who took joy in tormenting them. When they had been thoroughly doused head to foot, the sailors took steps backward, leaving the three men standing in the middle of the circle of crewmen. The boatswain's mate made his way through the ring and glared at the captors silently. He and the rest of the crew were smartly dressed in the sailor togs of the Royal Navy of the time. The crew referred to the boatswain's mate as "Chubb."

In the Navy seaman's brogue of the time, Chubb addressed the three soaked men matter-of-factly, without malice. They each answered "aye" when he asked if they had sea experience. He then assigned them their sleeping quarters, their workmates, and work hours. Because of his young age and strong back, Rob was immediately put to work scrubbing decks and polishing brass. Tasks needing more skill and experience were doled out to the seasoned sailors, which the officers soon discovered included Rob's father and uncle.

Chubb also told them he didn't care anything about how and why they happened to be on the ship. He told them bluntly that they were in the Royal Navy now, and as long as they conducted themselves as responsible men, did their duties without shirking, they would be treated as any other member of the crew.

So it was. All they could do now was to contend with their circumstances as they were, here on the ocean aboard the HMS *Hawke,* their world for now. They fell in with the crew, dressed in the Navy togs, learned their duties and timing, as well as their duties when called to battle stations. They learned to load and fire the 18-pounder cannon on the main gun deck. Rob was also assigned to carry powder and shot from the magazine to the gun crews during engagements.

Once the crew discovered Rob's father and uncle were experienced merchant seamen—first mate and captain, respectively—they assigned the two men duties in the rigging and as steersmen. Although young Rob was more experienced than some of the young lads serving aboard, his youth still kept him on the more mundane, dirty jobs involved in running a ship.

There were some thirty Royal Marines on board as well. Their commanding officer was the youthful major who had captured the family. For the most part, he stayed away from them, but it was impossible to never see one another on a ship of that size. Still, he never spoke to them, never acknowledged their presence, and always averted his eyes when they were close by. They found out his name was Smith—Major Andre Smith.

The master of the *Hawke* was Capt. Matthew Whitston, an experienced seaman with some success against the French and Dutch in recent wars. He was also very much a gentleman, well read and very hands-on. He was neither aloof nor condescending to his men but rather like a father, stern yet approachable. He did not leave everything to his subordinates. Instead of staying in his cabin with a few of his officers, he roamed the ship top to bottom, stem to stern. He seldom called for formal inspection. He made one every day without ceremony.

He spoke to the men directly and respectfully. Sometimes he would find something not to his liking, and then he would order it corrected, and move on. He seldom used flogging to discipline his sailors. In return, his men respected him and bent over backward to please him. It was a system that worked very well.

The master of the *Hawke* set a course southwest, dropping down to catch the more favorable winds in the southern latitudes. The first few days of the voyage had been hectic, everyone adjusting to their duties, while the weather turned into several successive days of overcast clouds, gray skies, mist, and periods of rain.

Captain Whitston called everyone to battle stations or gunnery practice every other day, regardless of the weather. Most days, the men didn't actually put shot and powder in the guns to fire them, but instead went through the motions to ensure a smooth and practiced system. By the time they were halfway to the Caribbean, the gun crews were performing to near perfection.

As the days passed and they settled into their routine of eating, sleeping, and working on board ship, Rob seldom saw his father and uncle. He had been assigned sleeping quarters forward, while theirs were nearer the stern.

Fifteen days out, a sail was sighted, barely visible, to the west just after daylight. It soon dipped below the horizon and was gone. Two days later, two sails were sighted due south of the *Hawke*. For most of the day, the ships were in sight, close enough to see that they were three-masted ships and roughly on the same southwesterly course as the *Hawke*.

Shortly before nightfall, clouds and misty rain moved in again. Most of the night, the *Hawke* had to contend with squalls and lightning. Dawn brought glorious sunshine, however, and the high, white clouds and favorable winds were a welcome respite. The two ships were no longer in sight. The *Hawke* was once again by herself on the great Atlantic, and Captain Whitston changed her course to due west.

Rob had been up most of the night during the stormy weather, shortening sail, pulling ropes taut—whatever the second mate ordered him to do. Just before going on watch, the first mate made some changes with the crew assignments in terms of watches and sleeping arrangements. A young man whom Rob had seen on board from time to time but had not yet had opportunity to speak with had been reassigned to Rob's watch. He slung his hammock right next to Rob's as ordered, and exchanged pleasantries and greetings. They warmed to each other immediately and talked right up until it was time for their watch on deck.

Verdin Girard was his name, and he was the same age as Rob. He was a couple of inches under six feet tall, the same height as Rob, but not quite as stocky, a little leaner with longer arms and legs. His hair was long, straight, and light blond in color, and he tied it in a queue at the back of his head. His eyes were liquid-clear light blue. Whatever his background, there was no denying his Anglo-Saxon ancestors somewhere back there.

Born in Savannah, the port city of the Royal Colony of Georgia, Verdin had his own story to tell about how he'd ended up on the ship, a story which he shared with Rob during that first night after reassignment. His father had been a successful merchant in York, but two years before Verdin's birth, he had moved to Savannah. At first, things had gone well for Mr. Girard in Savannah. But by the time Verdin was twelve years old, his father's finances had become rather shaky. His real estate holdings had been reduced to the family home in Savannah, a somewhat modest structure, but large enough to accommodate a big family.

It was about then, Verdin said, that his father "made a pact with the devil," an agreement with none other than Lord Burntthorne! Yes, the same Burntthorne of Lancashire whom Rob knew. Verdin said his father became a changed man after that "agreement," whatever it had entailed. He eventually abandoned Verdin's education. For three long years, Verdin watched as his father became sad and melancholy, often muttering under his breath. Verdin's youngest sister eventually went to live at the Burntthorne's country home just southwest of Savannah to work as a maid at age fifteen. The estate, as well as most of Lord Burntthorne's business affairs overseas, was in the care of none other than his son, Oden Burntthorne.

Rob listened to the tale, dismayed by the coincidences, and heartbroken for his new friend. He dared not interrupt Verdin and leaned forward in anticipation of the rest of the sad story.

And indeed it got sadder. Verdin's father, mother, and three of his siblings fell victim to yellow fever. It didn't take long before his entire family was dead and gone, save for his oldest brother, who had not been heard from in three or four months, and his eighteen-year-old sister, whom he had not seen since she left for Thornewell, the name of the Burntthorne's country estate.

Verdin's fate was soon sealed when, the day after he buried his parents and siblings, there came a loud knocking on the door. Oden Burntthorne stood beside an officer of the Royal Marines, one Lt. Andre Smith. Oden was blunt and to the point. Verdin's father still owed the Burntthornes a large sum of money, and despite his death, Oden expected the debt to be paid—for starters, through the mortgage that the Burntthorne's held on the Girard family home. Oden intended to take possession.

The devil had come for his due.

As if that bad news wasn't enough for Verdin, Oden was quick to add that the Girard family home was not worth enough to fully cover the sizable debt, and he held Verdin responsible for the balance. Therefore, he suggested Verdin could enter into a seven-year period of servitude to pay the balance . . . or join the Royal Navy. Lieutenant Smith would receive a bounty for recruiting him, which he would then split with Burntthorne to satisfy the debt. In turn, Verdin would serve three years at sea.

"The whole situation smelled rotten as rotten could be," Verdin said emphatically, and Rob nodded. "Indeed," Rob said but could think of nothing more comforting to say. Verdin had asked after his sister, and Oden assured him she was well and cared for, still in his employ, and would be provided for. Left with no real alternative, Verdin agreed to go to sea.

He had been on board the *Hawke* ever since, for months on end, not on dry land even once. Rob shuddered slightly, wondering exactly how long his own stay would be.

***

Their first night on duty together was met with rough seas and gale-force winds. The second officer, Lt. Jamie Edwards, kept the crewmembers jumping as the first officer and steersman battled to stay on course and upright. Up and down the rigging the crew went, despite the wind and rain, to shorten sail or unfurl it. It was a long night that anyone on that watch would not soon forget.

The storm finally blew itself out just before daybreak. Verdin and Rob had gone aloft, as they had been trained, to once again shorten sail. They had collapsed and furled the sail and had just secured it, when suddenly the yardarm shot out from under them. Rob reached out quickly, caught hold of a lanyard, and pulled himself to safety. Verdin also grabbed the yardarm, but was unable to hang on. Before Rob's horrified eyes, Verdin was yanked away from the yardarm, falling backward toward the deck some fifteen feet below them. The two young men screamed as the action unfolded. Suddenly, Verdin stopped falling, precariously dangling by one foot from a lanyard attached to the end of the yardarm. The lanyard had become slack for a split second on the downroll of the ship, and a loop had coiled around Verdin's right ankle. As Rob watched without breathing, the ship then rolled the other way, pulling the lanyard taut, dragging a terrified Verdin away from the yardarm, leaving him dangling upside down.

Verdin was in a predicament; his bare ankle could be severed by the pressure of the rope if it became too great. At the same time, enough slack on the rope would cause his ankle to come free, and he would plummet headfirst onto the deck below, or into the foam-flecked waves of the Atlantic, depending on the roll of the ship.

Rob's mind shot back into gear as he came up with a plan to save his friend. He slid to the end of the yardarm and looked down. Though milder weather, there was still the wind, some rain, and darkness alleviated only by lightning. Careful not to fall victim to similar events, he could see that Verdin's ankle was caught in the loop about four feet down from the yardarm. Gripping the horizontal lanyard on the yardarm with his left hand, Rob swung his legs free. His knees struck Verdin in the midriff. Grimly, he hung on with one hand, wrapping his legs around his dangling friend.

Verdin instinctively stopped flailing around and wrapped his arms around Rob's legs. Then Rob yelled for Verdin to bend his arm at the elbow to link with Rob's arm. Straining mightily, Rob was able to lift Verdin's body upward enough to take the pressure off the loop in the rope. The moment Verdin felt the slack, he flipped the rope free of his ankle.

Now they were both suspended by Rob's one arm and hand still grasping the horizontal lanyard. Verdin was able to bend upward at the waist, grasp Rob's arm, and move quickly, hand over hand, to the rope. Once he had a firm hold, he let go of Rob altogether and grabbed hold of the rope with both hands. He huffed mightily till he realized he now needed to return the favor: Rob needed his assistance.

Rob still dangled by his left arm and hand, in excruciating pain and too exhausted to bring his right arm up. Verdin had presence of mind then to let go of the blessed rope with one hand, grab Rob's right hand, and bring them both back up to the rope.

After that success, they sort of hung there for a few moments, gathering their strength to crawl up on the yardarm, slide to the rope rigging, and climb down to the deck below.

Lieutenant Edwards had seen the whole thing from his position aft. He took off amidships to where the boys were, relieved to see they were all right. "That was a close call, my lads. Close call indeed!" he croaked in his gravelly seaman's brogue, eyeing them from head to toe, making sure there were no missing body parts or blood pouring from gaping wounds. Spying none, he let loose a loud sigh and ran his hand over his mouth. "Quick thinking, lads! You both kept your noggins! Close call it was!"

Their injuries were painful nonetheless. Verdin's right ankle was raw and purple; Rob's left arm burned and throbbed, and the flesh on his left hand was raw and bleeding from rope burn.

Lieutenant Edwards sent them on to sickbay. The doctor wasn't there, though they waited several minutes. Finally, they poked around in the sick bay until they found some salve, which they generously applied. Then they went to their mess, which was just breaking up, got some biscuits and pork, and munched hungrily on the way to their hammocks.

They slept like babies.

When they awoke later in the day, they found they had achieved some sort of celebrity status due to their little overhead adventure. Edwards told the story over and over as he had observed it. Soon their shipmates were asking them about it, and all they could do was modestly confirm the story.

From that day forward, it seemed Rob and Verdin had gained a new level of respect from everyone on board. They were treated more as seamen rather than young, inexperienced landlubbers. And a strong bond of friendship was created between the two of them. Something they didn't speak about, but a powerful camaraderie that they each knew existed and quietly acknowledged deep inside.

The HMS *Hawke* plowed westerly on. Most days were sunny and hot with big white clouds or very few clouds at all. During the forty-five days it took to reach the Bahamas, they had to tough it out with some storms on a few occasions, but the crossing was mainly uneventful and routine.

They encountered a particularly nasty blow about three days from Nassau. All hands were called on deck for a short while to do battle with the storm. Suddenly, someone sounded the alarm "Ship to starboard!", and everyone quickly looked up to see a brigantine-type ship not half a mile distant, slugging through the same storm they were battling.

When the weather at last eased and the sun was streaking through the gray clouds to the west, she ran out her colors. The union jack unfurled at her stern and everyone breathed a sigh of relief. Her crew may have experienced the same relief when the *Hawke* unfurled her own colors of the British navy.

The other ship only acknowledged the *Hawke*'s presence by unfurling its colors, but never offered to come closer or rendezvous. As the winds became more favorable and the seas calmer, she plied on more canvas and began to pull away. Being smaller and lighter, she was faster than the frigate. By dark, her lights were still visible over the warm southern waters. By morning, however, she was just out of sight.

As it turned out, she'd been on the same course as the *Hawke*, as they saw her riding at anchor in the harbor at Nassau, along with several other ships. The ship was the HMS *Vanquish,* and she carried new orders from the Admiralty of England for several vessels operating in the vicinity. New orders were included for the *Hawke* as well—to report to Boston, the port city of Massachusetts, which was being such a nuisance to parliament and His Majesty, King George III.

The *Hawke* anchored a few hundred yards away from the *Vanquish,* farther west and away from Fort Montagu. The *Hawke* rested under the guns of the fort, having entered the channel east of Hog Island. Now she was nestled in the harbor with Hog Island behind her and the Fort off her port bow. Close ashore was Bay Road and Government House.

For the next few days, Captain Whitston remained at Nassau, repairing, and restocking food and water supplies. He also allowed the crew liberty to go ashore for a few hours, while he met with Royal Governor Montford Brown. Some of the men headed for the brothels and taverns along the wharf front, establishments designed just for a sailor's business.

Lieutenant Chubb, the first officer, took Rob and Verdin with him. It was the first time Verdin had been on land for over a year, and it took some time for him to regain his land legs.

Rob's father and uncle were allowed to go with a different group at a different time. Major Smith was probably the author of that arrangement, reasoning that they were less likely to try to escape if kept apart from young Rob. They spent a little time in one of the taverns and mainly walked around looking at the wares of the shops.

Rob and Verdin followed along behind Lieutenant Chubb and a couple of other sailors. They went straight to the One Eyed Rooster, a tavern down near the waterfront. The sun was an hour or so above the western horizon as they went in. Rob and Verdin were familiar with spirits, but only slightly. They took their mug of ale that Chubb bought for them and quietly sat at a table near the back, as out of the way as possible.

Looking around them at the patrons of the fine establishment, they could have been in a den of thieves and pirates. Kerchiefs and tricorns with feathers and scarves, long hair, some unkempt, some plaited at the back. Sunburnt, wrinkled faces from long exposure to the sun. Loud, boisterous voices of men seeking release from the pent-up life on board ship.

As they watched and listened to those around them, they heard more than the sailor's brand of English. They heard the dialect of the Caribbean, the Irish and Scottish brogues, and the sounds of both the Yankee sailors and those from the southern colonies. They heard French, Dutch and Portuguese, and even Spanish tongues. They were fascinated by the din around them and the differences in dress, attitudes, and expressions. Such a potpourri collection of the world right there in that tavern.

Even the women were represented. Raven-haired beauties, blondes, redheads, some with scarves on their heads, most of them in low-cut blouses and long skirts. Skinny, fat, pretty, plain, and downright ugly. Even a few dressed as men! Some of them serving the customers, some there as customers, some there plying their trades in the world's oldest profession.

Rob and Verdin got an eyeful that day. They were enthralled with every minute of it.

*** 

Trouble can erupt sometimes when spirits, men, and women are all mixed together. When tempers flare, like a volcano, the explosion that takes place is deadly. There was something in the atmosphere that night that may have helped bring it on. Off to the south, dark ominous clouds were looming. A brisk breeze out of the east had sprung up midafternoon and was now coming in strong gusts that whipped up sand and made the harbor choppy and foam-flecked.

The dark clouds seemed to suddenly snuff out the brightness of the sun, and darkness seemed to fall like a curtain. Those outdoors could see the orange glow of the sun breaking through the clouds that were trying to cover it like a shroud. It continued to glow like a hot coal on a bed of black ash until it sank out of sight in the west.

The clouds overhead continued to get thicker and darker, coming out of the southeast now. At first during the afternoon, they were high white streaks of clouds, moving east to west. As the clouds to the west finally claimed the sun, it began to become completely overcast by darker, low, fast-moving clouds out of the south. Lightning flashes could be seen low on the southwest horizon.

Inside, the lamps had to be turned up. An indescribable tension filled the air, although no one inside could really tell what the weather was doing outside. Conversation and laughter filled the room. Wind gusts made the oil lamps waver and flicker.

Suddenly, someone screamed something unintelligible, followed by a thud and the deep roar of a man going into battle. Rob and Verdin never knew what caused it, but in the next moment, an "every man for himself" fight broke out. Fists were being used to pummel one another; mugs full or empty were being thrown or used to whack someone. Shoes were in the air, and a headgear sailed across the room. Plates, knives, and bowls were being hurled. Bloodthirsty screams, enraged bellows, curses, and every sort of crashes and thuds could be heard.

For a long ten minutes, pandemonium ruled. Chubb, Verdin, Rob, and the other *Hawke* crewmembers sprang to their feet, and more or less formed a circle trying to get to the front door.

More than once, they were obliged to punch or push someone, or kick people out of their way. Eventually, all five of them made it out the door. They stood there watching the things still going on inside. Every now and then, someone would come sailing out the door or one of the windows. Some of them would disappear; others would go back in for more.

Chubb became aware of the wind, premature darkness, and the lightning flashes way off to the southwest. They heard him say something about it not looking good, and he started toward their launch to return to the *Hawke*. They quickly followed in the eerie light caused by the glare of the white sand and the foam-flecked, choppy waters of the harbor.

It was hurricane season and no sailor alive wanted to face one of those storms out on the sea. Chubb and his charges regained their ship in a few minutes to find their captain and the second officer on the navigation deck. They were watching the weather, looking from sky to sea anxiously. It was too late to change their anchorage, so the decision was made to drop a stern anchor, lash down everything exposed, and ride out the storm.

It turned out to be a sound decision. For two days and nights, the storm buffeted the island, the harbor, and the ships. The winds at first were out of the south and southeast, blowing so hard the air was full of sand, water, palm leaves, plants, and sometimes debris from a damaged building. The ship heeled over, pulling on the anchor hawsers, sometimes dragging the anchors a few feet. Thankfully, the lines didn't part and the anchors only slipped a few feet.

Eventually the winds lost some of their ferocity and became southwesterly and westerly. The crew had ridden out the storms mostly below decks, eating cold meals. As the rain and wind abated, more men ventured on deck. They could still see the huge, angry cloud mass punctuated with nearly continuous lightning flashes to the northwest. All that second night they watched the storm moving on northeasterly as the skies above them eventually became high streaks of clouds moving the same direction, following the storm. Stars began to twinkle and the moon appeared overhead, giving way to a tranquil and beautiful predawn. Morning brought clear, blue skies and soothing breezes, with the harbor waters placid and the color of a translucent robin's egg.

The galley fired up the stoves and hot food was prepared for the first time in three days. The captain and the mates inspected the ship top to bottom, stem to stern. The magazines were inspected; the guns, their carriages, and everything put back into shipshape. All in all, it had been a very trying time, but not nearly as trying as it would have been if they were at open sea. For Rob, it was almost enjoyable because he got to spend a lot of that time with his father and uncle.

The other ships in the harbor had all fared fairly well. One merchant vessel had begun taking on water, the storm causing some damage that the ship had suffered before to become even worse. One sloop had run hard aground and sat keeled over to portside in shallow water, close to shore.

Shortly after midday, a British naval brigantine came limping into the harbor. Damage to her sails, stays, and rigging could be easily seen. She also had a cracked rudder that they had temporarily repaired. Worse, she had lost four seamen to the sea during her fight with the storm. Already short-handed, the loss of these four had created a serious manpower problem for her. The captain of the HMS *Crescent* came aboard the *Hawke* early the next morning, retiring to the captain's quarters for a conference.

Several crewmembers were detailed to help with the work on the *Crescent,* including Rob's father and uncle. For two days, the *Crescent* was repaired, re-provisioned, and resupplied. The officers had met with the royal governor of Nassau and had worked out a solution to solve the manpower problem of the *Crescent*. Three sailors from the *Hawke* and five others from other ships in the harbor were to be transferred to the *Crescent*. Two of the sailors from the *Hawke* were Rob's father, Robert Glynne, and his uncle, Jonathan Loxley.

They were brought back briefly to the *Hawke* for their very few personal belongings. Rob was barely able to tell them goodbye as they rushed back to the longboat waiting to take the three sailors from the *Hawke*. All three were nearly in tears, though they dared not show it. Jonathan smiled and called out as he went over the side, "Farewell, Rob! Never grow faint-hearted, me lad! We'll see you when the tide changes, for sure!"

Verdin joined Rob in waving goodbye, standing atop the gunwale; the two older men waved back briefly until they were obliged to clamber up the side of the *Crescent*. They disappeared into their new home, which immediately weighed anchor—destination: Savannah, Georgia. It would be a while before Rob saw them again. He would miss them, as he had been missing his mother and sister. He had also been thinking of Hannah.

The captain of the *Hawke* finished up some last details ashore, and once back on board, gave order to set sail for Boston. They weighed anchor a few hours later, taking the tide out the western channel, cleared Hog Island and the harbor, and turned northwesterly.

A squall overtook them two days out, and the crew had to contend with the wind, rain, lightning, thunder, and rough seas for most of the night. They were both on duty with the second mate when they witnessed St. Elmo's fire.

They both had heard about it before, from other sailors describing it vividly. They had also conveyed the fear and fright that superstitious sailors could do so well. Both boys had fallen to their knees in fright as they beheld the strange phenomenon. The eerie light flickered, clearly outlining the ship's upper appendages. They had bravely watched it, not covering their eyes and cowering as some of the other sailors who were on watch did. The pale light revealed Chubb, thoughtfully and calmly watching, arms akimbo. They decided if he could do it, so could they.

Helped along with the currents, the *Hawke* made good time. Her experienced captain and navigator soon had them in the waters off Cape Cod of the Massachusetts Colony. The crew was kept busy trimming sail or putting more on, tacking and turning, always using the wind to their advantage. It wasn't long until they were at anchor in the waters of Boston, and their arrival made known to the British naval and army commanders.

Soon some of the British naval officers who knew Captain Whitston had come on board. Naval Commander Arlister sent for him, requesting his presence for dinner and a conference.

The ship had been ordered to be in top shape, ready for inspection. Everyone was busy, cleaning, washing, shining, repairing. The ship was a virtual showpiece—every sailor and the Marines, clean, properly uniformed. Gun crews practiced to perfection, every gun and carriage virtually sparkling.

# Chapter Five
## BOSTON

Their arrival in Boston in late October 1775 marked a change in Rob and Verdin's lives. They had a little more idle time, but their day was mostly filled with the monotonous routine of cleaning and scrubbing. Clothes were washed and hung on lines on deck to dry. Drills were carried out daily to keep the gun crews sharp. Maj. Andre Smith and most of his Marines were ordered ashore to help patrol Boston's streets and guard stores of supplies belonging to the Crown.

A contingent of ten Marines were left on board in the charge of a sergeant, one Darcey Wurlee, a career soldier. He was in his thirties, gruff at times, but very religious. Therefore, his language during his angry tirades directed at the Marines in his charge was without the usual profanity of other sergeants. He had learned to read and write as a young lad, educating himself by reading everything he could lay his hands on. He borrowed books on any subject. He read circulars, newspapers, pamphlets. As a result of all this, he knew a great deal about what was going on between the colonies and parliament and the king.

For some reason not overtly clear to either Rob or Verdin, Sergeant Wurlee took a liking to them. Perhaps he knew the circumstances under which they happened to be in the king's service. He had probably seen that sort of thing happen before, and while he was powerless to do anything about it, he could be kind to those victims who happened to be within his sphere of influence. It was through quiet evening conversations with him that the two boys learned more about the events known as the Boston Tea Party and Boston Massacre. Wurlee became a good friend to them, and they to him. Their leisure time while confined aboard ship was made more enjoyable and interesting due to their time with Sergeant Wurlee. He had relatives living in the colonies in North Carolina, and the two quietly noted that Wurlee was somewhat sympathetic with the colonials' disagreement with the British government. Of course, so were they!

The time seemed to drag by as the fall months slowly turned colder and the bitter chill ushered in by the month of December was suddenly upon them. They had finally been allowed shore leave and, with Sgt. Wurlee, visited the shops and stores along the Boston waterfront. On one walk, they passed by the business of one Paul Revere, a name they would hear again. They eventually walked around most of Boston's streets just to see the sights and places of Boston . . . to do just about anything but stay on board ship all the time.

Thanks to Sergeant Wurlee, the boys had access to all kinds of books and spent most of their leisure time in some place out of the way where there was light for reading. Sometimes they would read by candlelight if they could get their hands on one. They even read the British army's manual for soldiers, which was furnished to them by Wurlee.

It was during this time in Boston that Verdin made a discovery, one that lifted Rob's spirits to no end. They had been instructed to go down to the brig, which was empty at the time, and clean the area thoroughly. As they went about their assignment, Verdin discovered some canvas bags in the forward hold. Opening the first one, he found a haversack, two unstrung bows, and a quiver of arrows. On both of the bows, carefully carved in the English ash were the initials RLG. A good-sized hunting knife in the haversack had the same initial in the wooden handle.

He called out to Rob, excited, "Come look at this stuff!"

As Rob scampered to his side, Verdin opened another canvas bag containing two more haversacks. He motioned for Rob to bring a candle closer.

"What's going on?" Rob asked, then his eyes went wide when his gaze fell upon Verdin's find. The bows, arrows, and haversack were his very own! Overjoyed, Rob squealed with pleasure, but Verdin quickly put a hand over his mouth, motioning for him to keep it down. Rob nodded, but the smile did not leave his face.

Quietly now, lest they be discovered, they inspected the other two haversacks which Rob recognized as his father's and uncle's. Among the smaller personal items, there were knives very similar to Rob's—one belonging to his father also had a smaller knife and scabbard. Jonathan's also held a smaller knife and, much to the boys' excitement, a pistol, complete with flints, a powder cask, and lead balls, along with a small pouch with the tools to care for the gun.

A startling find, and uplifting too! Their captors had carelessly thrown the two canvas bags and some others that were empty into the cramped little space, probably intending to come back later and remove what they wanted.

Quickly and carefully, the boys concealed the articles into the even tighter area of the bow, placing the empty canvas bags in a stack to carefully conceal the opening. Anyone looking in the dim light would see only a stack of folded, neatly stored canvas bags.

The boys were thrilled. Just knowing these personal items were there was reassuring somehow, and gave them a sense of hope.

***

Every three weeks or so, Captain Whitston would cancel all shore leave and take the *Hawke* out to sea for a day or two. There was always a bustle of activity when this happened, preparing the vessel for the outing. The time at sea was spent in gunnery drills and ship maneuvers to give the seamen and midshipmen experience in handling the ship. One outing, just before Christmas, was a cold, blustery affair and not received with favor by the crew. Captain Whitston was not moved, reminding the crew that the *Hawke* was a vessel of war and, as such, could be called upon at any moment to conduct its deadly business, regardless of the weather.

During this Christmastime outing, the frigate's gun crews practiced firing at targets consisting of empty casks and even small boats outfitted with masts that were made by the ship's carpenter and his mates. Verdin and Rob had worked with them on some of the wooden replicas. The ship circled the targets as the men practiced coming to quarters, being called to battle stations, and running the 18-pounders out in unison and firing broadside, either all at once or one after another as the guns come to bear. This was exciting stuff, especially after the day-in-day-out boredom of sitting in port. Orders from the captain or his chosen officer in charge were called out to the helmsman and the sailors to change sail and direction, come into the wind, run with the wind, quarter into the wind, speed up, slow down, come about, and so on. There were orders to the gun crews to fire, reload, fire on the up roll. Marines fired at targets from rigging or behind the gunwales. "All hands prepare for boarding." "All hands prepare to repel boarders." It was a constant scene of organized chaos, yet serious with deadly undertones.

Christmas was quietly observed on board by the crew with the captain ordering two beefs and a hog slaughtered for Christmas dinner. Verdin and Rob passed the holiday missing their families and bitterly remembering the events that caused them to be apart.

Most of January and February were spent close to port, the men staying warm below deck around the galley fires or on the upper deck around fires in cast iron pots, one located forward and one near stern. Rob and Verdin were sometimes ordered to help in keeping those fires fueled and were sent ashore to bring firewood aboard that the British purchased from vendors, usually Loyalists who still lived in the countryside. Their farmhands would cut the wood and cart it into the city to be purchased by the navy or the army.

\*\*\*

These uneventful months on the *Hawke*, staying warm and close to port, would soon give way to another opportunity for Rob and Verdin, involving a new ship and a new plan—to patrol the lower coastlines for smuggler ships. The king's navy was constantly on the lookout for smugglers, who were considered not much more than pirates.

Small ships such as schooners were usually detailed for this close coastal work. Some months earlier, a very handsome, well-built Yankee sloop was captured by the Royal Navy. She had been tied up in Boston, unused since then. The last week of February, the British fleet commander ordered the ship to be rechristened the HMS *Osprey*, resupplied, manned by a selected crew, and put to work watching for smugglers.

Accordingly, Captain Whitston selected two of his own crew to provide his quota for the crew of fifteen that were to put the *Osprey* into British service. For the next ten days, interrupted by heavy snowfall and a winter storm, they labored to prepare the little sloop for her duties.

She was fitted with six 12-pounders, three to a side. Gun ports were cut amidships in the gunwales to accommodate them. Two swivel guns were mounted, one fore and one aft. A magazine area was outfitted below decks with double bulwarks and stocked with the required gunpowder and shot.

The men on board the *Hawke* were given the choice—two men would be chosen by lots, or two could volunteer. Seasoned sailors did not relish the thought of living and working on a smaller vessel in cramped quarters and doing the smuggling recon planned for the *Osprey*. However, Verdin and Rob jumped at the offer and volunteered, anticipating new and exciting adventures, and avoiding the possibility of being separated if the men were chosen by lots. No one else bothered to volunteer.

So it was, the two were put on board the *Osprey*, along with sixteen other sailors. A lieutenant of sufficient age and experience was named master and commander, along with a younger lieutenant and two midshipmen to complete the ship's roster of officers. Rob and Verdin were told this would be a temporary assignment; they would return to the *Hawke* eventually.

Not wanting to take a chance with their newly found possessions, in case they actually never did make it back to the *Hawke*, they endeavored to sneak the goods on board the *Osprey*. As it turned out, it was a rather simple matter to bundle the bags containing the items in with some other canvas bags being transferred to the *Osprey*. Storing the items wasn't much of a problem either, as the boys just shoved them in with other items in the forward hold. Only Verdin and Rob knew what was in those bags and where they were stored.

Sleeping space below the main deck was more cramped in the bow of the ship. Those sailors who were not sleeping stored their hammocks while those who were off duty slung theirs to sleep. Lt. Daniel Arlister, their commander, was in his late twenties, arrogant, and overbearing, trying to make sure he proved himself capable of handling his first solo command. He had chosen twenty-four-year-old Peter Brickland as second-in-command. They had been friends before coming together on the *Osprey*, and Brickland modeled himself in the same stiff, arrogant way as Arlister.

The two midshipmen, Ellis Rofford and Norwin Chaddham, however, were quite amiable, disposed to showing the curt side of their authority only when the senior officers were around. They were both nineteen years old, well educated, from good families. They considered the Royal Navy to be the best position available, but neither were heart-and-soul sailors. Instead, Rofford and Chaddham, both fair with blue eyes, were rather cheerful and full of youthful vigor, fun, and curiosity.

In the second week of March 1775, Rob and Verdin were officially and physically on board their new vessel. During the first two days, the master organized his gun crews, and battle stations were assigned. Then they drilled—the gun crews practicing their routines, while the officers and sailors assigned to steering and maneuvering the ship carried out various orders. It was the same orchestrated confusion as on the *Hawke*, yet on a smaller scale. At first, things were disjointed and awkward as the men were not accustomed to working with each other. By the end of the second day, however, the crew began to mesh, and their commander felt good enough about their lot to put to sea in pursuit of smugglers.

The third day was foggy at daybreak and remained so up until midmorning. As soon as the fog lifted, they would leave the harbor, so the crew on duty at the time was kept busy in preparation. Rob and Verdin had been assigned battle stations in the rigging and were on duty watch when the ship got underway.

Catching the seaward breeze, the little *Osprey* gallantly turned eastward out of her Charles River berth and darted away. She was fast, sleek, and easy to handle. Fairly skimming the water with the slightest breeze, she was like a bounding deer compared to the beef cow of a frigate.

The fog was completely gone by noon, leaving gray wintry skies and sea. They ran easterly out of Boston Harbor until they cleared Deer Island. They set a course north/northwest into the wide expanse of Massachusetts Bay. Once out of sight of his superior officers and the anchored fleet, their commander put the little ship and his crew though several maneuvers and drills, letting himself and the crew get used to her. He worked everyone hard, including Rob and Verdin, who grudgingly had to admit Lieutenant Arlister apparently knew how to handle a ship. Surprisingly, the odd crew of misfits and youngsters did well on their first journey together.

The *Osprey* settled into a routine as did her crew, and they zigzagged up Broad Sound between Oak Island and Bass Point. On the fourth day out, the weather took a turn for the worse, with snow spitting and the wind blowing in strong gusts.

Arlister was seriously thinking of returning to Boston to ride out the cold weather, when, to his pleasure, the sun came out that next morning, and the wind turned gentle. They were close up to the north end of Broad Sound when Lt. Brickland relayed Arlister's orders to bring her about and head for Bass Point. Once there, they turned eastward, past East Point, then northwesterly into Nahant Bay.

For two or three days, they patrolled the area but only saw small fishing craft from time to time. The weather was unusually warm for the end of March. Lieutenant Arlister took that as a sign of being too good to last. After a short jaunt easterly past Galloupes Point, he ordered a southeasterly course for Boston Harbor. They rounded Deer Island and were poised to enter Boston Harbor itself when the young eyes of Midshipman Norwin Chaddham caught sight of a sail in the dark off the port bow.

The cry of "sail ho!" brought a response from the officer on deck, Lieutenant Brickland. Chaddham called Brickland at once, and he hurried to Chaddham's position at the bow and pulled his ship's glass to his eye. Adjusting and straining his eyes at the little white puffs on the horizon, he gazed for a full sixty seconds trying to make out what size ship it was.

Finally, he removed the glass from his eye and said, "Chaddham, report to Commander Arlister that we have sighted what appears to be a sloop one and one-half to two miles away on our heading, south/southeast."

Chaddham responded with a salute and "Aye, aye, sir!" then about-faced and bounded away, going aft.

Brickland shouted directions to the sailors, which included Rob at the time, to throw on more sail to give chase.

Chaddham then returned to his position aft, next to the helmsman. Lieutenant Arlister soon joined them on deck and Midshipman Brickland returned to the bow.

They had already closed the distance enough to make out the sails a little better. She had not thrown on more canvas to try to run—not yet anyway. The moon nearly full but intermittent clouds, heavy at times, were not allowing it to be a constant help.

The gap closed more . . . enough to see it was a ship similar in size to their own *Osprey.* By now, the excitement had run through the ship and crewmen not on duty had come up on deck into the cold to watch.

Almost leisurely it seemed, the ship ahead shook out more sail. She was close enough now to see in the intermittent glow of the moon overhead that figures were bustling about on deck. Commander Arlister issued orders to sound battle stations, and the shrill pipes made Rob and Verdin jump as all hands rushed on deck to their gun positions. He ordered "Stand by your guns," so the men crouched or stood by the gun ports watching the ship ahead. They were not to load them or run them out yet. Just stand by them ready when ordered.

The *Osprey* had gone for two miles since sighting the ship that was clearly running from them now, down the east side of Long Island and past it. Another two miles and suddenly the little schooner ahead had thrown the helm over and turned nearly due east. By the lantern light near the helmsman on the flat table, Arlister and Brickland were studying a chart and talking. Brickland soon bellowed out the orders necessary to conform to the chase.

The new course would take them between Peddocks Island and Houghs Neck on the mainland about two to two and one-half miles east. The island's low-lying hulk was visible to their left and the northernmost point of Hough's Neck to their right. Three miles or so after turning east, the schooner gradually resumed a southeasterly course, which the *Osprey* soon followed.

Arlister told Brickland, "She's heading into one of those coves south of the neck!" Arlister drove the *Osprey* on after the runner, sure that he almost had a smuggler at bay. They could tell the ship had taken down some sail and slowed as she headed between two protruding points into Town River Bay. Arlister stayed his course following her, confident of the channel since the other ship had made it through already.

The intermittent clouds gave way suddenly to clear, sparkling, star-filled skies. Their foe had apparently come to a stop and was now lying athwart their course, curiously looking as though she were waiting on them. Her bow was turned to their left, downwind, just past the narrowest part of the entrance to the little bay.

Arlister gave the order to load all guns and run them out, which the men did quietly for some reason, without the usual shouting and noise.

Brickland was clearly calling out directions to drop sails and turn downwind, and for the colors to be run out. The Union Jack of the British Empire soon flew above the stern.

The ship turned parallel to their adversary and came to a stop. All was quiet for a few moments except for the sound of the flag fluttering in the breeze and water dripping off the ship. All eyes were starboard, staring intently at the dark ship that was now silent and still.

At orders from Arlister, Brickland bellowed loudly, "Ahoy! Ahoy!" to the ship across the way. "This is His Majesty's ship, The *Osprey*! Please make yourself ready to receive a boarding party for inspection of your cargo!"

The quiet sound of a muffled oar and the dull thud of a smaller boat against the hull of the HMS *Osprey* went unnoticed as all hands were training their eyes on the ship they had run down and was now about to board and capture.

Rob was perched on the starboard gunwale near the bow. Verdin was standing on the deck at his side. Rob and Verdin had been whispering back and forth all along. Verdin had been the first to ask, "Is she running from us or leading us somewhere?" She just didn't act concerned. "It was almost as though she slowed down to make sure we gave chase," he said.

As they drew closer and closer and finally stopped in the little narrow strait, Rob and Verdin were sure of it. This was a trap, and Arlister and Brickland had fallen for it.

When there was no response to the loud bellow thrown across the water by Brickland, they were sure of it. They looked at each other then warily around.

Suddenly a loud voice from the ship across the way roared, "This is the sloop *Nantasket* of Massachusetts! Throw down your arms and surrender! Put your hands on top of your heads! NOW!"

At that instant, a large number of heads appeared along the port gunwale of the *Osprey*, followed by arms and hands holding muskets. While all hands were looking starboard, four boats, each with eight to ten men had quietly come out of the darkness, attached themselves to the portside, and at the word "NOW," popped up and over the side, all armed with muskets loaded and primed.

Someone yelled "ready!" and thirty rifles were all cocked at once. A startling and deadly sound to the shocked sailors of the Royal Navy. At the same time, eight gunports on the *Nantasket*'s portside popped open and eight 12-pounders were run out in unison.

\*\*\*

No one on the *Osprey* bothered to look at their commander. With jaws dropped open in shock, the whole ship simply complied with the *Nantasket*'s orders by placing their hands on their heads. Arlister and Brickland were no exception. Immediately the colonials moved among the silent men, removing weapons and piling them on deck. All of the men were then herded into a single file amidships.

Their captors stood in lines on either side, weapons at the ready while some of their comrades expertly dropped anchor. One young man, slender and composed, spoke to Commander Arlister loud enough for his whole crew to hear. He gave simple instructions for two men at a time to be taken below to retrieve any personal belongings. They would then be taken ashore, given directions to Boston, at which point they were free to go. That was it!

When their time came, Rob and Verdin went below together, followed by two men with pistols. Rob quickly gathered the two linen bags containing his belongings, as well as those of his father and uncle. Verdin grabbed another bag to place his few things in, and they returned topside with their escorts.

Together with their belongings, the two boys were helped over the side into what appeared to be a longboat. When everyone had been seated in the longboat with their possessions, they were instructed to pick up oars and start rowing. They all did so, rowing in unison to the instructions of a colonial steering in the stern.

It was just a short distance to the dark shoreline where the craft was run into the shallow water until the bow struck the sandy bottom. Each one of the crew was hurried out of the boat into the cold, knee-deep water and up onto the sandy shore. They were placed in single file again, and marched about a hundred and fifty yards in the bright moonlight through the sparse vegetation that grew in the sandy, rolling terrain.

Then they staggered into what appeared to be a sandy clearing, which was in reality a lane or road running north and south. One of their captors pointed each of them northward toward Boston, about twelve miles away.

There was no need for lanterns in the clear, cold, moonlit predawn. Holding their possessions, the nineteen men of the *Osprey* began trudging northward, passing by quiet, tight-lipped men posted at intervals along the road with muskets at the ready.

Rob and Verdin took one last look to their left at the *Osprey*. Her new owners had already gotten her underway, and she headed southward with her companion ship following.

When the line of men had gone almost a mile by Rob's reckoning, the track joined another coming from the right, and they were obliged to turn left. A man on horseback stood in the road just to the right of the intersection, pointing them in the direction they must go. Rob and Verdin recognized him as the young man from the *Nantasket*, who seemed to be the leader of their captors.

His sandy-blond hair was neatly pulled back and tied with a ribbon at his neck. A dark brown tricorn rested above clear-cut, handsome features—dark eyes, strong mouth, and chiseled chin. His long coat was also a solid dark brown with a buff-colored waistcoat, breeches, and stockings. He sat upon his dark bay horse easily, yet erect and imposing. Arlister and Brickland had stepped aside to speak to him. As Rob and Verdin approached, they heard the young man say, "Gentlemen, from this point you're on your own. We apologize for the inconvenience, but we felt it necessary to recover property that was rightfully ours. Just continue northward to Boston, and you'll be fine." He gestured for them to rejoin the line and dismissed them from further protest or conversation.

Rob and Verdin were near the end of the single file, and as they approached the gentleman on horseback, a thought came to Rob. Maybe this was their chance to get away from the Royal Navy. They had both been unlawfully pressed into service under trumped-up charges, after all.

Rob came to the turn in the road, even with the horse's head. He stepped to the right, out of the way of those behind him, and nodded his head at Verdin to follow, which he did. He said, "Sir, might we have a word with you, sir?" He stood stock still, arms full with the sea bag of his possessions. Verdin stopped next to him, his arms also full. They both looked up into the eyes of the man on horseback, plainly visible in the light of the moon, now low on the western horizon. The breath of the horse and rider were white vapors in the cold, crisp air.

He looked first at Rob, then to Verdin, then back to Rob. He quickly glanced up at the last couple of men in line who had hesitated when Rob and Verdin stepped away. "Move along there, gentlemen. Move along!" he said with authority, and they moved on as directed.

When they were out of hearing, his eyes again focused on Rob, and he said quietly, "What can I do for you, young man?" His eyes and mouth held firm, unmoving, void of any emotion.

Rob straightened his posture and, glancing back once, said quietly. "Sir, we don't belong with these men. We both were forced into the king's navy. We were pressed into it . . . against our will . . . along with my father and uncle who are on another ship now." He glanced quickly in Verdin's direction for reassurance, then continued. "We wish to be free from having to go back, sir, if you have no objection."

The man on horseback looked at the two boys pensively. Rob spoke up again. "Sir, we have no money, but we can work. We're willing and able to work."

Verdin nodded emphatically.

Rob added, "Sir, we have no love for King George and his parliament, if that's bothering you, and we are in favor of what you're doing here in Boston, putting up a fight and all. Right, Verd?"

Verdin responded immediately, "Right! Right you are, Rob! Right! And we are hard workers!" he blurted to the sitting horseman.

Suddenly the man shifted forward a bit, smiled down at the two faces staring intently up at him. "Well, boys, I certainly do not mind having a hand at taking two fine, capable young sailors out of His Majesty's service." He paused a bit, then said, "Maybe I can find you some sleeping quarters for the night. Are you both sure you want to do this? You know the king has a very bad disposition toward deserters. The king's navy may come looking for you so they can give you some rope on a yardarm," he said seriously.

The boys assured him they were prepared to proceed, and the man on horseback sat still a minute more, quietly assessing them both. Finally, he said, "Gentlemen, we may be in need of a great many young men like you before it's over. I'll see what I can do. Just come along with me now." Then he slowly leaned forward. "Say, do you boys think any more of your crew think the way you do?"

Verd and Rob looked at one another, then Verd spoke up. "Sir, we were very careful about what we said and who we said it to, but I believe two or three of our crew feel the same, especially the two midshipmen."

The young gentleman looked over their heads at another horseman, who had approached quietly during the conversation. He said to the newcomer, "Tom, why don't you see what they have to say about it, while I take these young men with me?"

Tom responded, "Aye, aye, sir!" and turned his horse toward the backs of the men marching northward.

The man on horseback deftly dismounted, holding his reins in his left hand. He stepped forward with his right arm extended to shake hands, first with Rob, then Verdin. "Gentlemen," he said, "let me introduce myself. I am George Wolloston, formerly of Charlestown near Boston, but thanks to our current situation with the British, I am presently living elsewhere."

The boys eagerly introduced themselves, and before they got into more conversation, George said, "Let's find a place to rest our weary heads for a while, boys. It's been a long, eventful night. Just follow me, and we'll be there shortly." Pulling his horse behind him, with the two boys on either side, he started walking up the track in the direction the others had taken. For several minutes, they walked quietly, hearing only their own footsteps and the muffled clomp of the horse. After traveling two hundred yards or so, George turned down a small path that was clearly leading them back to the small bay. In the waning moonlight, the boys made out a similar vessel at anchor close to shore . . . similar to the one on the *Osprey.* As they got closer, they could tell there were a couple of figures huddled around a nice fire, apparently waiting on George. There were two horses tied to a boat pulled up on shore.

George halloo'd to let the people know it was him. They walked eagerly toward them to take the reins of George's horse while he briefly explained who Rob and Verdin were and why they were with him. The small group stood briefly in the welcome warmth and light of the fire. Then George turned toward the boat and gestured for them to follow. "Come on, boys. Let's get some sleep!" He led the way to a small boat in the shallow water and boarded. The boys threw themselves and their bags in as well, after pushing away from the shore.

They had just settled down, found their oars, and dropped them in place when a shout from the shore told them to hold up. Tom had appeared with three figures energetically following along. They all three stampeded out into the shallow water and clambered aboard the small boat. Their eyes and body language clearly indicated they were jubilant about not going back. George smiled at them and said, "Glad to have you with us, gentlemen!"

Rob and Verdin smiled at their companions as they headed for the schooner. Ellis Rofford and Norwin Chaddham had jumped ship too. They wanted a chance to live as free men in the colonies. The other freedom lover was a quiet, slender, rather small redheaded, freckled young man they reckoned to be about thirty years old. They only knew him as Twig, but soon found out his full name was Twig Hayven. They later learned a lot more about this surprisingly talented and gifted young man.

George Wolloston led them aboard his *Osprey,* showed them where hammocks were, and where to suspend them in the crew's sleeping quarters. He bade them goodnight and went aft to his own cabin. They all five quickly made themselves at home, snug in their beds, and went sound to sleep.

It was midafternoon before they stirred. They found the day to be a bright, sunny, and brisk one. George had told his men to leave the new charges undisturbed until they awoke on their own. Then he invited them all to his quarters to have a meal prepared by the cook on board.

The young man, Tom, came aboard with news of the crewmen reaching Boston. The British naval commander had gone into an absolute rage, according to an informant. Poor Arlister and Brickland were ordered back to their former stations, confined to quarters with only bread and water for three days. Duped into surrendering one of His Majesty's vessels without firing a shot was inexcusable. They were lucky His Majesty didn't have them shot, according to their superior. The news didn't completely surprise Rob and Verdin, and they were delighted not to be a part of that sordid story any longer.

Their host proved to be a charming, articulate gentleman and a man of his word. The next morning they left for George's father's farm located some twelve miles west of Boston near the Charles River. Isaac Wolloston was in his mid-fifties, full of energy, and full of hatred for the British Crown and parliament. He was a devout American just as his son was and over the next several days, filled them in on a concise history of what had taken place over the last several years to cause the current state of affairs.

# Chapter Six
## ALL THE KING'S MEN

The comfortable two-story farmhouse had a two-story addition on the back with four modest-sized bedrooms upstairs and three downstairs, one being used as an office and storage room, therefore not available as a bedroom.

All but two of the bedrooms were being used by house servants and other farmworkers. So the five were assigned the two bedrooms available on the top floor. Rofford and Chaddham were housed in one room, and Twig elected to bunk with Rob and Verdin.

There were only two beds in each room, and these were military barracks style beds, only large enough for one person. Twig quickly volunteered to Mr. Wolloston to make another bed. He enlisted Rob and Verdin's help and, using the farm's carpenter shop, crafted a handsome bed matching those already in place. In addition, he made a bedside chest of drawers for clothing.

Twig's carpentry expertise was the first inkling that Rob and Verdin had of Twig's many skills. Over the next three weeks, the five men bonded as they fell into a routine of work on the farm. They also met the three other farmhands, who cheerfully welcomed them into the fold.

George came to the farm about a week after their arrival. Isaac was glad to see his cheerful, handsome son, as was everybody on the farm. The evening meal was more exciting and noisy with conversation. George brought the latest gossip and news about the British in Boston. He explained the reasons for the increased tension in the air: the British were expected any day to try to seize some of the Patriot leaders and powder stores that were being collected by the local militia in outlying areas.

He spoke to the five of them about their willingness to serve in the local militia unit and to fight the king's soldiers if necessary. Without hesitation, they said they would.

The next day, after some of the early morning chores had been done, George assembled the five men together and produced five muskets that looked similar to those of the former seamen of the British navy. They obviously had been "borrowed" from British military stores. He also provided a shot pouch, powder horn, and musket balls for each. George took his men out to the edge of a wooded area alongside an open field not far from the house, where they could demonstrate their abilities in loading and firing the weapons.

They were all sufficiently adept at the process due to their training on board ship. Once George was convinced of their abilities, he queried them about their knowledge of the *Manual of Arms and Marching Maneuvers*. Of this, they were ignorant, and George at once systematically began correcting that.

For three hours at a time, he drilled them on how to handle their weapons, follow commands in formation for loading and firing, how to march in columns of two, counter march, and to file left and right. He stayed with them at the farm for three days, each day filled with marching and drills.

Then late in the evening of April 18, Tom came to the farm on horseback. The men heard the horse and then the dogs barking, so they went out on the balcony in time to see Tom dismount and greet George and Isaac at the back door of the main house. The Wollostons disappeared inside for a short while, then reappeared fully dressed, ready to travel, in dark brown coats, tricorn hats, buff breeches, and waistcoats. Tom caught up the reins to his horse and walked to the barn behind the house to prepare George's horse. He soon had the large bay bridled and saddled, and both swung easily into their saddles.

They returned to the house, George's horse snorting and prancing, eager to run; Tom's horse was too, caught up in the air of excitement from the other horse. Rob and his buddies were at the railing now, and George lifted a hand in farewell when he saw them. He hollered, "The British may be trying to capture some military stores in Concord. Looks like they're marching tonight. If so, I'll send word for you to join up with a militia company not far from here . . . as soon as we know for sure what's happening."

They all somberly wished them well and waved goodbye. The gravity of the situation suddenly struck them, as the possibility of going to war with England became very real and imminent. They all agreed to turn in and try to get some rest in the event they were called.

Before turning in, Rob, Verdin, and Twig readied their weapons and supplies. Without much conversation between them, they cleaned and oiled their weapons, including Uncle Jonathan's pistol. They packed their haversacks with extra shirts and their smaller personal items, laid out their garments and shoes to wear—these given to them by Isaac and George in place of their Royal Navy togs—and crawled into bed in their long undershirts. They went to sleep quickly in spite of their nerves. Thanks to their youth and perhaps their faith in God's guiding hand, they drifted off to sleep and slept soundly until just before daylight.

Rofford and Chaddham pounded on their door, yelling, "Get up! It's time!" The three quickly pulled on their clothes and sprang to the door, running onto the balcony.

There sat Tom on his horse below, looking weary and concerned. He bellowed, "The British have marched and are probably at Lexington now! Bring your weapons and ammunition and go to Concord as fast as you can. The militia and the minutemen have all been called out. No time to waste. Go as fast as you can!" He then wheeled his horse around and sped away to warn others and to urge them to go to Concord to fight.

Isaac Wolloston instructed them to go to the kitchen first for food—

enough for three days. The cook prepared pieces of ham, biscuits, and apples from the cellar, all wrapped in a cloth that could be placed in their haversacks. The five men quickly voiced their thanks, heading back upstairs for their arms. Just before they were out of earshot, Isaac yelled for them to each take a canteen. These were hanging just outside the kitchen, recently filled with fresh spring water.

When all were ready, Isaac led the way on horseback, the five young men half-walking, half-running alongside and behind. The sun was just peeking over the eastern horizon to their right, as they started northward.

***

It was midmorning when they finally topped a small hill and looked down into smoke-filled Concord. They could see the scarlet and white of the British troops at the south and north bridges, and in Concord itself. The militia from numerous surrounding small towns was mostly centered on a hill overlooking Concord.

There had been fighting at the north bridge because several wounded and dead militiamen were being tended to by some of their comrades.

Isaac led them to the body of militia on the hill watching the British, waiting to see what they would do. No one seemed to be in overall command and making decisions.

The British soon began to close their columns and bring in all details, looking for arms and powder stores. The sun had just passed its zenith in the sky when the British began moving eastward, back toward Lexington. The five, along with Isaac on horseback, soon began moving along on the north side of the British column.

Suddenly the rear guard wheeled around in file and fired a volley at the militia. The balls zipped and whined through the militia, some of them finding flesh and bone with a thud. A few of the men crumpled to the ground. Others stopped to look to their aid and comfort, if possible.

Without a sound, without looking back, the militia, to a man, surged forward toward the Redcoats. Each of them had an angry, determined look on his face. That last volley was like a spiteful, mean-spirited slap in the face. There was no more indecision or hesitation on anyone's part. Their goal was now gloriously simple: kill as many of these murdering, home invaders and looters as possible before they got back to Boston.

Rob and his companions moved with the rest of the militia. Suddenly, one man knelt behind a tree and fired at the column. Then another fired, then another . . . without orders they also began to systematically load and fire.

When the British wheeled and fired back, Isaac Wolloston's hat went flying off. A small, splintered groove was knocked in the wood piece below the barrel of Rob's musket, which he held at an angle, left hand under the barrel, right hand on the trip of the stock. Another musket ball tugged at Rofford's coat sleeve near the shoulder.

Luckily, none of them were wounded or slain. Twig recovered Isaac's tricorn, now with a bullet hole, and Isaac firmly placed it on his head. They looked to their weapons, ready for firing, and then with set lips, looked for a place from which to fire.

Rob ran forward to a boulder-strewn area, knelt behind one that afforded good cover, sighted the musket, and fired at targets about eighty yards away. The ball hit no one, as the smoothbore muskets were accurate from only forty or fifty yards, or less. He dropped to one knee and quickly reloaded.

Meanwhile, Verdin and Twig dropped behind other boulders and some bushes and began to fire, choosing to stay close to Rob. Rob ran closer to the column, musket balls whistling overhead as the harried British soldiers returned fire.

About forty yards away, Rob aimed at the chest of a red-faced soldier about to fire. The musket ball hit the stock of the soldier's musket and tore into his right arm just below his shoulder, tearing out a big piece of flesh and scarlet coat sleeve. Another man crumpled to the ground with a loud scream, clearly heard by Rob who was about forty yards away.

The air was filled with shouts and curses from the ranks of the Redcoats, the crash of the gunfire, and now moans and screams. The colonials were fairly quiet in comparison as they went about their deadly business with silent determination.

Now and then, one of the militia would be hit as the Redcoats wheeled and fired. Their moans and screams began to mix with the others.

What a sight. The militiamen moved along with the column, firing and loading. Scarlet-clad soldiers were firing individually as they drove onward. Sometimes an officer would pull a squad out of formation, and they would blast a volley at the pursuing militia, who would dive behind rocks or trees to reload and fire.

Puffs of smoke were showing on both sides of the column in increasing numbers. More and more colonials were arriving from surrounding farms and villages.

Rob, Verdin, and Twig stayed together as they ran, stopped to fire, reloaded, then ran some more to repeat the cycle. A middle-aged man near them stopped to raise his flintlock rifle and fire. Just as he fired, a musket ball caught him below the knee, and he dropped to the ground. A younger man ran to his side to help. He, too, had a rifle.

The young man suddenly looked up at Verdin, who had quickly approached. "Here, take our rifles and ammunition!" he yelled, handing the weaponry to Verdin. "This here's my pa, and we ain't gonna be using 'em no more today. I gotta get him home!"

When Twig reached them, he dropped on the ground below a slight rise out of the line of fire. He examined the newly acquired rifles and said, "These are some sure fine rifles. Well-made and taken good care of. Thanks for the use of 'em," he said.

The young man nodded his head in acknowledgement and turned to his father. Rob joined Verdin and Twig, and they moved on to find cover so they could load the rifles. Rob reloaded his musket and stealthily half-crawled, half-ran to within forty yards of the column. He aimed and fired, watching as the grenadier winced in pain and doubled over, grabbing his left thigh. A crimson stain was already showing on the white breeches. Suddenly, he straightened up and bellowed, grabbed his musket bayonet, and started running toward Rob. About ten of his harassed companions charged along with him, screaming and cursing, bayonets pointed at their enemy.

Rob had dropped to reload and didn't see them at first. The group of charging Redcoats had covered almost fifteen yards before he looked up and saw them. Verdin and Twig were just a few yards behind him and had just reloaded their rifles. They saw the charging men in red immediately, quickly stood, and fired simultaneously.

Two Redcoats to the left of the one Rob had wounded went sprawling backward as though hit in the chest by a mad bull. Their weapons came flying forward out of their lifeless hands, one of them sticking in the ground, bayonet first, just a few feet from Rob. The Redcoat he wounded had zeroed in on him and kept coming, brandishing his bayonet. Rob immediately squared up to meet the charge, using his musket to knock the bayonet aside.

The angry, wounded Redcoat kept bellowing and coming. He tried to hit Rob with his rifle stock, which Rob was able to parry with his own. The man's momentum bowled Rob over, and soon the Redcoat had pinned Rob to the ground with his musket.

By this time, other militiamen had come to face this charge, including Isaac, Rofford, and Chaddham. Isaac, still on horseback, fired his pistols calmly, as if on a bird hunt. His first shot hit one of the charging Redcoats in the forehead. The man's musket discharged in his twitching fingers as he slowly sank to his knees. Isaac's hat again went sailing from his head, knocked off by a flying bullet.

Luckily, enough men had responded to the charge to quickly take them out of action. Rob was still in the clutches of a rage-filled, desperate bear of a man, however. He was able to finally force the Redcoat into a roll to one side. He sprang back on top of Rob, knocking his musket out of his hands. Rob grabbed hold of the Redcoat's musket, and for a few minutes, it was a desperate push and pull match to gain control of it. Suddenly, the Redcoat changed tactics and pulled the bayonet free from the end of the barrel. He grabbed the ring end of the weapon and drove the point at Rob's face. Rob moved at the last minute, rolling to his left, clearing the scabbard of his hunting knife, which he removed in one deft motion, driving it up under the attacker's ribs and into his heart before the enraged Redcoat could even react. The man died instantly, and Rob threw his lifeless body backward, away from him.

By the time Twig and Verdin had raised their rifle butts to hit the man, Rob's swift move with the knife was the only action needed, thankfully fast enough to keep the bayonet from plunging into his face or throat.

Rob sat still a moment, pulled his canteen around from his side, and took a long slow drink. The others huddled close by, reloading their rifles, catching their breaths. The end of the column had moved on toward Lexington. Colonials were still firing from both sides of the column. Men raced past Rob and his group. Some paused to take the dead and wounded Redcoats' weapons, cartridge boxes, rations, canteens—even their bearskin hats and boots.

The three men noticed some of the colonials were going home when they'd run out of shot or powder. Some of them left plainly because they had been scared by what they saw . . . blood, brains, whizzing bullets, screams, dead bodies, wounded, bloody men crawling, dragging legs . . . The sights and sounds of war were horrible beyond belief, yet glorious in a strange, gut-wrenching way.

Rob propped his musket against a small tree, took off his powder horns and shot pouches, and then handed them out to whoever wanted them. He unslung the longbow and the quiver of arrows from his shoulder. "I can do better with this than that stupid old musket," he said to anyone listening.

Isaac held out his hand. "Here, give it to me! I'll use it."

Twig grabbed up the horns, pouches, and musket, and handed them up to Isaac. A trickle of now dried blood ran over Isaac's right eye. The fourth bullet to knock his tricorn off had taken a little swath of hair and skin. His hat had been recovered each time and sat jauntily on his gray-haired head.

They kept to the north side of the column as they ran to catch up and then pass the end of the Redcoat column. Rob chose a small clump of trees for cover, then pulled and notched an arrow and let it fly. He was off the mark a little—out of practice—and the arrow sailed over his target's head and lodged in a tree on the other side of the road.

Isaac and the others also found cover in the clump of trees and fired at the column. Suddenly, the last company came to shoulder arms, and formed two uniform files, or ranks. Grimly and methodically, they loaded their rifles in the face of smoke and whizzing bullets. The front rank dropped to one knee, and both ranks followed their sergeant's orders and let loose a volley. Nearly a hundred muskets fired at once—flame, smoke, and deadly metal bellowing out of them.

Some of their comrades around them fell bleeding; some dying, some wounded. It didn't stop the colonials though. They kept firing as the Redcoat company began reloading. Rob and his group took the advantage to spring forward and run on toward the front and middle of the long column of harried Redcoats.

Suddenly, the Redcoat company that had stopped to fire began taking on heavy casualties. Their sergeant, the only officer with them, had been shot through the mouth and was being helped along by two of his men.

As the two ranks tried to reload, some of the men were hit, falling over and knocking other men down. Suddenly some of them realized there was a growing gap between them; they stopped at the end of the column, and the rest of the column moved on toward Lexington. They were being left behind! Isolated!

The same thing must have come to the minds of many of the Continentals because the firing at the stopped company by militiamen on both sides of the road picked up.

Bullets whizzed through the air. The hats of the beleaguered Redcoats flew off. Bullets splintered rifle stocks, glanced off the barrels. Hot lead balls sometimes broke into little tiny fragments of hot, stinging lead when they glanced off rocks, metal rifle barrels, bayonets, sword hilts. Bodies stumbled and fell. The smoke, the noise, the screams of the wounded, the stinging lead fragments, no officers to direct them, an enemy that just kept on and on—it all became too much, even for these seasoned, well-trained soldiers in red. Panic set in.

They began throwing away their firearms, ammunition pouches, powder pouches, and canteens. Anything that would slow them down, they threw away. They ran hard and soon enveloped the company on the road ahead of them. Then the panic spread to those men. They paid no heed to their officers. They trampled one another. They, too, began throwing away their equipment.

It spread to the entire column. Soon a tangled mass of panic-stricken men filled the road as they broke and ran for Lexington a short distance away. All the while, the militiamen kept firing and yelling, smelling blood.

As the mass of running men passed Rob, he let loose three arrows from his longbow from almost seventy yards away. One arrow struck a man in the left side of his chest and came out on the other side. The man fell and was trampled by his panicked comrades-in-arms. Another arrow penetrated the left arm of a man, going through the skin and muscle on the lower side of the upper arm, the steel point passing on into the man's side, pinioning his arm there. He kept running with blood streaming down his side onto his white pants. Rob's third arrow went through a soldier's hat. Somehow, the hat stayed on the man's head, the arrow comically protruding on both sides as he raced after his comrades. To the man's credit, he still had his weapon and equipment.

The column raced into Lexington and kept heading east on the road, suddenly colliding with a relief column marching from Boston. The pandemonium ceased, and soon the reorganized ranks of the advance column and the relief column were trudging easterly.

The fire from the farmers and shopkeepers had died down while the British were in Lexington, but it never entirely stopped. Once the columns of British soldiers moved out again, the onslaught continued.

Rob and his companions halted for a bit in Lexington to catch their breath and eat something. Suddenly, George Wolloston, along with Tom and a few other men, came riding up to them. Their horses were hot, sweaty, and dusty.

George greeted his father enthusiastically, both men obviously glad to see the other alive. George then greeted the rest of them with a nod and weary smile. "Gentlemen, you all must know that this means war. My father and I could fight as soldiers but with our experience as merchants and seamen, our country will benefit from our services in that capacity. Our elected leaders have requested that we assist them in forming a navy. I ask any of you who wish to serve with me to go with us now."

Rob, Verdin, and Twig glanced at each other—all in agreement, shaking their heads. They would stay. Rofford and Chaddham, on the other hand, nodded their assent to head out with George.

"Sir," Chaddham said to George, "we will serve with you." He looked at the trio of Rob, Verdin, and Twig, and said, "We've come to be close friends to the three of ye. Will be a real pain in the heart to go without ye."

The men shook hands, slapping each other on the back in strong hugs, mumbling things like, "You've been good friends and mates," and "We'll miss our mates."

George thus recognized that Rob, Twig, and Verdin preferred to be on land. Still, he was gaining two fine, capable young sailors in Ellis Rofford and Norwin Chaddham. He was pleased. Before they headed out, George put his hand out, and one by one, they stacked their hands one on top of the other. George said a brief, emotional prayer asking for God's care and watchfulness and if it be His will, let them all live to see one another again in peaceful times.

George pulled Rofford up behind him, and Isaac took Rofford on his horse. They slowly turned south toward the farm.

The three stood and watched them go, aware that the fighting and shooting had been going on all the while, getting farther away from Lexington.

They took off at a trot after the column of Redcoats. They could still see men arriving and others leaving. Thankfully, more were arriving than leaving. The boys swung to the north side of the road and soon were caught up in the melee again.

Twig dropped down behind a low rock wall about a hundred and thirty yards from the road, which was also slightly ahead of the column, thanks to their brisk pace. Rob and Verdin followed suit.

All but Rob, who stuck with his longbow, loaded and primed their rifles. Soon the column came abreast of their position, and two rifle shots sounded. Two Redcoats fell, their hats and weapons going in different directions.

Rob let go an arrow, but he hadn't aimed high enough, and it passed between his intended victim's legs. The man, it turned out, was an officer, and he jumped high in the air, even though the arrow had already passed through without hitting any part of him.

This made the officer madder than a wet hen, and he began shouting orders. Suddenly, two companies came to a halt and let loose a volley of murderous fire. Luckily for Rob and his comrades, the wall provided suitable protection.

Just before the volley of bullets, Rob had noticed a man dressed in deerskin hunting clothes come out of the woods behind them and approach the wall, preparing to join them in the battle. A comrade-in-arms, and he'd had been hit from the enemy's gunfire. As the man slowly fell to the ground, his long rifle still clutched in his hands, Rob crawled along the wall to reach him.

A small, neat bullet hole between the man's eyebrows marked the entrance of the musket ball that ended his life. The ball had been fired from far enough away that it just entered his skull and brain, but did not exit. Rob closed the eyelids of the man's staring, unblinking eyes. They were a startling, clear gray, prominent against his sun-browned, dark-whiskered face.

Without hesitation, Rob removed the man's powder horns, leather shot pouch, and haversack. He also removed a hatchet and knife from the man's belt. Then, taking the rifle, he rolled away and took up position again behind the wall.

The rifle was ready to fire, hammer cocked. Rob looked down the barrel to pick a target. His sights settled on the cross straps of a soldier, and he squeezed the trigger. The Redcoat staggered back and fell out of sight in the rutted road. At the same time, his comrades came up out of the road in a line that was about two hundred men wide in two files—a total of four hundred or so men. The drums beat out the signal to advance with bayonets, and these harassed and bedraggled scarlet-clad killers advanced quickly.

The enemy headed straight toward the wall that had so far successfully protected Rob and the rest of the militia, whose numbers had increased at this locale to around a hundred riflemen. The Redcoat officers ordered their men to stop about fifty yards from the wall and then fire a volley. Most of the militiamen were able to time things well enough to dive for cover and not get hit, but not all of them.

Twig was one of the less fortunate, though not in a deadly sense. Indeed he'd hit the ground for cover, but his rear end stuck up just enough that a lead ball plowed a neat furrow across the most protruding part of both butt cheeks. It was a furrow about as deep as a man's finger was thick, and ran clear across one hip, skipped the cleft in between, and continued across the other.

The injury involved no bone at all, just a flesh wound, though it wasn't confirmed until later. When it happened, Twig screamed in agony and shock as the hot lead seared that furrow in his tender flesh. He now lay face down, both hands exploring the two holes in the right and left side of the seat of his breeches. Through the pain, he hollered, "I've been shot! Help me, Rob! Verd! Where are you? Owww! I been shot in my backside!"

His hands became soaked with the blood from his wound as he probed the injury. When he suddenly realized how wet his hands felt, he held them in front of his face. A strange sound came from his pale lips, his eyes grew wide in sheer horror, his face turned white as snow . . . and he passed out. His head slowly settled on his outstretched forearm tilted to one side as though he were asleep.

Fearing the worst, Rob and Verdin turned to the business at hand. After all, there would be nothing they could do to help Twig if they, too, were shot.

After the first volley, the colonials along the wall thought they would be facing a bayonet charge. The officer who had ordered the volley, though, could clearly see many more men through the trees than just what was behind the wall. Instead of a bayonet charge, he ordered the men to reload. The first rank fired from a kneeling position, then faded back to reload while the second rank came forward, firing. They continued in this manner, allowing them a faster rate of fire, until they finally began to run out of ammunition.

As the gunfire died down, Rob and Verdin tried to determine the extent of Twig's wounds—if they were mortal wounds, where they were located. They finally traced the blood to the bullet holes in the seat of his pants, and though they could only guess at the true nature of the wounds, they opted for "not too serious."

They turned back to pay attention to the British soldiers and to snap off a few shots between the diminishing volleys.

The head of the column had passed on behind these two companies who were protecting their left flank. When their ammo got low, they wheeled back in line and took up the march. Finally, the end of the column passed Rob and his fellow fighters, moving eastward. The firing from either side had ceased.

Breathing heavily, Rob and Verdin laid aside their rifles and looked again to Twig. Rob took his canteen and splashed a generous amount of water on his friend's head.

Twig moaned and rolled his head side to side slowly. Meanwhile, Verdin looked at Twig's backside. Carefully, he took Rob's knife and inserted it in one of the bullet holes of Twig's breeches. Then he cut a slit in the material, from one bullet hole to the other. Pulling apart the blood-soaked material, he could see a gooey mess of flesh in the groove that cut across both buttocks.

Twig had completely come to his senses by that time, though he still groaned from the pain, and he lay still while Verdin and Rob examined his backside. They determined the wound was to the flesh only, not a life-ending shot—assuming infection did not set in, which was always a serious possibility.

With the examination complete and the urgency diminished, Rob and Verdin sat back and looked at each other—and started to snicker. The comical part of the situation hit them at the same time. Though they tried hard to stifle their laughter at first, for their comrade's sake, they failed miserably, and their snickers soon became outright hoots of laughter. Twig lifted his head briefly, smirked, then went back to his moaning, now mixed with an occasional chuckle as well.

Verdin said, "Well, my friend, it's a grievous wound for sure, but you're gonna make it fine."

Twig raised his head again, his face serious. "You sure? Are you for certain sure, 'cause it hurts like my backside done been half shot off."

That last part set Rob and Verdin into another fit of raucous laughter.

Twig yelled, "I ain't kidding! Are you sure it's gonna be okay?"

Rob and Verdin shut it down and assumed a mock seriousness that neither of them felt.

Rob offered, "Relax, mate. Your hind end is still there." He patted Twig on the back gently. "Except . . . it's just got a groove in it now." He looked at Verdin, who had his hand over his mouth now to keep from snickering. Rob grinned but gave him a warning look not to start up again.

Verdin composed himself and added, "Yeah, but now we got to figure out how to clean it up and bandage it."

Twig just hung his head in pain-shrouded disbelief, mumbling something about "of all the places to get shot, I had to get shot in the butt!"

Rob and Verdin pulled out some cloth they had in their haversacks and, using water from the canteens, were able to clean up the areas above and below the wound. The wound itself had mostly stopped bleeding, just leaving a line of clotting blood and tissue across his behind.

The searing pain had subsided a great deal by now, and Twig was able to bear it much better, except when he tried to raise up. Not knowing what else to do, they left his pants pulled apart at the slit and his shirttail pulled up on his back. A very strange sight to behold, and Rob and Verdin worked hard to control their snickering yet again. Twig just gave them the evil eye, though he, too, wore a half-grin amidst his grimace.

Some of the residents in the area had been tending to the fallen and wounded, and an older gentleman with a black leather medical bag eventually approached the trio.

He looked at Twig's wound, shook his head . . . and chuckled. "Ye'll be fine, laddie!" he said in a fine Scottish brogue. Then he knelt down at the boy's backside and removed some clean cloths and ointment from the bag. "Now grit your teeth a bit, lad. This is goin' to hurt a mite."

He cleaned the wounds and applied a generous portion of the ointment. Then, using a knife, he literally cut away Twig's breeches, removing them completely. He bandaged the wound, wrapping the strips of cloth completely around Twig's body, as there was no other way to hold the bandages in place.

Finally, with the assistance of his friends and the doctor, Twig was able to stand on his feet. Walking was another story—the pain was just too intense.

The doctor said, "Aye, lads, you're gonna have to carry your comrade or find transportation for him. He canna walk." He raised Twig's shirttail to double-check the bandage. No blood had seeped through, at least not yet.

"Tek this lad home," he continued, "and make sure he stays off his feet 'til this heals, so he won't pull it open and make it bleed again. Remove these bandages in a week, then place this poultice on it, bandage it up tight, and leave it 'til it quits itching, for two or three days, I'd guess.

Then, he'll be good as new." He handed Verdin a cloth-bound bundle, and the boys thanked him for his advice.

Without further ado, he closed up his pouch and moved on to the next victim. In this case, it was the buckskin-clad man with the bullet hole between his eyes. The elderly doctor knelt down beside the body, saw the bullet wound, sadly shook his head, patted the dead man softly on the forehead, and said something softly about the "great physician above taking care of you now."

He got up, grasped his bag, and looked around for another fallen warrior. He went hurriedly on through the trees, moving easterly. The boys had gathered their weapons and, with Twig between them, his arms over each boy's shoulders, began dragging him down to the road. At first, the movement unnerved Twig, and he moaned loudly. He then picked his feet up by bending at the knees and thus kept his feet from dragging and bumping, hurting his backside.

When they reached the road, they didn't know which was the best option: turn back to Lexington or press on toward Boston. Twig decided it for them. "Let's go on to Boston. Maybe we can fight them bloody bastards some more!" So eastward they went, stopping often for breathers, and to let Twig rest his arms and straighten his legs.

They followed the refuse-strewn road where the retreating Redcoat column had gone for a couple of miles when they came upon an older gentleman on an old white horse, which was attached to an old grayed and weathered, two-wheeled farm cart. He had been picking up discarded weapons and other military equipment left behind by both sides.

He gestured for the boys to place Twig in the cart when he saw them. Relief swelled over them as they waved their appreciation and slowly made their way toward the cart, placing Twig on his stomach at the rear of the rickety vehicle. The old man started the horse slowly eastward without a word. The boys had placed their weapons alongside Twig in the cart, which they now walked beside, picking up discarded items of military equipment for the old man so he wouldn't have to dismount. In this manner, they kept plodding toward Boston without stopping, the sounds of gunfire coming from up ahead, where the beleaguered column of angry, exhausted soldiers struggled on.

It was well after sundown when they stopped next. A group of continentals had stopped to make a fire beside the road not far from a farmhouse back from the road. They gestured for the boys and the elderly gentleman to join them at the fire for a meal.

Grateful for the offer, Rob and Verdin quickly warmed their fare by the fire. Twig had thankfully slept most of the time in the cart, and he now ate a few morsels and drank some water. The old man got down from the white horse—the boys still didn't know his name—and politely refused their offer to share their food with him. Instead, he broke out his own food and shared some of his bread pudding. After they'd eaten, the boys rested a bit, realizing they had been on the go since before sunup this morning. They were beyond tired!

The long column of scarlet-clad men was exhausted and was still being plagued and harassed by the unrelenting rebels. The colonials still fired at them from behind rocks, trees, clumps of brush, and farmers' rock fences. The fire had slacked somewhat with the coming of darkness, the ammunition running low, and just plain exhaustion. Still, they kept up the guerilla tactics, never coming to grips with the enemy in a formal stand-up, rank-against-rank, European-style shootout. They just kept peppering away, fading back, and taking cover when the organized columns returned fire in massed volleys.

On and on, the spent Redcoats marched until finally they passed through the narrow Charlestown neck under the safety of the navy's big guns. They sought the high ground of Bunker Hill, Breed's Hill, and Moulton's Hill and succumbed to exhaustion after nearly twenty-four hours of marching, fighting, and no sleep. The tired but jubilant colonial militia stayed back out of range of the naval guns and slept on their arms.

Rob and Verdin had followed Twig and the old man's cart as far as the Charlestown neck. Once there, the man pulled off the road at a suitable spot and got down from the horse, which he unhitched and then fed with a feedbag that he hung over the horse's head. He pulled some blankets from under the cart seat, handed a couple to Verdin without a word, then calmly crawled under the cart, wrapped up in his blankets, and was soon sound asleep.

The boys gingerly pulled Twig off the cart onto half of a blanket on the ground, and folded the other half over him. They lay down on either side of him, using their haversacks as pillows, and covered all three of them with the remaining blanket. In this manner, they became quite snug and warm against the chill of the early spring night. They slept soundly, although at first their minds raced with the thoughts of the days' events, the sights, sounds, and questions about "what now?"

# Chapter Seven
## "I'M BACK NOW!"

From April 20 to June 17, the boys remained on duty, becoming a part of the Colonial army battling the Redcoats up in Boston. They followed the doctor's instructions in caring for Twig's battle wound, and he healed quickly without complications. They practiced drilling, marching, and doing the manual of arms. They learned to make a shelter with log walls and a tent roof, and how to dig fortifications. They came to know and respect many of their comrades-in-arms. The three of them shared quarters, rations, conversation, thoughts, hopes, fears, memories, and experiences. Their friendship continued to grow, steadfast and true.

Twig's recovery brought about a side of him that Rob and Verdin hadn't seen before. He became active in the camp life—correcting flaws in the shelters so they withstood the elements better, helping with procuring and preparing food, repairing equipment, clothes and guns. The man was a genius with guns, and they found out he was actually a trained gunsmith, among other things. He found the nearest blacksmith shop, which was just a short walk from their camp on a farm. He was able to work wonders repairing weapons and putting them back into service. Some officers on the regimental level learned of this service he was able to render, and soon he was swamped with work, so much so that the officers assigned men with similar talents to help him. Twig naturally asked for Verdin and Rob to be part of the operation, and they worked closely alongside Twig and his little group.

Early in the morning on June 17, Verdin and Rob left with the rest of their company to fortify the hills overlooking Charlestown and Boston. Twig bade them farewell, as he had been ordered to stay and continue his ordnance duties. He enjoyed the work he performed and received a great sense of gratification doing it. Still, he didn't want to part with his close friends. Rob and Verdin were also crestfallen at the three of them being broken up, but there was little they could do about it. They reassured each other: "We'll be able to serve together in this army again someday soon."

***

Rob's mind twirled and twisted as he remembered the details of his recent life: the anguish of separation from his home and family, his hatred for those responsible, his warm friendship with Verdin and Twig . . . and his meeting with Hannah Burntthorne.

Then suddenly his mind began a careful yet speedy recollection of the events of the day at Breed's Hill, right up to the point where everything had gone black. His mind asked the questions: *"What is past this black veil?" "Surely there's more to see." "This isn't the end, is it?"*

In his mind and with his real, physical being, he reached out his left hand, caught hold of the edge of the dark curtain, and slowly moved it back to reveal the light. His arm and hand moved as they should, his fingers grasped the edge of the black veil. He could feel the coarse fabric and the edge of it with his fingers. He felt his hand move to take the veil away. He expected to see light, but there was none.

*Oh wait! One other thing to do before he could see the light. He had to open his eyes!*

He did, and the light rushed in. He could see his arm and hand extended as if pushing the veil away, but the veil was not there. He let his arm drop.

And then he saw Verdin looking at him with quizzical eyes. Rob smiled and said, "Don't worry, Verd. I'm back now."

"Well, hi there, ole Rob!" Verdin's smile was as wide as his face would allow, and his eyes sparkled with delight at hearing Rob's voice. "We had just about sure enough given up on you!"

They heard steps quickly coming up the stairway. Jenna Anne, the seventeen-year-old daughter of the Medfords, came bounding into the space and stopped stock still at the foot of Rob's bed. Her big brown eyes were alive and dancing, full of joy at the sight of Rob now leaning on his side, talking with his friend. She clasped her hands together at her throat, which flushed slightly when Rob turned his gaze upon her beaming face.

"Well, hello there, young lady!" he said impulsively, realizing he didn't know her but sensing that his comment was appropriate. She apparently knew him. She didn't say anything for several moments, taking in his handsome face and glowing eyes, although he was pale and haggard from his wounds. She didn't say anything in response at first, but finally she blurted out, "Hello, Mr. Glynne!" An awkward silence followed as they just looked at each other.

She then averted his eyes to look at Verdin, who watched her with amusement. Her eyes darted from one man to another for a few seconds, then she laughed aloud, a happy, tingling, young woman's laugh of relief and genuine merriment. "Hello, Mr. Glynne" she said again, "and welcome to the world of living people!"

She then came up alongside each of them, standing in the space between the two beds. "Let me check your bandages there, Mr.—"

Verdin quickly broke in, saying, "Miss Jenna Anne, let me introduce the two of you properly, if you don't mind."

She looked at him shyly, dropping her hands to clasp them behind her back. Then Verdin said calmly and with enforced politeness, "Miss Jenna Anne Medford, I would like to present Mr. Robert Loxley Glynne of the township Claysdale, of Lancashire, England." He turned toward Rob. "Mr. Glynne, I am pleased to present to you, Miss Jenna Anne Medford, whose father owns these beds, this house, and this farm where we found refuge."

She quickly did a little half-curtsy then said, "Jenna Anne … just call me JenAnne for short. That's what all my family and friends do."

They smiled at each other, and Robert said sincerely, "Very pleased to meet you, Miss JenAnne."

She smiled a dimpled smile. "Pleased to meet you, Mr. Rob."

Then she turned serious and began bustling about. "Let me check your dressings, then I have to tell Mother and Pa." She checked Rob's thigh wound then the bandages around his head. She briefly looked at Verdin's shoulder bandage, then hurried down the stairs, calling for Mother and Pa and the rest of her family.

In no time at all, the Medford family—including JenAnne, her two sisters, two brothers, and Mother and Pa—had assembled at the foot of the mens' beds. They all said hello as Rob propped up weakly, yet bright-eyed, happy to meet this family who had probably saved his and Verdin's lives. As he tried to thank them, everyone seemed to speak at once, a jumble of conversation, especially when Verdin joined in. No matter—they all understood the joy and relief behind their words, no matter how it came out.

Then just as suddenly, they all fell silent as the grateful Verdin and Rob looked at the friendly faces of the Medford family and grinned.

Mr. Medford broke the silence by saying, "Let us bow our heads in thankful prayer!" As heads bowed and eyes closed, the kindly Mr. Medford lifted his voice and heart in prayer to the Lord Jesus Christ, thanking Him for His blessings and requesting His continued protection for these two fine young men, his family, and his countrymen. The patriarch ended the emotional prayer with a solemn, "Amen."

Mrs. Medford at once took charge, getting everyone back downstairs and addressing Rob's need for some food with substance and drink. She reminded him to begin eating just a little of the solid food slowly, as he had been existing only on broth for three days. She herded everyone downstairs, and Verdin and Rob were left alone. Rob fell back onto the bed, clearly fatigued by the prolonged propping up.

Verdin smiled at his friend and moved over to prop him up again so he could be comfortable while eating his first meal. He asked Rob, "Well, my friend, do you remember what happened?"

Rob smiled and said, "Right up to the volley that hit us!" he gritted out. "So they got you too, eh?"

Verdin touched his own shoulder and grimaced. "Yes, but I'm lucky. It was a musket ball that ricocheted or was partially spent, and lodged in the muscle of my upper shoulder. Didn't go through the bone, just nestled up next to it real close. They were able to dig it out of me while I was passed out. I lost a lot of blood, but I'm recovering now with the good liver and other things the Medfords have fed me. Still hurts badly at times, and I don't sleep well, but Mrs. Medford even has something for that too."

Rob gingerly touched the bandages on his head. "What's the damage here, ol' friend?"

"Just a nasty bang on the head and a bone-deep groove for two or three inches along the side of that thick head of yours!" Verdin said. His brows shot up as he spoke, apparently still in disbelief that the wound hadn't been worse. "Your thigh was shot clean through. The ball went in, through, and out, but didn't touch any bone . . . or at least Mr. Medford doesn't think so. He said you'll be able to tell yourself once you try moving around and standing again."

In a few moments, they heard steps on the stairs, and JenAnne appeared with a tray of food and beverage for them both. Rob let the pretty young lass feed him small morsels of beef and tasty pieces of buttered biscuit. She also gave him apple cider to drink, which had been stored in the springhouse to keep it cool.

Verdin had been struggling to eat with one hand, so she next turned her kind attentions on him. "I'm sorry, Mr. Verdin," she said softly, "but I knew Robert wouldn't eat much his first time to eat solid food."

Verdin shook his head. "I've no problem with that at all. I'm grateful for your help."

After eating, when they were alone again, Rob asked Verdin if Twig knew where they were. Verdin assured him that as of yesterday Mr. Medford had sent a messenger to look up Twig, and also one to the Wolloston farm.

"Good, good!" said Rob as he lay back and closed his eyes. He was anxious to get back to living again, and he suspected Verdin was too.

The next thing Rob knew, the mid-morning sun was streaming in the window, and it was almost past time to head for the outhouse or chamber pot. Verdin laughed and helped him get out of bed and astride one of the little pots that had been left in the room for just that purpose, partially filled with water. The effort caused Rob a lot of pain in his thigh, but he made it.

"There's lots of sweet relief in life, and that there is one of them," Rob joked. Verdin had to agree, nodding and laughing at Rob's outlook on life.

Just after a hearty breakfast, they heard a commotion and clattering of hooves outside the home. They looked at each other expectantly.

"Could it be?" Verdin asked.

Footsteps pounding on the stairs, and in no time, there at the foot of their beds stood Twig Hayven and their captain, Arvil Claxton, who was clad in a new uniform of white breeches, blue waistcoat, and blue outer coat with burgundy facings. Both men were perspiring in the late June heat as they beheld the two wounded young men.

Rob and Verdin whooped with joy at seeing Twig, and he them. Eyes misted over as the three friends greeted each other and shook hands. They were glad to see their captain, too, who soon brought them up to date on the situation with the British in Boston. He told them about the pending arrival of Gen. George Washington, who was appointed commander of the army by Congress on June 15. There had been horrible losses by the British army that day on Charlestown Peninsula and how dear the British "victory" had been. Their informants described how deeply mortified and chagrined the British commanders had been regarding the horrendous numbers of casualties dealt their forces at the hands of the ragtag, supposedly pusillanimous, little army of scabrous rebels. And both sides would never forget it.

Captain Claxton also had letters with him addressed to Rob and Verdin, commending them on their bravery and heroic deeds in the face of overwhelming odds, and winning the thanks and gratitude of their fellow soldiers and countrymen. The letters were signed by a group of officers who had witnessed their fighting that day, including Captain Claxton.

While they talked, a message arrived from the Wollostons telling them that neither George nor Isaac were there, but the message of Rob and Verdin's whereabouts would soon reach them. The four men talked until the noon hour. The captain then gave them all a farewell to return to the noose around Boston, which they were drawing tighter and tighter. Twig was free to stay with them on a few days leave, but the captain reminded him that they sure wanted him back to continue his ordnance work. Twig assured him that his associates could handle things very well now, with or without him.

The Medfords welcomed Twig to stay at their home with his friends and accepted him at their table. He, in turn, helped around the farm, repairing and improving on things. The Medfords didn't have an extra bedroom, but he didn't mind. He preferred bunking with his friends anyway, and with the blankets and bedding the family provided, he had a very comfortable place to sleep on the floor under the window.

On the morning of the second day after Twig arrived, the three men awoke to the gentle patter of footsteps on the stairs. Into the room came a pretty, slim, well-proportioned young lady with straight, sandy red hair, freckles, long eyelashes, and deep green eyes. The eyes of all three young men snapped open, now wide-awake with curiosity as to who this lass was—someone new, bearing the breakfast tray for Rob and Verdin.

She bade them a cheerful good morning, then explained. "I'm the daughter you haven't met yet. I'm Louisa. So pleased to meet you all," she said with a bright smile. With that, she helped them prop up and get settled down to eat. She set the tray on the table between them and commenced to ply them with food and drink. All the while she softly prattled on about how she knew who they were, how pretty it was outside, and that she had been away helping a dear friend who had just had a baby boy, whose husband had been at Concord and Lexington and was now in the Rebel army encircling Boston. She was constantly on the move as she spoke, fixing them drink, or food, straightening their pillows and bedclothes.

She would often turn toward Twig's bed at the end of the room under the window, still talking nonstop, asking if she could get him anything, smoothing his bedclothes, fluffing his pillows, taking his clothes off the floor and neatly refolding and stacking them. She placed his tricorn gingerly on top of his clothes, then asked again if she could get him anything.

Just as quickly as she arrived and spoke, she then turned and took off briskly down the stairs with a happy "goodbye for now."

Rob and Verdin looked over at Twig. He had sat up in bed just before her entrance and had started to remove his nightshirt. It was halfway over his head when she came in. Now the nightshirt was half on one arm with the other half laying on his other shoulder, the tail up around his chest, and the bottom half of his body nearly exposed.

He had frozen at her sudden bursting on the scene, and then merely sat there, stunned and mesmerized by the whirlwind of this woman. The whole time she was in the small room, his eyes stayed wide open and unblinking, his mouth half open, a look of surprise and bewilderment on his face.

Verdin snapped a finger to bring Twig out of his trance.

Rob said, "Hey, Twig! You all right, Twig?" When Twig didn't respond, Rob and Verdin both shouted at him, "Twig!"

Slowly he turned his head to look at them while he mechanically completed removing his nightshirt. His lips moved, saying something under his breath.

"What's that, Twig? Couldn't hear you!" Rob said.

Twig remained silent, just moving his lips and looking kind of unseeingly at Rob, then at Verdin.

Rob and Verdin looked at each other and shrugged, then turned their sights back to Twig. For a few moments, they watched this man who was capable of so much, now sitting like a lost lamb, bewildered by a woman he had never seen before.

Twig shook himself and, with noticeable effort, returned to this world and the present. His eyes began to focus on his surroundings again, his gaze darting around the room, and the color returned to his face. Without a word, he continued removing his nightshirt and getting dressed. He stood there next to his makeshift bed and blurted out, "I'm in love with her!"

Stunned, Verdin and Rob glanced at one another, swallowed hard, then began to grin. Their friend was smitten!

Not another word was mentioned about this sudden change of heart in Twig, though everyone wore a smile on his face. Instead, they busied themselves with typical morning "things to do" until JenAnne came bouncing up the steps. She grabbed the tray and eating utensils as she said a friendly good morning to all.

Then she specifically turned to Twig and repeated, "Good morning!" She quickly added, "Can I help you with anything, perhaps with removing your nightshirt?" And with that, she started laughing hysterically, exiting quickly down the stairs. The boys could hear her giggles, which were quickly joined by others downstairs.

Twig sat, mortified and red-faced. Finally he fell over on his pallet and covered his head.

Rob and Verdin tried hard not to break into laughter themselves, and didn't trust themselves to utter one word of comfort, lest they double over, howling at the hilarity of the morning.

Verdin had been getting up and walking around on his own for a couple of days. Between Twig and himself, they decided to get Rob out of bed and moving around on his feet. Although it would be painful for Rob, they instinctively knew he needed to start using that thigh and leg. So slowly and surely, Rob began hobbling around, at first aided by his friends. Soon he was able to go downstairs, and they all began to take their meals at the table and enjoy some time on the porch each day with the rest of the family.

One night they decided since it was cooler on the porch than in the upstairs bedroom, they would prefer to sleep there. So with the

Medfords' blessing, they took to sleeping on the porch on makeshift beds.

Verdin's shoulder wound still pained him, and the damage to the muscle was significant enough that he had to keep it in a sling to immobilize the arm so the wound could heal. It began to drain but then it quit. One night as they were sleeping on the porch, Verdin began running a fever. By the early morning hours, he was nearly delirious with fever, burning up, moaning, and groaning. Wilbraham Medford examined the wound, which he determined was indeed infected.

Rather than moving Verdin back upstairs and possibly aggravating the situation, the Medfords tried to keep him comfortable on the porch, redressing the wound as needed.

Shortly after daybreak, the boys saw a figure turn onto the lane leading to the Medfords' house, walking toward them. He had a doctor's bag slung by a strap across his shoulder. As he approached and came more clearly into focus, they all three recognized the man who had first cared for Twig's buttocks wound.

The gentleman greeted them with a subdued, "Good morning, gentlemen," then set his eyes on Verdin, who lay limply on a blanket. The fever was still evident on his face; his eyes glassy. The doctor gently placed his hand on Verdin's forehead, then said, "Here, lad, let me look at your shoulder." He opened the dressing and looked at the clearly infected wound.

He removed a bottle from his bag and told Verdin to drink it. The liquid immediately burned Verdin's throat, and he coughed and sputtered, but the man insisted, so Verdin took a few long draws on the bottle. Then the gentleman poured some on the wound itself and removed a small knife from his bag. Smoothly and quickly, he opened up the wound and removed the scabbed-over pocket of pus and blood. He pushed on the tissue surrounding the wound to encourage drainage.

He kept that up for probably an hour, talking quietly to Verdin about how he got the wound, how he got here, and this and that. Then he told Verdin to take another long drink from the bottle. He waited a bit to let the full effects of the spirits take hold. Then he again sprinkled a generous portion of the drink into and around the wound. From his bag, he removed a powder and cloth-covered poultice, which he stuffed into and over the wound. He carefully re-bandaged the wound, making sure it stayed tight.

"Laddie, leave this poultice there, just as it is, until about a week after your wound stops itching," he said. "Don't bandage the wound after that. If it drains, leave it be. Clean it, but leave the bandages off. Ye'll be fine, laddie. Ye'll be fine."

He then turned to Rob, placed a hand on his head, and tilted his head up to look in his eyes. He examined Rob's bandaged thigh, poking at it gently, then took hold of the leg, pushing the knee upward toward Rob's chest. Rob grimaced from the intense pain. The doctor held it there for a moment, then released the leg, instructing Rob to do that exercise several times a day. The kindly Scottish gentleman added, "And you must walk on it. Find a hill to walk up . . . every day, laddie. Every day. Ignore the pain. Keep on, even after the pain has stopped being so bad. Ye'll do just fine, laddie."

Giving a nod to Twig, the doctor then gathered his things, closed up his bag, and turned and walked to the road. He was gone, just like that. They never did see which way he went. It was if he'd appeared from nowhere, and left the same way.

For a time, the three young men just sat there staring after him without a word spoken between them—sort of basking in a soothing aura for having seen him again, and being taken care of by such a gentle soul.

They snapped out of their dreamlike state when Louisa appeared at the door and bade them all good morning. She looked at Twig and said, "Kind sir, would you help me with a door on the chicken coop? Papa said you were good at repairing things."

Twig immediately stood, straightened his clothes, and donned his tricorn. He gave her a serious look and nodded, too nervous to speak. She reached out and took his hand as if it were the most natural thing in the world, led him down the steps and around the end of the house, holding onto his arm and hand, telling him what she thought was wrong with the door. Rob and Verdin didn't see him until much later in the afternoon, and he seemed as calm and collected as usual, but also with a happy glow that wasn't there before.

They noticed the same thing about Louisa. She still was full of energy but didn't talk nearly as much. Somehow, she had a look of contentment and a glow about her that had not been there before. In just a few days, while always a pretty girl, she seemed to blossom into a beauty not fully realized until now.

Verdin and Rob noticed other changes in Twig too. He had always appeared thin and sinewy, but now he was a little more robust, stood a little straighter, kept his clothes cleaner and straighter on his frame. He took to carefully folding his neck cloth to fit just right and proper.

Louisa's parents noticed all this, too, and were inwardly pleased for her. She was already twenty-one years of age. She had never looked at anyone seriously, always seemed to spurn the young men who came calling. Most young women her age were already married and having children. She never seemed to worry or to be despondent about it. She once told her mother that she knew the right one would come along one day, and they both would know it immediately. Well, Twig had come along indeed, and they both seemed to know it—it just all seemed so natural and easy.

***

They soon got a visit from Isaac Wolloston, who came riding up to the Medfords' home one day with Tom. They got down off their horses and shook hands all around. The Medfords knew them well, and everyone drew chairs up on the porch with the boys. Though he was usually out working on the farm, repairing this or that, Twig happened to be there that morning to take part in the visit and hear updates on the war.

Isaac talked about some of the latest news from Boston, Washington's efforts to organize the army, and the struggle to get sufficient supplies. He talked about his son George and his endeavors to help supply Washington's army by ship. Using his contacts up and down the coast, George Wolloston was able to flit in and out with two or three ships, bringing stores close to Boston, where the goods were transported overland to Washington's army. The young Wolloston would be leaving soon for Savannah and Charleston, where he would get supplies of much-needed gunpowder.

Verdin heard the word "Savannah" and asked, "When is George leaving?"

Isaac shook his head. "Maybe a couple of weeks, maybe a month. I'm not sure yet, but I can let you know."

Rob looked at his friend suspiciously, wondering what he had in mind.

That night, long after dark when the household was asleep, Rob asked Verdin, "You want to go to Savannah, Verd? Is that what you're thinking?"

Verdin hesitated a moment, finally replying with, "Yes. Yes, I do. I want to see what I can do to get my family away from Burntthorne. I can't do it sitting here. I've been thinking about this a lot lately."

Rob said, "All right, Verdin, we'll go to Savannah."

Twig pushed himself up on his elbows. "Just as soon as you two are up to it, and not a moment before." Then he returned his head to the blanket.

The days went by slowly. Verdin's shoulder was doing better and his fever was gone. Rob was walking, as the Scottish doctor had told him to do, and with Jen-Anne's help, he was soon climbing the hill that was behind the barn. Really, the hill was just a knoll that was weedy, rather bare, and strewn with rocks. But it was a good start, and he would rest on a rock at the top before starting down.

One day after he had returned to the porch with JenAnne on his arm, laughing and talking, Rob said his goodbyes to JenAnne and plopped down next to Verdin.

Verdin raised his eyebrows. "Robert, you know that young lady has fallen for you."

"What? Oh no, you're all wrong. She's just a nice lady looking after a wounded soldier, that's all," Rob said with a dismissive wave of his hand.

"Oh no, you're the one who is wrong. I've seen her looking at you when no one else is watching her. She's in love with you, all right."

But Rob would have nothing of it. He dismissed Verdin's observations as being much mistaken. Verdin simply smiled at his friend with a look that said he knew better. Rob laughed and shook his head in an emphatic "no"—because he could think of only one person that way, and she was in England. Her name was Hannah Burntthorne.

Meanwhile Twig and Louisa were getting along splendidly. The two became more and more inseparable, helping each other with their chores. They got a lot of things done. In fact, so much that Wilbraham had Twig doing things he had always wanted to do but never had time to do around the farm.

One day Rob was walking to exercise his leg and came upon them kissing just inside the hall of the barn. It was a long, passionate kiss, followed by the two of them looking into one another's eyes tenderly while still embraced. Rob smiled at the sweet, touching moment, full of tenderness and honest love between this man and woman. The lovebirds soon became aware of his presence, but did not part. They smiled back, still in an embrace, then went back to gazing at each other. Rob wished he hadn't happened upon them, intruding on the moment, but at the same time, he was glad he had—to see them like this gave him a warm sense of wellbeing. In this world of suffering, war, cruelty, and savagery, the proof that love of this magnitude could exist was reassuring. He was glad he got to witness it.

The allotted time had passed for Verdin's poultice to finally be thrown away, and though his shoulder was still sore, the wound was healing well from the inside out. It was a long way from being completely healed, but it was much better.

At the same time, Rob's head wound had scabbed over and was just about gone. There would be a scar for the rest of his life, but it wouldn't show through his long hair. His thigh wound drained from the lower exit wound on the back of his thigh, but Wilbraham said that was best, since it was healing inside first and would be less likely to abscess. The exercise and walking kept the thigh limber.

On Rob's seventeenth birthday, July 4, they quietly celebrated with a nice meal and an apple pie made from apples fresh off the tree. It was the best apple pie he had eaten in a long time, if ever, and the party made him miss his own mother and his siblings. He couldn't help but relive the last moments he had seen them before they were separated. Oh, how he longed to do something about that tragedy!

Tom appeared again around the first of August to see how the boys were doing. He told them that George and Isaac were leaving Town River Bay for Savannah within two weeks. Rob, Verdin, and Twig approached him then about going along. They explained Verdin's family situation there, and their desire to do what they could to help. Tom, of course, knew they had experience as both sailors and soldiers, and conceded that their abilities would be an asset for George and Isaac. He felt certain the Wolloston men would agree to the boys coming along; indeed, they could use their help. If George and Isaac agreed, Tom would send a carriage for the three young men and their belongings.

They conveyed their pending departure to the Medfords, who were saddened by the news but admitted they knew it would come one day. JenAnne had tears running down her face as she disappeared in the other direction. Louisa and Twig held hands and looked somberly into each other's eyes. They slowly walked to the rear porch steps and sat down, her head on his shoulder, his arm around her.

Brothers Silas and Luke Medford started pestering the young men to let them go too. Being only fifteen and eleven, of course the three friends told them emphatically "no," although Silas was the same age they were when their lives were ripped apart and manhood forced upon them. The Medfords wouldn't hear of it anyway; they were needed at the farm.

The upcoming departure was an emotional time for all.

The next few days were filled with preparations for their leaving. The Medfords had been working on a complete set of clothes for each one of them, and proudly presented them with newly made white linen breeches, hose, white undershirts, buff outer shirt, buff waistcoats, navy blue coats, and matching tricorn hats.

The three young men looked splendid indeed in their matching uniforms. All three profusely thanked the Medfords for all they had done and for their new clothing. They were moved to tears with gratitude.

A letter was sent to their captain in the colonial lines around Boston. They explained their mission and why they needed to go. He sent a reply at once, wishing them well and that they always had a place waiting for them in any troops he might be serving with. Of course, they were strictly volunteers, had never been mustered into any unit, even of militia, so they were free of any military regulations or obligations.

Tom was true to his word, and an open carriage arrived a few mornings later to collect them and their things. The carriage was driven by a sailor who had a colorful head cloth tied over his hair, a full beard, and a large red sash tied around his waist with a pistol and dagger wedged in it.

He bustled about, helping stow their belongings on board the carriage while they said their sad farewells. JenAnne had rushed up to Rob, kissed him on the cheek first, then quickly on the mouth before tearfully turning to the others to hug them goodbye. Affectionate hugs and farewells were spoken all around. Rob told the Medfords he hoped to repay them someday for all they had done. They shushed him, telling him they did not need or want payment of any kind.

Twig and Louisa hugged, kissed, and clung to each other up until time to leave. They were sad at parting, but both seemed to have an inner peace and conviction that it would be for just a small space of time. They would be together again and not long from now. Just before he left, Twig spoke with Wilbraham, quietly asking for Louisa's hand in marriage. Wilbraham had said, "My boy, if there were ever two people meant for each other, it is you and Louisa. You're both grown and know your own heart and mind. You have our blessing, her mother and I, and we believe a Divine blessing prevails also."

So, at some point in the future, Louisa and Twig were to be wed. But for now, a war was raging. Things had to be done.

Their journey in the two-horse open carriage with Raphael, the sailor, was bumpy and painful to their wounds, but they finally made it to the bay. There they found at anchor two schooners outfitted for war. They both had eighteen guns, eight 16-pounders on each side, and fore and aft swivel guns. The schooners were nearly identical with modified captain's quarters under an abbreviated quarterdeck not usually built on a schooner. A captain's mess and officers' quarters were below the quarterdeck, which was the main deck.

The two ships were named the *Edisto* and the *Roanoke*, and these names were hand carved on a large oak board, seemingly imbedded in the handsome woodwork of the stern. They were both American made, handsome with oiled and gleaming wood, well crafted, and well manned.

The captain of the *Edisto* was none other than George Wolloston; Isaac was master of the *Roanoke*. They had consolidated their fleet of smaller vessels for these two vessels, which were armed and provisioned at the Wollostons' own expense and efforts.

George was not present upon their arrival, but Isaac was. He placed the boys and their belongings according to George's instructions. Rob was to serve on board the *Edisto* with George in the capacity of a cabin boy/midshipman/aide and was to bunk with the first and second officers. Twig was to work with the carpenter and help with ordnance. Verdin was to serve on board the *Roanoke* in the same capacity as Rob served on board the Edisto. He quartered with four other officers.

The boys didn't like being separated, but they understood George's logic and judgment in the matter. They settled in their quarters and awaited George's arrival to get underway. They were delighted to see Ellis Rofford and Norwin Chaddham again, each serving as second officers.

It was at sundown when George and Tom appeared on horseback and then rowed out to the *Edisto* riding at anchor. A man rowed the boat back to shore, mounted one of the horses, and led the other, riding off to the north and out of sight.

Capt. George Wolloston welcomed Twig and Rob aboard and waved to his father and Verdin on the *Roanoke*. Then he took command, getting the ship underway, carrying letters from General Washington to Congress at Philadelphia as well as dispatches to other colonial leaders in Williamsburg, Virginia; Wilmington, North Carolina; Charleston, South Carolina; and Savannah, Georgia.

They were soon headed east out of the bay, ever watchful of British warships, and into the Atlantic to clear Cape Cod and turn south, then southwesterly.

Thomas "Tom" Rone was on board the *Edisto*, serving as first officer. Rob finally found out from George that Tom had been a twelve-year-old orphan that his father had taken in and raised. That was fourteen years ago. Both of Tom's parents had died of smallpox. Tom had come close but somehow survived. He had been born and raised in the Overmountain settlements. His father and mother had followed Tom's widowed grandfather over the mountains. He had died when Tom was nearly twelve and Tom's parents had decided to return to the coast to provide their son with a good education.

They had made their way to Savannah and had fallen ill with the smallpox a day or two after their arrival. A kindly servant woman of Indian and black blood had taken the child away from his parent's deathbed. She nursed him back to health and, knowing Isaac Wolloston herself, she brought the boy to him. Isaac happened to be in Savannah on business at the time, and he took the boy on board ship as his own. A decade and a half had nearly passed since then, and now Tom was a faithful, hard-working, smart, handsome, well-educated young man. He viewed his role in life as being there for Isaac and George. They in turn felt the same way toward the young man.

George Wolloston was four years older than Tom, and he assumed the role of older brother for the boy easily and naturally. The three of them had been through a lot together and, if necessary, would die for the other.

George headed the ships cautiously into Delaware Bay to turn north into the Delaware River and on to Philadelphia. A couple of small vessels hailed them and told them the bay was clear of British vessels for now. Signal fires had been laid out along the coast to warn Philadelphia in case any approached.

Tom was given the dispatches to take to the State House where Congress met. He returned quickly, and they immediately departed for waters farther south.

The two ships entered the Great Chesapeake Bay on a beautiful sunny afternoon the fourth week of August 1775. Rob and Verdin enjoyed their duties and studies under George and Isaac. They helped plot the ships' locations and courses, made journal entries, tracked the ships' stores of food and water and ammunition, amongst other seafaring duties.

George and Isaac were wary of entering the bay and getting bottled up by British warships. But they needed to put in at Yorktown to drop off dispatches for Williamsburg and to pick up supplies to send to Boston. George decided to stand out to sea until after dark and then run into the tobacco port town of Yorktown.

They were just dallying around, all hands keeping a watch for sails, when just to their south, one was spotted. A single ship headed toward them on a northwesterly course. George turned his ships westerly, closer to Cape Charles, hoping the oncoming vessel would pass to their west into the bay or stay off to the east and up the coast.

The ship turned neither way. It just kept coming, making adjustments to the sails to keep the wind to her advantage as much as possible. George put on more canvas and turned northwesterly again. The ship kept coming.

Tom had been watching through a glass, standing next to George. Suddenly he said in a low voice, "Sir, it's a frigate, and I'm very sure she's a British ship, just from the way she looks."

George instantly gave the order for all hands to report to battle stations and for the guns to be loaded and run out. Isaac followed suit as soon as he saw what George was doing. He also ordered shortened sail to get a little distance between their two ships so they wouldn't interfere with the other's breeze and to give room to maneuver.

George began watching the frigate through his glass as she drew closer. He could make out the British colors flying at the stern. He at once had his ship's Massachusetts flag run up, the only one he had, and brought her about to take on the adversary and rake her with cannon fire.

The *Edisto* turned southeasterly, the wind a little front of amidships; the *Roanoke* about half a mile behind. As the enemy continued her northwesterly course, the *Edisto* opened fire first with the fore swivel gun. Then each gun fired as they came to bear. Their order to fire had been five seconds before the enemy's.

That brief amount of time made a significant difference in favor of the Wolloston ships. The *Edisto*'s first shot from the swivel hit the forwardmost gun of the starboard battery, killing part of the gun crew, so it couldn't be fired. The gun carriage was splintered and knocked to the right into the next gun carriage and crew. Some of that crew was killed also, but the gun went off as the rear of the gun was knocked to the right. The shot sailed harmlessly over the stern of the *Edisto*.

The ten shots fired by the *Edisto* yielded eight direct hits on the enemy's cannon and gun crew. The 28-gun frigate had thirteen guns on each side and two in the bow. Ten were taken out, the gun crews mutilated, and blood, guts, brains, and limbs sprawled across the deck. Three guns on the other side were also hit by the same shot and were devastated, and out of commission.

The British captain changed course to due east, in order to turn between the two ships. Each ship let loose a barrage at the same time, the *Roanoke* firing just at the start of the upswell. The shot created carnage again on the deck of the British ship, but the British gunners had fired quickly enough this time to inflict some damage of their own.

The shot killed the *Roanoke*'s helmsman, knocked out two of the guns and their crews, and damaged the gaff and boom of the mainsail. The hit tore rigging and blew holes in the mainsail.

Verdin and Isaac rushed to the helm. Isaac told him to take over while he tried to clear the mess on deck. Verdin wiped the blood off the wheel and listened for Isaac's commands.

Meanwhile, the *Edisto* reloaded her guns and opened fire again, striking more of the enemy's guns and gunners. Rigging and sails were shot away too. The British ship was basically without any firepower. Only two cannons could be fired, still in position on the starboard side. Small arms fire was the greatest danger she presented to the men on the *Edisto* and *Roanoke*.

But the two 16-pounders were still there, and fire they did, causing damage to the sails and rigging of the *Edisto*. The British ship drew away from its two adversaries, taking the favorable wind out of range and then slowly out of sight to the south.

Both the *Edisto* and *Roanoke* had fired their swivel guns at the departing, wounded ship. They had been able to fire six or eight times while she was still in range, hitting the stern several times, damaging the officers' and captain's quarters. The three ships were also exchanging small arms fire, which exacted a toll on all.

When the British ship's stern could be seen, they could see her name—HMS *Hawke*. Little did the colonials know they had killed her captain, first officer, and a great deal of the crew. Rob or Verdin had not been able to read the ship's name at the time, being otherwise occupied. They only heard about it later.

Apparently, their old commander, Captain Whitston, had seen the two smaller, less-armed Rebel ships and thought his superior frigate of the Royal Navy would blast them into submission. Instead, he was killed, and his ship had to slip away to keep from being blown to bits with a much decimated crew.

The *Edisto* and *Roanoke* let her go. The crews were already clearing away the damaged rigging and sails. George immediately turned both ships toward Yorktown and repairs.

The *Roanoke* had taken the worst damage to her sails, rigging, gaff, and boom. They were able to put up enough sail to get into Yorktown slowly. Eight crewmembers were wounded, and one dead.

The *Edisto* had lost eleven of her crew. The damage to her sides, sails, and rigging were none too severe and, with Twig's help, were repaired to good condition in just three days.

George's friends and business acquaintances in Yorktown helped him acquire materials and parts for the repairs to the *Roanoke*. Twig and the ship's carpenters and crew went to work, doing what they could with what they had, but they would have to wait for some of the parts, such as the gaff and the boom.

It was a difficult time for the *Roanoke* to be sidelined for repairs, but once all the needed materials were available, Twig and the ship's carpenters and crew would have her shipshape in a very short time.

The dispatches to the Patriots of Virginia were sent by courier. They learned that the royal governor had fled to Norfolk, a city infested by Loyalists. Most of the Patriots had fled to Yorktown, Williamsburg, and other areas away from Norfolk.

# Chapter Eight
## HEROIC DEEDS

C apt. George Wolloston was in a quandary. Should he wait with both ships until the *Roanoke* was repaired, or should he depart with the *Edisto* to deliver the letters and pick up the supplies?

Not wanting further delays, he made the decision to go on with the *Edisto*. He left all three of them, Verdin, Rob, and Twig, on board the *Roanoke* with Isaac. Also on board was Ellis Rofford as first officer. Tom went with George as his first officer.

On the sixth of September, in the darkness of night with the favorable tide, the *Edisto* slipped away, headed for Wilmington, Charleston, and Savannah. All the *Roanoke* and her crew could do was bid her farewell and wait.

The problems with the Loyalists became evident two days later. Some of the rigging and wood needed for repairs was coming from the Williamsburg area in a wagon that was part of a small wagon train filled with various supplies bound for Yorktown. A contingent of Loyalists waylaid the wagons and took them to Norfolk.

This infuriated the Patriots of Yorktown and the crew of the *Roanoke*, in particular. There was little anyone could do, though, as the royal governor had five hundred or more Loyalists at arms. The Virginians lacked equal manpower. They couldn't move against them at that time.

Some inconclusive skirmishing took place, but nothing else for two or three weeks. Then the weather turned foul for a week or more with strong winds and rain, and even waterspouts out in the bay.

In the meantime, Twig, the carpenters, and mates performed all the repairs they could with the materials they had available to them. They repaired cannon carriages, ramrods, and wheels. They repaired muskets and rifles, oiled them, cleaned them, and shined them. They repaired every little chunk of wood on the *Roanoke*, oiled the wood, re-pitched the decks. The ship was picture-perfect, except for those repairs they couldn't make until the necessary materials were delivered to them.

Finally some intelligence arrived that the wagons were sitting in a certain warehouse down near the waterfront. Captain Isaac Wolloston's ears perked up at this bit of information. *Perhaps the supplies could be slipped down to a boat under cover of darkness?*

Looking about the waterfront at Yorktown, they finally found a boat that might facilitate Isaac's plan—it was like a longboat with a mast for a small sail, oars, and a capacity for enough men and the supplies. But the weather did not cooperate and news came that another source for the supplies had been found. So they waited. Then came a rumor that the Loyalists were on their way to burn Yorktown, which ultimately proved to be false. Then came word of fighting around Norfolk.

Finally, out of nowhere, a group of wagons arrived from up river with the needed supplies. In four days, the *Roanoke* was re-rigged, re-sailed, and in shipshape. The jubilant crew restocked water and food stores, and the jaunty little ship was put out to sea—that is, after first successfully clearing Cape Charles and Chesapeake Bay to gain the open sea.

It wasn't meant to be. They had swiftly made the approximately thirty miles to the mouth of the bay in the dark, running with no lights. Suddenly the lights of three ships could be seen under sail but certainly not under a full complement. They were slowly moving to the south about one-half mile apart. Isaac surmised these had to be British ships patrolling the entrance to Chesapeake Bay.

Captain Isaac had no choice but to bring the ship around and run.

They made it back to Yorktown where they spread the news. The next day, a small craft came in bearing news that three British ships, a frigate, and two sloops of war were patrolling the bay in concert with the Loyalists' activities in and around Norfolk. The Virginians decided it was time to do something about that bunch of hornets, to knock down the nest and burn it.

A new regiment of Virginia troops was moving down the James, skirmishing with the Loyalists as they went. Their commander was a Colonel Woods, who was determined to exterminate the threat of the hated royal governor and his Loyalist army and followers.

Isaac agreed to let Rob, Verdin, Twig, and a couple of other crewmen join in with the Patriots to help anyway they could. After all, what else could they do, with the British keeping them bottled up?

So, with some of the locals, the five men from the Wolloston crew set out on foot to cross to the bank of the James, thence by boat to the opposite shore on which Norfolk lay to the southeast. Rob had his bow and arrows slung across his back, and they were otherwise armed with their rifles, knives, powder horns, shot pouches, haversacks, blankets, rations, and canteens.

They were dressed in white hose, white breeches, white linen undershirts, white linen outer shirt and neck cloth, buff-colored waistcoats, and solid blue long coats of wool with matching tricorn hat. Their shoes were the usual hobnailed, black buckle shoes.

They were welcomed by Colonel Woods himself, who was told by one of his esteemed countrymen of their coming. He was also told of their connection with the Wollostons and of their military experiences. The colonel was glad indeed to have fighting men of this caliber.

They were taken in by a young man serving as sergeant. He had only militia drill experience, but was sincere and capable. Sgt. Ross Chandler was from a fine Virginia family farther up the Potomac, who knew George Washington and his family. He was made aware of who they were and their experiences. Despite the difference in age, as he was near thirty, he became a friend and companion to the younger boys, who seemed much older than their years. He and Twig, near the same age, hit it off from the start.

Despite some residual pain, both Rob and Verdin had essentially recovered from their wounds and were able to walk, march, and endure the rigors of military life. Within just a few days, under Sergeant Chandler's tutelage, they were fitting right in.

They spent only two days with the Virginians when they were on the move. Colonel Woods was intent on pushing the Loyalists back to Norfolk, where he could bring them to bay and annihilate them. There were some five hundred Loyalists and close to six hundred Patriots jockeying for position on the limited road network of the Virginia coastal lowlands.

Rob and Verdin's company was out front that third day when some of the Loyalists came barreling around a slight bend of the road. They were in a line that overlapped the road on either side by about fifty yards. Instead of fading back on the main column, the captain ordered the sergeants to bring the men into line across the road. This they did, but left both flanks woefully exposed to the overlapping lines of the enemy. Rob and Verdin watched the smartly dressed, green-uniformed men advancing, their longer lines about to envelope their flanks.

The long green line stopped and fired just as the Virginia Company was ordered to fire. Mass confusion broke out among the Virginians left standing. A good quarter of them were down, wounded, or dead. Rob and his companions had suffered no harm, but they didn't mean to start here and just be run over. They could see poor officership and soldiering on their side, and their captain didn't seem to know what he was doing.

The only saving grace at that point was that the Loyalists were somewhat in disarray too. The Patriot volley had hit a number of them, including some of their officers.

Motioning for the other four to follow, Rob led them to the right of the road. Stooping low in the waist-high grass, he angled toward and to the right of the extended left of the Loyalists. Suddenly they came to a small stream with the banks sloping down on either side. Rob kept following the stream, popping up his head every few moments to see where the enemy was. He could see them slowly walking forward, shooting at the Patriots across the road, and stopping to reload.

Rob was finally satisfied with their position, and he whispered, "Let me see if I can hit one or two with arrows before we alarm them." The others nodded in agreement, spread out in a line along the creek bank, checking their rifles and squatting down to stay out of sight.

Rob took off his hat, removed the bow from his back, selected an arrow, and notched it. When he stood up to look for the enemy, the nearest one at the end of the line was no more than fifteen yards away. He pulled back and let fly the arrow! He heard the man grunt when the arrow hit him in the side, and he disappeared in the grass. Rob quickly notched another arrow and fired at the next man, who was busy loading his musket. The arrow hit him in the middle of the back just to the left of the backbone, and the point protruded through his chest after piercing his heart. He, too, fell and disappeared in the tall grass.

The next in line was standing to fire his musket when Rob's next arrow hit him in the left armpit. He screamed and fell into the grass, thrashing around. This time his comrade to his right wheeled around to look directly at Rob, just as Rob let fly the next arrow. It hit the Loyalist in the chest, and he staggered back into the next man in line, who caught him and slowly laid him in the grass. He then shouted the alarm to his comrades: "Rebels on the left!" He repeated this several times.

Finally, eight of the Loyalists turned and formed a line facing Rob, who was no more than forty yards from them. He stepped back into the little depression of the creek, just as they let loose a volley that lopped off the grass about chest high.

Immediately, Rob and his companions sprang up and, on Rob's directions, let loose a volley of their own. Four of the Loyalists in the line were killed outright. The others panicked and began running toward the road. It was catching, and soon nearly all the Loyalists in the grass to the left of the road fell back as well.

Rob and his companions reloaded and again stood and fired in unison. Again, they found their marks; this time, five more Loyalists fell into the high grass. Rob let loose an arrow quickly on the heels of the volley, and another one went down.

That did it. The remaining Loyalists on the left and even some on the road in the center began streaming to the rear. Some were downright panic-stricken and hysterical, throwing away firearms and ammunition.

Rob and his group did all they could do to keep up the scare. He told them to fire one after another in order to keep up a continuous fire while they advanced. This they did, popping up to fire, ducking down to reload and run forward, then fire again.

This so confused the Loyalists as to how many were rolling up their left flank that the officer in charge of the advance sounded recall. The panic then set in full bore, and in a matter of minutes, the remainder of the two hundred or so men was gone—running down the road toward the main body about a mile away.

The major who had led the column was the last one to leave, disgustedly trotting back down the road. Rob ran into the road with his loaded rifle, drew a bead, and fired. The major tumbled and sprawled in the road, dead.

Colonel Woods was highly praising the captain of the advance column on sending the enemy running. A couple of lieutenants and sergeants had a quiet conversation with the colonel that evening and told him about Rob leading his companions out to the enemy flank and how their fire had caused the enemy to collapse, ultimately creating the panic of the enemy.

Colonel Woods never openly chastised the young inexperienced captain, but praised him for utilizing brave young men and tactics severely detrimental to enemy forces. He praised young Rob and his companions, held a banquet in their honor, and awarded them all with the rank of lieutenant in the Virginia military forces.

Fighting resumed the next day as Colonel Woods kept up the pressure, using all in his power to gain control of the delicate road system in the soft, low-lying terrain. The second week of December, he feinted down a narrow corridor between the river and a marshy area to the right of the road. These troops attacked the advance column of Loyalists, which contained many of the same troops that had panicked earlier. The Patriots feigned defeat and disaster and began retreating down the road back toward the Virginia camp and main body. The enemy charged down the road in pursuit, soon strung out along the road in the narrow corridor.

Two companies of Virginians, including Rob and his companions, were hidden in the grassy marsh well out of sight of the road. As the Loyalists got to the right place, the Virginians came stomping out of the marsh and fell upon the unsuspecting Tories. At first, the Tories tried to make a stand and their officers actually got some of them in line, and they began firing. But they were too strung out and outnumbered, too unorganized, and soon too panicked to offer a real defense.

The Virginians came out of the marsh, fired one volley at close range, then began firing individually as soon as they could load and fire. The young new lieutenants, Rob, Verdin, Twig, and their other two companions, as well as a few Virginians, had been selected to close the trap door. They formed a defensive line across the road, barring the way to safety for the trapped Tories.

The Loyalists were being shot to pieces in the road, and soon, several of them turned and tried to storm the Rebel line across the road. Rob fired at one of the bearskin-capped officers, who fell at their feet after running full speed toward them. In a moment, it turned into hand-to-hand combat, as there was no time to load and fire.

Soon the whole Rebel line was engaged in hand-to-hand combat, using knuckles, fists, and knives, kicking, gouging, and hair pulling, throwing of tomahawks, using rifles as clubs . . . and some had bayonets.

Rob pulled his knife from the scabbard and, standing with Twig and Verdin, who were also brandishing knives, cut and slashed at the onrushing Tories, trying to either kill them or run over them. No quarter was asked . . . and none was given.

For what seemed a lifetime, the Virginians fought tooth and nail. The surrounded, trapped, outnumbered Tories were soon all down, dead or wounded. A few broke and ran for the river or the marsh. While most of them were mowed down, some did make it back to Norfolk.

Covered in blood from slashes and cuts of their own and of their enemy, Rob and his companions rounded up a few prisoners, mostly walking wounded. The enemy's advance column had been obliterated.

By mid-December 1775, the last of the serious fighting around Norfolk was over. The royal governor and his Tory friends torched the city to celebrate the New Year and their departure by ship. At last, Virginia was free of the royal governor and this bunch of Tory hornets. The nest had been burned.

Gone were the British warships, and so Rob and his friends were back aboard the *Roanoke*, heading after the *Edisto*. They were going straight to Savannah in hopes of reaching her there. Captain Isaac drove her hard, and in spite of the cold, spitting snow and rainy weather they encountered soon after leaving, they made good time.

In early January, they slowly slid past Tybee Island into the Savannah River channel and soon tied up in the crowded riverfront of Savannah. Captain Isaac had been there before and carefully and safely guided them in.

The little port was bustling with activity as Captain Isaac and the boys walked the cobblestone streets to find out where the *Edisto* had gone, as she was nowhere to be seen in Savannah. He went to the offices of one Elisha Seagate up the hill from the waterfront. From Mr. Seagate, he learned that the *Edisto* had delivered her letters and loaded the military goods going to Boston, then departed. The captain asked if the stores for them to take were still available, and when told they were, he at once determined to have them loaded and be on his way.

Mr. Seagate called him aside and talked to him earnestly for a moment. He was an avid Patriot and had done and would do more for the Patriot cause than many men . . . and it went unnoticed except by those with whom he worked and by the Patriots who benefitted from it.

"Captain Wolloston," he said, "while we all appreciate the

Bostonians' efforts and their need of our support, I can't help but bring
to your attention the desperate need of some of our countrymen near
Wilmington. The Tories there have been exceptionally hard and cruel to
our brethren of the cause, and they need these supplies desperately.
Would you kindly deliver them to Wilmington and return here for your
supplies to go to Boston? I will replenish them while you're gone."

Isaac could hardly refuse. Mr. Seagate informed them where the
supplies were located in a warehouse and sent a man with the crew to
show them the way and unlock the warehouse.

While the stores were being transferred to the *Roanoke*, Seagate
filled him in on the latest news. A great blow had been dealt the Loyalists
in South Carolina when fifteen hundred Rangers under Colonel
Thomson had captured a host of trouble-making Loyalists at Great
Canebrake in South Carolina. Also, during the last week of December,
another blow had been landed on the Tories during the so-called SNOW
Campaign in South Carolina, where they had fifteen inches of snow. He
also told of the news he heard about the Patriots running the Loyalists
out of Norfolk. That was when Captain Wolloston stopped him to let him
know that he knew of the Norfolk fighting firsthand. He, too, shared
what he knew—including the exploits and heroic deeds of his very own
crewmembers who were integral in making that a favorable campaign.

It was cold and getting colder as the military stores were brought on
board. That evening, the *Roanoke* stood out in the river and took the
receding tide out past Tybee Island, turning northward toward
Wilmington, about three hundred miles away.

The weather turned on them: cold, blustery, overcast skies, contrary
head winds, rough seas, rain, freezing rain, snow flurries. They passed
Charleston in the dark, barely seeing some lights twinkling on the distant
shore. They kept on trudging along and were nearing Cape Fear when
they suddenly saw a sail. A ship had apparently come around the Cape,
running with a good, favorable wind and now was upon them.
Immediately, they could see another smaller vessel behind her as well.

Capt. Isaac Wolloston called all hands to battle stations, and the

*Roanoke* came alive. He shouted to the helmsman to turn with the wind to run, and he called for more sail. Ellis Rofford, the first officer, had been watching with a ship's glass and suddenly bellowed, "She's British, and she's at battle stations!"

Captain Isaac watched as his heavy-laden ship sluggishly came about and began running with the wind to her portside, a quarter off the stern. He watched the two ships a few minutes and realized his ship was too heavy with supplies to outrun the bigger ship.

He decided the best thing to do, and immediately put it into execution. He ordered the sailors aloft to stand by to drop all sail. He ordered the helmsman to back off the wind a little—not noticeably—just enough to let the frigate more quickly catch up. For a while, it looked as though there would be a long chase, but eventually the frigate closed in, her escort in close pursuit. Just as the frigate came into gun range, Captain Isaac gave the signal to drop sail and stand by the helm. The ship bowed up and stopped like a horse with a bit in its mouth. The frigate reacted like someone with his mouth flying open. She was in danger of running past her quarry. The helmsman brought the ship out of the wind while sailors scrambled aloft.

That was when Captain Isaac ordered the starboard batteries to fire as the British ship turned straight into the wind. The belch of flame, smoke, and cannon shot hit some of the gun crew, a couple of cannons, and did some damage to the rigging of the British frigate, but it wasn't near enough this time. The answering broadside from the enemy swept the deck of the *Roanoke*, sweeping aside guns and littering the deck with dead and wounded, blood and gore. Captain Isaac gave the order to run up sail and to turn with the wind. "Let her luff!" he roared. Luckily, there was no real damage to the sails and rigging.

Now another serious danger faced the British frigate. As she dropped her sails and lost headway, firing her guns, the escort close behind and slightly on her starboard side came bearing down on her. The frigate began to turn slightly starboard, tail to the wind, and the recoil of the broadside helped. But the escort was running toward the starboard bow of the ship, which was barely underway now, going with the wind across the bow of the escort. When the captain of the escort realized what was taking place, he ordered the ship to turn right, to the starboard, and to run with the wind past the bow of the larger frigate.

She had such good headway that she answered the helm at once, but as with all ships, it was not instantaneous. She began turning, but her bowsprit had already penetrated airspace above the deck of the frigate and began ripping into rigging and sails forward of the main mast. Her bowsprit snapped against the mizzenmast, but the stub continued to do damage as it turned windward.

Then the escort began to glide by the bows of the frigate, and the bowsprit of the frigate began ripping the rigging, sailors, and sails off the escort as she continued under sail with wind. The captain of the escort finally got enough seamen aloft to drop the sails. When the two ships were both at rest, they were quite a jangled-up, tangled mess.

The *Roanoke* surged forward across the bow of the frigate and downwind. This tactic was unexpected by the captain of the frigate, and he could do nothing in the way of maneuver to stop it. There was one serious flaw in the movement though. It exposed the *Roanoke* to the unfired starboard battery very briefly. The gun crews took it upon themselves to fire, and they did.

Again, men and guns were hit, and this time, the stern of the ship and the area where the officers stood around the helm were hit as well. But there was very little damage to sails or rigging and none to the helm itself. The *Roanoke* crowded on all the sail she could and left the two damaged ships in her wake as she ran for Wilmington.

Only after she was out of danger and the men began assessing the damage, did they discover a tragic casualty. Their much respected and beloved captain, Isaac Wolloston, was dead. One of the last cannon blasts from the enemy to the stern of the *Roanoke* had hit the gunwale at the back of the deck. Large oak splinters had gone everywhere, one piercing the good captain's chest and heart. He had died instantly and painlessly. Ellis Rofford was the first to find him and was overcome with tears as he bent over his captain. Soon, Norwin Chaddham, Rob, Verdin, Twig, and many others were by his side, tears streaming down their saddened countenances.

There would not be much time for grieving, however, as there was much to be done after such a battle. They had Isaac's body removed below decks and then quietly went about their duties. Other dead and wounded needed attention. The decks were cleared and cleaned, guns uprighted, carriages repaired. They had seen the chaos the last maneuver by Captain Isaac had caused the enemy. Their two damaged, motionless ships, with rigging torn, sails flapping and lying in the water, looked forlorn and much like two wounded birds.

The *Roanoke* raced away from the scene toward Wilmington. Without their captain, the crew didn't know the right people to contact, the harbor approaches, or the hundreds of other little things that only his experiences could bring them. Ellis Rofford assumed command of the ship, and Norwin Chaddham, first officer. Both men proved capable and enterprising in their new roles. They soon discovered the charts, Isaac's notes, and names of people important to their mission. Captain Rofford easily brought the *Roanoke* to anchorage at the port, following Isaac's written notes. The weather turned foul during their journey, so they were glad to finally drop anchor in a safe refuge. The weary crew went to sleep with a minimum watch guard revolving every two hours.

The next morning, Colonel Abner Treadstone rowed out to come on board. The Patriots were eager to get those badly needed munitions and weapons. He got the ship a berth at a wharf, with crews unloading the ship and loading up the wagons.

Supplies from other ships and locales had been loaded on the large freight wagons pulled by four horses each—a total of thirty-five wagons in all. Rob, Verdin, and Twig were ashore with Captain Rofford at the time, and watched them noisily pull out.

# Chapter Nine
## RETURN TO SAVANNAH

With the mission accomplished, Rob, Verdin, and Twig were free to return to Savannah and assume their previous roles. This time, however, Verdin intended to find his sister and get her out of the clutches of the Burntthornes. If the *Roanoke* had to sail without him, so be it.

Meanwhile, there was the issue of burying their dead. The crew had talked it over and decided to not bury their dead at sea. They asked Colonel Treadstone about someone to help them with the internment of Capt. Isaac Wolloston and the others killed in that last battle. If George Wolloston wanted to disinter his father later and move the body to Massachusetts, then he could do that. Families of the other crewmen could do that also. So, a brief yet emotional service was held, and the bodies were buried in the North Carolina soil. That was all they could do for them . . . and their families. Sorrowfully, the crew walked down off the hill cemetery back into town.

Later that evening, pandemonium broke loose. Back on board, the crew of the *Roanoke* had been preparing to get underway when they heard a bunch of shouting and ruckus outside the ship. Captain Rofford sent a few men to investigate.

They soon returned with news that the wagon train was back without getting the supplies to the Patriots. While en route to the Patriots' camp, the wagons were ambushed by Loyalists and were fortunate enough to hightail it out of there without loss of man, horse, or wagon. It was assumed that the Tories' motivation was not so much to kill or seize, but to have the wagons turn back.

Colonel Treadstone was beside himself with rage. So were Rob and his mates. Risking life and limb and losing dear friends and shipmates to bring the badly needed supplies only to have this happen? It just wouldn't do. So, Captain Rofford at once determined to use his crew as an escort to get the wagons to their destination.

Three hours later, Rob, Verdin, Twig, and nearly half the crew—twenty men, armed, provisioned, and warmly dressed—reported to Treadstone. He was pleasantly surprised to have this support. He decided to pull out just before daybreak the next morning so that, barring any problems, they could conceivably cover the twenty miles by nightfall.

After a cold, windy night when few slept, the wagons began moving out just a little before the eastern sky began to redden. The dirt road on the northeast side of the Black River was typically bad in the winter. It was slow going, and a cold day, but they kept plodding forward. Taking turns riding and walking, Rob and the boys actually enjoyed the change of task. The lead wagons began pulling into the Patriot camp near Moore's Creek just as the sun was touching the tops of the trees on the western horizon. This time, the trip was without incident.

The supplies were immediately dispersed to the thousand or so Patriot soldiers, who were now all on the east side of the creek, the planks having been taken off the bridge in their front. Word from scouts and informants told them that some sixteen hundred Tories, mostly from North Carolina, were advancing on their front, looking to do battle.

During the night, the Patriots had shored up their defensive works and tried to ease their nerves about the advancing enemy. The next morning, cookfires were lit, and the troops ate a good hot meal, finishing up even as the drums, bagpipes, and fifes began blaring. The enemy had arrived to take its position and to destroy the Patriot army.

The main enemy attack came at the bridge across the creek, which only had runners now, greased by the Patriots, and no planks. The Tories tried to cross and kept coming despite mass gunfire, fire from a cannon at point blank range, and the grease. Soon, about fifty bodies were in the creek—shot down or had slipped off the greased runners. All drowned.

Rob had been watching the right flank of the Patriots with his men. While sneaking around in the growth of bush and trees along the creek, they actually found a ford to cross it. Some Tories on the west side of the creek were unaware of their presence, and they, too, were looking for a place to ford.

Losing no time to thwart this, Rob led his men in attacking the Tories, approximately sixty of them coming out of the brush and trees screaming and bellowing, firing all the while. The shocked Tories stood their ground, unsure of just who these wild attackers were or how many. Rob instructed his men to fire individually, in teams and from cover, so that when one man was firing, the other man was loading. This way, they could power on with three or four shots a minute. In response, the Tories massed and unleashed a single volley. Rob had his men jump behind trees or hug the ground at the last minute, and not one of them was hit. While the Loyalists struggled to reload while in line standing up, they made excellent targets for Rob and his companions.

Rob pulled his bow off his back and, with Verdin and Twig alongside him, crept closer to the enemy, staying concealed by brush and trees. From thirty yards away, Rob began sending his quiet messengers of death into the enemy. His first arrow struck one of their officers in the eye and came out the back of his head. He fell to his knees, head back, with the arrow still in his skull, and slowly his body hit the ground fully, his dead eyes looking up.

Verdin and Twig worked as a team, one firing, then the other. Both were excellent shots and, by now, just like Rob, were seasoned, battle-tested veterans, cold-blooded killers in war. They began taking a serious toll on the Tories nearby. The rest of the crew wasn't doing badly either.

The Tories suddenly got maybe thirty reinforcements in that sector, and the officers decided to mount an attack to drive these deadly Rebels from their flank. They fixed bayonets and charged. Rob and his comrades began firing and picking them off, taking a deadly toll on the Loyalists. Fading back from the greater numbers pressing them, they were soon faced with the prospect of turning, fleeing, and fording the creek in nearly chest-high water while under fire, or standing their ground. Standing their ground, it was.

The Patriots sprang among the enemy, firing, slashing, smashing, and ripping. Rob fired an arrow point-blank at another officer and struck him in the throat. The man fell with the arrow jutting front and back, blood gushing from his nose and mouth. This officer had a cavalryman's sabre in his hand, and Rob snatched it from the dead man without hesitation. He then went to slashing right and left. Soon, he was covered with blood as he severed arms and hands, and slashed necks and heads. Verdin and Twig went with him, protecting his flanks, hitting the enemy with their rifle stocks, firing when they could. Like a madman, yet very methodically, Rob savagely went after the enemy.

It was more than the enemy could take. They broke and ran. The exhausted Rob and his companions found themselves firing at the backs of the fleeing men, hitting their marks with deadly accuracy.

The center of the Loyalist line began retreating, too, following their repulse at the bridge, which was all too bloody and horrible for them. They turned and headed back west from which they came in fairly good order. The Patriots soon had enough men across the creek in pursuit, that the good order fell apart somewhat. It still wasn't a complete panic and rout, but men began throwing down their arms and surrendering in ever-larger numbers. Over the next few days, the disorganized Tory army was depleted by almost nine hundred prisoners. The great Loyalist offensive and takeover of the Carolinas had been brought to a screeching halt.

One of the last shots of the battle was fired at Rob. He, Verdin, and Twig had been in pursuit of the enemy when one of the officers turned and fired his pistol at Rob. The lead ball passed completely through his left thigh, much like the previous wound. This time, the ball didn't leave the bone unscathed. It didn't sever the thighbone, but it did graze it, driving the piece of bone out with the ball. The ball and piece of bone were later found matted to the inside of his breeches leg, as it did not have the velocity after passing through his thigh to penetrate the cloth of the pants leg.

Rob crumpled to the ground, and Verdin and Twig fired simultaneously, instantly killing the enemy officer. They turned to Rob immediately and picked him up to carry him to the surgeon. Their shipmates followed, sensing their business was done here.

The wound was intensely painful to Rob, and there was little the surgeon could do for it but apply medication to the two holes in the thigh, and bandage it. Colonel Treadstone arranged for a wagon to transport Rob and the other crewmembers back to their ship. He also provided Rob with the only medication for pain known at that time: a full bottle of Scotch whiskey made in the highlands of North Carolina.

Rob seldom touched spirits, but he was in a good deal of pain and the journey over twenty miles of rough road in a wagon called for medicinal help. By the time they were well underway, he had passed out, holding the bottle of "medicine" resolutely under his arm. His companions let him sleep.

They arrived during the night, got Rob and all their equipment on board, and cast off. Daylight found them luffing along, well on their way to Savannah. Rob was in sickbay, being cared for by the ship's doctor. He wasn't really a doctor, but an aspiring young man who had apprenticed with a doctor in Boston for six years, since he was sixteen years of age. Still, he was really quite gifted . . . and studious, constantly reading to learn all he could. For now, Rob was in good hands: the good hands of Dr. Maury Kensly.

# Chapter Ten

# THORNEWELL AND A BOBCAT

March 1776 found them once again in Savannah. Spring was around the corner, but the weather was pleasant and warm already. The *Edisto* had not been seen or heard from since their last visit. Capt. Ellis Rofford told Elisha Seagate of the death of Captain Isaac Wolloston and the other seamen who were interred in Wilmington. Seagate said he would inform Capt. George Wolloston the minute he arrived.

Quickly, the supplies for Boston were loaded aboard the *Roanoke*. Captain Rofford was set on leaving at once. Verdin and Twig reminded him of their plans to stay in Savannah to see what they could do about Verdin's sister. He was very sad to see the three men go. They had become cherished friends during the past year.

Rob and all their personal belongings were brought ashore and taken to the nearby home of Elisha Seagate. He was a widower and lived alone except for a housekeeper/cook, a spry and kindly lady in her early senior years. She was known as Mrs. Bunnie—and that was all they ever knew as far as her full name.

The home had two small bedrooms on the back of the ground floor. Mrs. Bunnie occupied one, but she made Rob comfortable in the other. The others made the bedroom upstairs their quarters, across from that of Elisha Seagate.

Seagate was a man of many contacts and made it his business to find and have information. He knew of Oden Burntthorne and Oden's father, Lord Burson Burntthorne. He knew of their country estate southwest of Savannah called Thornewell. He knew they were rabid Loyalists who had extensive dealings with the Creeks and Cherokees. At the time, the whereabouts of both men were unknown. Seagate didn't know if they were in England, at sea, or at Thornewell, which was three or four days from Savannah. Another possibility was that one or both of them could be in Indian Territory. Seagate had heard that the men had been in towns such as Long Swamp and Coosawattee, stirring up the warriors against the Rebels. These towns were deep in the Indian nation and not easily reached.

As far as Verdin's sister, her whereabouts were unknown. She might be at Thornewell, as far as Seagate's informers knew, but servants seldom were discussed. Without talking with a recent visitor or to one of the other servants, no information was to be had.

Rob's wound caused him a good deal of pain and young Dr. Kensly had to cast about to find him more analgesic. The best place to find it was on the riverfront, and he was able to procure some bottles of good Jamaican rum. This was as good an analgesic as could be found for those times.

Verdin and Twig talked it over with Rob and Maury and decided they needed to go in search of Sylvia. Rob didn't like being left behind, but he knew it might be weeks again before he could undertake such a journey.

Leaving Rob in the care of young Dr. Maury Kensly and Mrs. Bunnie, Verdin and Twig left for Thornewell early one morning in the middle of March. Already the trees were budding, and some blooms were providing splashes of color. Armed with a map provided to them by an associate of Seagate's, they prepared for the journey with two borrowed horses, fully equipped.

From the ship's stores, they had kept two pieces of sailcloth and some rope and wood for pegs. They carried a blanket and their heavy, long coats rolled up behind their saddle in the sailcloth and strapped on very securely. They were dressed in the white stockings and breeches, black shoes with buckles, white undershirt, loose-sleeved outer shirt, and buff-colored waistcoat only, for coolness. They both wore their wool tricorn hats.

They had their haversacks hanging on their side along with the powder horn and shot pouch. In their haversacks were flint and dry tinder for making fires, meat and bread for food, whetrock and other tools for cleaning and oiling their weapons. Each wore a leather strap over one shoulder, which was attached to a leather scabbard holding a hunting knife. The knife hung more to the back over the hip and out of the way of the powder horns and haversacks. Hanging alongside the knife was a tomahawk. They had acquired these in North Carolina. Balanced across their saddles were the rifles they had acquired during fighting at Lexington.

Having said their goodbyes to Rob and Maury the night before, they saddled their horses in Mr. Seagate's carriage house and left just at dawn. Following the map given to them by their host, they had soon left the city of Savannah behind them. The sun was coming up, and they passed several houses, small farms, and some larger homes in the distance. Soon they came to a road that turned south about twelve miles from Seagate's, and so they headed south. Six or eight miles from there, they turned toward the Fleming Plantation to the west. It was early afternoon as they made their way past the big house, and by late afternoon, they decided to stop and rest for the night, feed their horses and themselves. They crossed a stream and turned right, following the stream to an area with grass and trees on a slight rise. A deer, followed by a fawn, bounded out of a thicket, startling them. They had seen all kinds of other wildlife. The creatures, particularly the squirrels and birds, kept up a jumble of noises all along the way, punctuated by the frogs singing along the creek. Every once in a while, they heard something snarling and crashing through the thick undergrowth.

They had followed their map to a tee. They crossed numerous little streams on rickety little bridges just wide enough for one wagon. They crossed one small river, or large creek, on a covered bridge. Their instructions indicated the road became a path after the Fleming Plantation, which was an Indian trading path that led to the Oconamaha River. Thornehill stood east of the river on a slight bluff overlooking a ford. Another north/south path, the Hatawwah trading path intersected the east/west path just east of the river. A likely spot for a man interested in the Indian trade.

They staked out their horses and slept under the stars in the cool, spring, night air. Just after they had gone to sleep, something spooked the horses. Twig held the horses by their halters and tried to soothe them. Verdin cocked his rifle and walked in a circle around the camp to see what had spooked the horses. He thought he heard something a little farther out, so he started walking toward a thicket. He could just make it out in the pale light of the moon and stars. Suddenly, he heard something snarl, and a sound like a scream came from behind him. He turned just in time to see a cat-like creature with little or no tail, screaming and starting toward him.

He whirled around and fired in one swift movement; a second later he was falling backward over a log. The cat-like creature had fallen over dead, but Verdin didn't know it until he was able to scramble to his feet and peer over the log. Still shaking from adrenaline, he walked back to the campfire and told Twig what had happened, so they took turns sleeping the rest of the night just to ward off any wild creatures.

Shortly after daylight, they walked over to the thicket where the cat creature lay. It was as big as a medium-sized dog, as Twig pointed out by way of comparison. The animal was like a house cat in the face, but had a short tail.

Twig said, "I've heard of these bobcats. That's what they're called by the people hereabouts. "Bobcats, because their tails are bobbed off."

Suddenly they heard a mewing sound, and following their ears, they looked over the log that Verdin had fallen over the night before. Twig reached down and picked up a baby cat who was meowing as though it was starved. He held it by the scruff of the neck, the way a mama cat picks up her babies. It was identically shaped and colored as the mama, only with very pronounced spots, and no bigger than a man's hand. They looked again at the dead cat and saw it was clearly a mama with milk for its young one.

Verdin said, "Oh my, Twig! What are we goin' to do with the baby?"

"Leave it to me," Twig reassured him. "I've raised critters before, and I reckon we'll make it all right with this one."

Verdin busied himself with the horses and breaking camp while Twig went down to the creek. Soon Verdin saw him mashing up two small fish, some biscuit, and water, which he then fed to the little cat. It must have suited the youngster because it gobbled down the thin gruel and was purring like an ordinary house cat in no time.

When they left, Twig laid the young cat across the saddle in front of him, and it promptly went to sleep. When it woke up, Twig put it on the ground and squeezed more of the mix into its mouth. It moved around a little, settling next to Twig, and soon was asleep again. So they moved on, discovering over time that the little cat would not leave Twig's side.

They camped a ways off the path near a small stream that night. During the night, they heard horses splashing across the creek, and men's voices speaking briefly to each other. Neither Verdin nor Twig could understand the words, so they surmised the riders may have been Creek Indians.

They fed the cat and themselves shortly after daybreak and made their way back to the path. Verdin held up his hand, and they stopped a few feet from the trail. A very real possibility came to them, almost simultaneously, as they looked at the horse hoof prints in the trail.

If they were on the trail, their footprints could be clearly seen. As far as they knew, that group of horsemen could have been trailing them and had just happened to run past their place of departure from the trail in the dark. They may be doubling back even now.

Slowly, the two young men backed their horses away from the trail and turned, riding from it until it was out of sight.

"What are we going to do?" asked Twig.

Verdin thought for a minute then pulled out their map. After studying it carefully, he said to Twig, "How far away from Thornewell do you think we are?"

Twig looked at the map, then reflected thoughtfully before saying, "Probably somewhere between five to eight miles."

"Close enough," said Verdin. "Twig, let's stay off the path, go due west to the river, then upriver to the estate."

Twig nodded his head in agreement then added, "Let's go up this creek a distance, away from the trail, then get in the creek and stay in it until we cross the trail. Then we can get out of the creek somewhere west of the trail."

Verdin nodded his head in silent agreement and followed Twig's lead.

They passed their campsite from the night before and pressed on for a quarter mile or so before angling into the stream. Then they turned downstream, westerly, slowly walking their horses in the dark water, which was sometimes knee or chest-deep on the horses. As they neared the Indian path, they slowed up, rifles at the ready. They peered both ways down the trail, but did not see or hear a soul. Still going slowly, they walked downstream past the crossing, and with one watching ahead and one watching behind, they moved out of sight of the trail.

They realized the stream was angling north to northwest; they guessed it emptied into the river. Some other smaller streams fed into it on both sides, and the creek was becoming deeper. Then it started gradually getting wider, about knee-deep on the horses. Twig noticed that a log seemed to be moving slowly away from them near the opposite bank—a log with eyes. Another was sitting motionless just a little farther downstream. Twig knew that logs with eyes were reptiles—alligators. He pointed nervously in their direction, and Verdin nodded his head knowingly.

A little farther down, a large green snake slithered along a tree limb dangling overhead. Another reptilian log watched from the south bank, and a dark colored snake wiggled across the water to disappear in the grass. Birds were calling in the forest canopy overhead. Squirrels chattered. Bobwhites whistled in some meadow not far away. Large bullfrogs and numerous smaller frogs splashed into the water just ahead of the moving horses' feet.

The land on each side of them was nearly as flat as the surface of the slow-moving, dark-colored stream. The larger trees were now in clumps on areas of higher ground. The creek was flowing through an area of mostly grasses, vines, and small bushes. They were basically in a swamp. They both could sense they had come downstream enough to be near the Oconomaha River.

Twig carefully guided his horse onto a slightly elevated, sandy rise, which was covered in tall, fat pines. With Verdin close behind, he began to weave through the trees. Moving almost due west for a hundred yards, they both could make out the confluence of the creek they had been following, and that of a much larger stream, which had to be the river.

It was only mid-morning when they turned their horses northwesterly to follow the river upstream, hopefully toward Thornewell, if their reckoning was right. They were still in the pines on a very slight ridge that ran parallel to the river. There was very little undergrowth in this virgin forest of massive pines.

In a couple of places, small streams cut into the ridge on its way to the river, and there were grasses and water plants to cross. None of these proved to be a serious obstacle, and they continued on their way.

Finally, on a curve in the river on a low-lying bluff, they could see Thornewell ahead. Surrounded by dark green, grassy fields, the two-story brick house loomed. The large house with its well-manicured, hand-cut grass lawn seemed grotesquely out of place, yet beautiful too. Facing south with no trees around it, the house looked across the river. To the back were barns and other outbuildings made of logs. Vegetable gardens, grapevines, and peach and apple trees were in orderly rows to the left of the house, between it and the river. To the right, along the very edge of the lawn next to the forest, was a row of ten small, one-story log cabins. The roof overhang covered a small wooden porch on the front of each cabin, while a small shed roof covered a porch on the rear of each.

The yards behind these smaller homes were clean, swept, with dirt surrounding them up to the trees. Each had a front door and a back door, but no windows.

"Mighty nice for slave cabins," Verdin commented, for that was what these were. And not just for African black people. There were red men slaves there, and some mixed too.

They considered their options. In the true impatient fashion of an eighteen-year-old male, Verdin wanted to go in, guns blazing, and haul away his sister. A decade older, Twig knew there was something to be said for proper planning. He reminded Verdin of an old carpenter's axiom: measure twice, cut once. Twig wanted to measure what they were up against before they did any cutting.

So, they melted back into the trees, out of sight. They scouted out a spot where they could see the house, the path leading off to the southeast, and the ford across the river. The north/south Hatawwah trading path was a little to the east, just out of sight.

By late afternoon, Twig chose a tree to climb for a better view, while Verdin lay down for a quick nap. Twig could see the figures of people working in the fields and orchards and around some of the buildings in back. Yet, no white people made their appearance, as far as he could see. He looked through a small spyglass that he'd brought with him from the ship.

An hour or so later, Verdin woke up to find Twig preparing a meal for his hungry cat. Twig muttered, "Maybe after dark, we can get this critter some cow's milk."

Just before sundown, they heard horses splashing across the river. Two mounted figures were dressed in deerskin, and one was taller, wearing a turban, much like the Creeks wore. The other figure was female with long, flowing, dark hair blowing in the wind, and she sat astride her horse in the fashion of a man. They rode up to the front of the house and dismounted, as a couple of servants, or slaves perhaps, appeared from the back of the house to lead the horses away. The two Indians entered the house, a servant holding the door open for them.

Twig and Verdin continued watching, unobserved, as darkness settled in. Then they mounted their horses for a ride that would take them east of the house and north. They had watched the slave quarters light up as the slaves came in from the fields and lit cookfires, candles or pine knots. Good smells began drifting in the wind as evening meals were prepared. The two boys put heels to their horses and began picking their way through the trees to the east.

Soon they had crossed the trading path and slowly moved on through the forest east of the slave quarters and the big house. They soon were at a vantage point from which they could see both the front and rear of the house. About thirty feet from the main house was a brick and rock kitchen building. From the back door on the main house was a plank walkway covered with a gabled roof.

Twig watched the house through the glass, but saw only an occasional servant. One went to what must have been a small rock springhouse down in a grassy gully behind the kitchen. The figure was carrying two buckets and returned to the house with both obviously filled.

On the opposite side of the house was what appeared to be a small garden area with wisteria growing on the trellises, and flowers planted on either side of a graveled walkway. Nestled in the well-kept, pruned garden were two outhouses.

Twig motioned for Verdin to stay where he was, to keep watching the house. Then he slowly disappeared through the trees moving north. After about thirty minutes, he reappeared beside Verdin as if by magic, moving as quietly through the forest as any savage. He related to Verdin that he found cornfields, goats, sheep, and lots of cattle. The Burntthornes had quite an operation going here, self-sufficient, and probably making money from the setup as well.

Suddenly a figure appeared between them, saying, "Shh! Shh! Stay quiet!", and holding a finger to his lips. The man was slightly stooped at the knees, obviously unthreatening, long rifle slung across his back with a leather sling. He seemed to be black but was dressed in deerskin clothing and moccasins with a stiff, round-brimmed, low-crowned hat.

To Twig's and Verdin's astonished expressions, he said in a low voice, "My name is Ambro and maybe we can talk a spell. I mean you no harm, if you mean none to me."

Verdin motioned for him to sit with them and said, "We mean you no harm."

Ambro hitched his rifle aside and sat cross-legged, facing them. He looked from one to the other, and they him. He said quietly, "I been watching you all day." Then he added, "Well, not all day. Just off and on, mind you." He went on to tell them he was a slave, belonged to Lord Burson Burntthorne as his game hunter and one who cared for his grapevines, making wine for him as well.

He stopped talking a moment then solemnly said, "Now, how can I help you gentlemen?"

Verdin glanced at Twig in the pale light, and Twig nodded the go-ahead. Verdin told Ambro about his sister, Sylvia, and that they had come to free her from Burntthorne and take her back with them. Twig shifted the sleeping baby cat from one arm to the other as he spoke. Seeing the cat, Ambro said "Oh, yes. I have something for you." He walked over to near where he had been standing, bent down to retrieve a bucket, and brought it to Twig. Handing it to him, he said, "Food and milk for the cat."

Pleasantly surprised, Twig thanked him.

Ambro said quietly, "Let us rest a while, and we will talk of this again."

With that, he propped against a tree and closed his eyes.

Twig and Verdin took turns sleeping, and just before daylight, Ambro told Twig, who was on watch at that time, that he would return. He then removed his rifle from his body, propped it against a tree, and faded into the forest.

***

Just after daylight, Ambro returned with hot breakfast food in a small pot. Fried eggs with hot biscuits and ham. Plenty for all three to eat, the food was delicious. In the light of day, Verdin and Twig could see their host much better. He was around five foot six, muscular with a narrow waist, and except for his hat, he was dressed like an Indian. He had on well-oiled deerskin leggings, breechclout, and vest. High top moccasins were on his feet. His wide leather belt held a tomahawk and large hunting knife. Powder horns and a shot pouch, held by leather thongs over his shoulder, hung at his sides along with a small leather pouch. His skin was dark red, but he had short, black and gray, kinky, curly hair, like an African. His head and face were rounded, and his nose was small, yet broad. He had a kind-looking face with coal-black eyes. His hat was of the same colored deerskin with a round, stiff brim, almost like a parson's hat with a larger crown. He looked like a very proper gentleman attired in the clothing of the forest. His belt, vest, leggings, and moccasins were all decorated with finely detailed beads, and the edges of his hat brim and all his clothing had leather stitching.

They soon learned his father was a half-breed Cherokee man named McGrivin, and his mother was a slave, half Creek and half black. His father and mother lived in the Cherokee Nation in Coosawattee, which was to the far northwest. His father and mother were getting quite old now. Ambro was forty-two. His wife was an Indian woman taken from her Seneca tribe in South Carolina and was also a slave of Burntthorne's.

Looking at this man, who was also so kind in demeanor, Verdin and Twig could sense he was a man with some education. His English was quite good, with a singsong accent of the Cherokee. At the same time, there was something lethal about his manner, his bearing, his strong shoulders, his compactness, his cat-like grace. Whatever else he was, he was a warrior. They learned later his Cherokee name was "The Cat."

After eating his own meal, Twig fed his cat and played with the little bundle of energy while he listened to Ambro's story. Ambro eventually looked Verdin in the eye and said, "Your sister is still here, Verdin. She still works for Burntthorne but no longer as a house maid."

Verdin's eyes lit up, and he looked at Ambro intently. "Yes, go on!"

"You remember the two riders you saw yesterday?"

Verdin nodded, trying hard to be patient as the explanation came.

Ambro went on, "Well, the woman you saw was your sister. And the man you saw with her is her husband. His name in the white world is Mangus McGriven. He is the overseer here at Thornewell, and your sister runs the house. Furthermore, we are cousins. His father and my father are brothers. His father lives in the Creek Nation in Coosatown."

While Verdin momentarily was silent, perhaps in shock, Twig asked, "Why is it you are a slave, yet your cousin is not?"

Ambro explained that his father had bought his mother from Burntthorne but he would not free her son Ambro. Burntthorne allowed Ambro to have some education and sent him to learn about raising grapes and making wine. Ambro had been allowed to hunt and roam the forests in his spare time. So, although Burntthorne refused Ambro his freedom, he granted him these things and leeway, either out of guilt or fear of Ambro's father . . . or both.

"I'll tell you," said Ambro, "Burson Burntthorne has some good in 'im. His son, Oden, has none, at least that I can see. My uncle, Angston McGrivin, is an evil man, as is his son, Mangus. And now, your sister is married to him! What I hate to tell you, but must, is that she seems to be in love with him and is involved in his and Oden's schemes and deals."

Verdin looked at Ambro with a sick look of alarm on his face. "I need to talk to her alone," he said, slamming his hat on the ground. He brushed his fingers through his hair in a fit of frustration, turning his dark gaze toward the ground.

Ambro sat still, looking up at the trees, deep in thought. Twig got up and silently walked away to check on the tethered horses in a grassy area. He put the sleeping kitten up on his horse's back and led both mounts down to the stream to water them.

When he returned, Ambro stood up and said, "I'll see what I can do. I want you two to go up this little stream until you come to Hatawwah Path. Cross it and go nearly two miles to White Sand Springs. Wait there out of sight until I come. Maybe tonight, maybe tomorrow night."

Without further ado, Ambro picked up his rifle and the food pot and disappeared in the direction of the slave cabins. Verdin and Twig saddled their horses, gathered their belongings, and did as instructed. Once they got to the springs, they decided to take a bath in the large, sandy-bottomed spring pool. The water bubbled out of the ground from under some large rocks at the east end of the pool, which was apparently manmade, perhaps by the natives.

The boys took turns taking a bath and cautiously splashing around in the cool water, a clear blue with a white sand bottom. Small crayfish could be seen on the bottom at times, and minnows darted through the water. The sides around the pool were also white sand, forming a beach around it, void of plant growth.

After drinking their fill of the water near the source, filling their canteens, and taking their baths, the boys let the horses out into the pool. Their mounts lay down in the water to completely immerse themselves, seeming to thoroughly enjoy their baths. Then Verdin led the horses to the lush grass growing along the stream just below the pool. Twig scooped out a bed for the kitten in the warm sand in the sun, stretched out his blanket, and after a little playtime with the kitten, they both went to sleep.

Meanwhile, Verdin kept watch and thought about his sister and the unexpected turn of events.

They waited the rest of the day, through the night, then through the next day and the night until just before dawn. They heard the faint splashing of a horse, or horses, coming up the stream. Seeing to their weapons and horses, they quietly led them back away from the spring into the forest gloom. From their hidden vantage points, they could see anyone coming to the pool or anyone around it.

As the sky gradually turned lighter in the east, two horses with riders came slowly up the stream. When they reached the sandy pool, both of them slid off their horses. Then one of the riders took the reins of both horses and led them to the grassy area so they could graze.

Verdin and Twig recognized Ambro immediately. Verdin recognized his sister, Sylvia, and nudged Twig to let him know that was who she was. They tied their horses and walked out to greet the newcomers. Sylvia stood still as Verdin approached her, then she ran forward and threw her arms around his neck, crying.

They hugged for a while, and then both began talking at once, laughing when that didn't work out.

Verdin said, "Sis, uh, Sylvia, I want you to meet my good friend, Twig Hayven."

They nodded at one another and smiled in greeting. Then Twig produced his blanket and made a seat for the siblings on the sand. He waved at Ambro before turning to the woods to retrieve their horses. He led them down to join Ambro and let them graze. Once the horses were tethered, Verdin and Ambro walked a little ways downstream.

Ambro said without prompting, "Sorry it took this long, but I had to wait to see her alone. She refused to come at first. She wanted me to send her brother away without seeing him. Then she changed her mind, but it was this morning before she could get away alone. Anyway, here she is now."

Twig smiled in appreciation then asked, "Yes, but what now?"

Meanwhile, Sylvia asked Verdin about his life. He brought her up-to-date on all he had done, where he had been, the fighting, the wound, the ships, and how he had gotten here with Twig.

Then she started talking about herself, how she had been so frightened and so humiliated to be thrust into a life of servitude. Then she had to fight off Oden's advances, which became more and more persistent. When he suddenly had to leave Savannah, he sent her here. She had been cruelly treated by the headmistress, even beaten, kicked, and made to live on bread and water and food scraps.

One night, she had been physically thrown out of the house when the headmistress and overseer got into a fight. The headmistress had nearly disrobed her, tearing at her clothes and throwing her out of the house on a cold winter's night, wearing practically nothing.

That was when Mangus found her. He clothed her, hid and protected her, made her feel human again, like a woman. She became his woman. She became devoted to him and his endeavors.

*** 

When Oden returned to Savannah and then to Thornewell, Mangus had ridden out to meet him secretly. He revealed to Oden what his overseer and housemistress had done to her, including that they were dishonest and had stolen from the Burntthornes. Oden had become enraged, and when Mangus said he could make his problem employees go away, Oden told him to do it. In return, Mangus and Sylvia would be allowed to wed, and to manage and oversee Thornewell for the Burntthornes.

As she talked, Sylvia paced up and down the sandy beach. Verdin watched her with interest, really seeing her for the first time since she had arrived to the spring. The rising sun now allowed him to see her and her clothes.

She had a bright-red head cloth wrapped and tied around her swept-back, long, black hair, which hung down past her waist. Her face was tan from being out in the sun, as were her neck and arms—so much so, she looked Indian. Her arms were bare to the shoulders, as she wore a sleeveless, low-cut, long white shirt over which she wore a deerskin vest, loosely tied with leather fasteners. She had matured into a grown woman at just seventeen years old, and her low-cut shirt revealed plenty of cleavage. Around her narrow waist was a wide belt or girdle of soft, light-colored deerskin, decorated with beadwork. She had on a breechclout just like a man that hung to her knees, leggings, and moccasins, all decorated with beads and porcupine quills. Around her neck was a necklace of large blue and white beads worn snugly against the skin. As she walked, her breechclout flapped and moved to reveal glimpses of her inner thighs, which were also brown.

She moved and talked like a mature woman, aware of how she looked and of her sensual appearance. She was also aware that she was her man's woman. She dressed this way for him—not willingly at first, but now she reveled in it. She would do anything for her husband. She would never return to society, where she would be unaccepted.

Verdin became aware that she had turned angry. She told of how she had prayed for deliverance at first. Then Oden began telling her how her father had gambled away his business and had sold her to cover his debts. Verdin tried to break in and tell her the truth, that their father was a good, decent man who had been duped by the Burntthornes, but she wouldn't have it, saying, "He must have been at least stupid or he wouldn't have lost all his money!"

Verdin gave up and just watched and listened.

"And now," she said, "my brother shows up to take me away from all this . . . away from my life, my husband. I'm not the meek, timid, scared little girl I was when I came here. I have something now. I have a life, a future. Go away and leave me be, Verdin!" As she spoke, she became more intense with her words. "My husband will kill you if he finds out you're here. You're one of the Rebels! You're fighting against the king! You've all taken leave of your senses. You have no chance, no chance of winning. Leave before my husband or the Burntthornes have you killed."

Verdin was silent, his mouth hanging open in disbelief.

Turning toward Ambro, Sylvia yelled, "My horse!" Then she looked at Verdin, her dark blue eyes darting angrily. "Get out of here at once, you damned Rebel. If you ever come back, it will be on your own head. Go away and leave me alone!"

With that, she vaulted into the saddle and turned her horse into the stream. She didn't look back as she slowly rode out of sight.

Ambro held the reins to his horse. He shrugged his shoulders, then turned to mount up. Balancing his rifle across the saddle, he said, "Well, gentlemen, I reckon that's how the missus sees it. That's the way she says it, anyway."

Verdin took a deep breath, then walked up to Ambro and shook his hand firmly. "Thank you, Ambro. Thank you for your help. I had to see her, and I guess I had to hear it from her. If there's ever anything I can do for you, let me know. Get word to Elisha Seagate in Savannah. Thanks again for everything."

Twig walked up to Ambro and also shook his hand. Ambro quickly untied a container in a leather pouch from his saddle and handed it to him. "More milk and food for the kitten," he smiled.

Twig touched his hat with his fingers in salute. "Thank you very much, kind sir."

Ambro said in return, "Think nothing of it, One Who Talks with Cats." He grinned, showing a stunning set of teeth.

Verdin and Twig gathered their belongings, mounted up, and started back. Four days and nights later, they dismounted behind Elisha Seagate's house and rubbed down, fed, and watered the horses. Their trip back involved spring rains, thunderstorms, lightning, and a close brush with a tornado; they were glad to have arrived. The housekeeper let them in. Rob was asleep, so they went upstairs and crashed as well.

Twig had brought the growing kitten in with him. Just before they blew out the candle, Twig said, "I think I'll call him Ambro." The cat purred contentedly, and Verdin smiled at the soft heart of his friend.

Elisha Seagate gave them the latest news of Henry Knox leading the expedition to bring the artillery from Fort Ticonderoga to Boston. He told of the British having to flee Boston as well as other news of battles in South Carolina and victories for the Patriot cause. British agents had been sent among the Cherokee and Creeks with guns, ammunition, provisions, bribes, and promises. They were cajoling the native tribes into declaring war on the rebellious colonies. Isolated attacks on a small scale were already taking place against outlying homesteads.

Rob's thigh wound was healing slowly, more painful than the previous one, and he had to keep weight off his leg as much as possible. He walked around with the help of some crutches Dr. Kensly had found through another doctor in town.

Rather involuntarily, Dr. Kensly had begun a medical practice in Seagate's offices. He had treated a sailor on the waterfront, and that sailor referred someone else, indicating Dr. Kensly could be found at Seagate's office. And so it went, until eventually Seagate gave the doctor a separate room at the office. Patients had been pouring in to see him since, including young Rob.

# Chapter Eleven
## NOW IN BETTER HANDS

**M**eanwhile, the *Roanoke* had been completely repaired and refurbished, sparkling like a gem, ready to go. The question was, where?

The weather was warm springtime, birds and blooms everywhere. Spring storms were frequent, some of them rather violent, much like those Twig and Verdin had encountered coming back from Thornewell. It was just after one of those storms that a shell-torn ship, none other than the *Edisto* herself, came slowly, yet jubilantly into port.

When the *Roanoke* heard she was coming in, they sent word to Seagate's office and to his house. Everyone rushed on board the *Edisto* when she arrived, joyously shaking hands with George, welcoming him back.

George told them he had waited as long as he dared before leaving with the munitions for Boston. He had some close calls with British ships before safely landing his cargo below Boston.

He had been unable to find safe passage to his usual places of refuge to replenish supplies and rest the crew. So he went farther north, where friends had helped in that regard. During that time, he learned that a squadron of seven British ships was leaving soon for Nassau. So, they planned to seize the military supplies there, and any ships or shipping possible, and then return to Connecticut with the spoils of war.

Their efforts were successful, and the captain of the *Edisto* and his crew were handsomely rewarded for their deeds. Even now, the *Edisto* was loaded with captured uniforms, foodstuffs, boots, shoes, muskets, powder, and lead. The good captain and his crew had unanimously voted to donate it all to the Patriot cause.

The reunion of the two crews was a happy one, indeed, but an underlying tension filled the air, as George would soon have to be told of the *Roanoke*'s adventures and the ultimate loss of his father, Isaac. Upon receiving the unfortunate news, George bowed his head, and tears began flowing as he removed his tricorn and kneeled down on the deck. He and his father had been very close. They had been through a lot together. It was a long while before he regained his feet, and his crew bowed with him in a show of solidarity and compassion.

George's sorrow over his father's death just brought it all back to the boys and the crewmembers. The next few days were rather somber as they revisited the grief of losing such a good man. George had moments of sadness for weeks afterward but he also shared some of the good times they had, including the humorous times.

George was pleased to hear of his father's burial in Wilmington. Someday, after the war, he hoped to move him to his farm and reinterred.

The big question in the air at this time was where the British would pounce next. Their fleet and army had left Boston and gone to Halifax. They could land at will anywhere they wished with their sea power. George studied the maps of the thirteen colonies and came to the decision that it would be New York. As it turned out, he was right.

In the meantime, life and commerce struggled on. The war supplies were most needed in Charleston at the time, so Capt. George Wolloston decided they would take supplies to Fort Moultrie. Elisha Seagate had a shipment of goods that needed to be shipped to Charleston. So the *Edisto* was repaired and put back into battle shape. Some of the powder supplies in her hold were used to replenish her own magazine, and some of the weaponry was replaced as well.

The captain thanked Ellis Rofford and Norwin Chaddham for their role in maintaining the *Roanoke* and their superb handling of her after the death of Captain Isaac. They were awarded positions of captain and first officer, respectively, for their efforts. Before the upgraded titles were given, George had asked his crew if anyone objected or had comments, encouraging them to speak openly. In response, the whole crew gave them three cheers. It was, after all, a natural choice. Rofford and Chaddham were well qualified and suited for the positions.

The crew also nominated Seaman Grey as second officer. The man was somewhat a mystery to the crew. He was friendly enough, but quiet about himself, a hard worker, clean and neat. He was of average size but strong, of sound body and mind, keeping a clear head in crises, somehow seeming to always know what to do. The crew was drawn to him because he was a natural leader of men. Clearly an educated man, he still chose to serve as a lowly seaman.

So the *Roanoke*'s new officers were listed as the officers of the ship instead of temporary positions. Second Lieutenant Grey accepted his new post quietly with a nod and wave of thanks to the crew. It was a sound decision, as events would later prove.

Rob was up to the voyage, despite his leg still in its healing stages, so with some help, he and his gear were brought aboard the *Edisto*. With both ships repaired, refitted, gleaming, and loaded, they sailed with the tide. They made the run to Charleston amidst springtime showers and thunderstorms. Once there, the *Roanoke* was to be unloaded in Charleston. The *Edisto* would take her war materials to Fort Moultrie.

Charleston was abuzz with preparations to defend against a British invasion attempt. Adm. Sir Peter Parker's invasion fleet was en route, along with twenty-five hundred troops under Sir Henry Clinton. The admiral had ten warships plus transports for the troops.

Captain Wolloston anchored as close to Sullivan's Island as possible, and his war materials were transferred by smaller boats to the shore. It was tedious work in the hot June sun. Meanwhile, the captain sent the *Roanoke* on out of the channel to the harbor to the north and east to watch for the enemy fleet.

Other vessels were patrolling as well, and when the fleet was sighted, warning signals were flashed for all Patriot vessels in the vicinity. Fast messenger vessels were sent scurrying to Charleston and the defensive forces.

As soon as the *Edisto* was unloaded, George took his two ships to the east, just barely in sight of the unfolding drama. He was out of danger of being bottled up in the harbor, yet close enough to dart in and harass the ten larger, slower British warships.

At first, Sir Henry Clinton's troops were unloaded on the island north of the log fort. Very unsuitable terrain and Patriot gunfire from soldiers sent to harass them from the fort soon caused the Redcoat soldiers to be recalled.

Then the British warships turned their whole attention upon the palmetto log and sand fort guarding the entrance to the channel. The defense was commanded by Colonel Moultrie, as his men methodically fired away at the British ships. The fire from the warships was fast and furious, seemingly continuous. The palmetto logs and sand of the fort absorbed the shots, protecting the defenders.

As the afternoon wore on, it was clear the British were taking a beating. Through the billowing smoke, flashing gun muzzles and flames from ships afire could be seen. Three of the British ships ran aground across the channel from the fort and were effectively out of the fight.

Capt. George Wolloston then brought his two ships close to the enemy fleet and unleashed his own broadsides at them. The shots found their marks, adding to the fort's damage. The enemy soon began returning fire, inflicting damage to his ships' sails and rigging. Thankfully, most of the enemy's shots were high and caused no casualties or damage to the guns.

One near casualty took place on the *Edisto*. The big kitten, Ambro, had jumped atop the gunnel right beside Twig. Suddenly it leapt into the air as a cannonball grazed the top of the wooden gunnel, passed clean over the ship, and splashed harmlessly in the sea. Somehow, the cat sensed the approaching cannonball in time to leap into the air, turn a somersault, and land on Twig's neck and shoulders. Twig had instinctively stooped and thrown his arm up to keep the cat from falling. This all took place in the space of a heartbeat and resulted in Twig's arm being removed from the path of the cannonball. Otherwise, Twig would have had only one arm and hand with which to hold the loyal feline. Twig looked at the marks the cannonball made on the wood and then looked at the cat, who he would swear was smiling at him. He could only shake his head in relief and smile back.

After dark, the fleet broke off the engagement and moved out to sea. The *Edisto* and *Roanoke* moved aside to keep out of their way. The enemy struggled to put up sail while fighting fires on board; the fleet had taken a beating.

George kept his ships well away from the wounded ones in case they decided to zero in on his two ships to unleash their fury. The fleet slipped into the darkness, leaving Charleston and her environs free from further threat. George watched them go gladly, a wan smile on his face.

They returned to Savannah a day or so afterward, where the military authorities in Charleston thanked them for their help and bade them adieu. What the British were up to after such a battle was anybody's guess.

Elisha Seagate had some stores that were needed by Rhode Island and Connecticut. One load of naval stores, such as pinewood and pitch, were natural products of the Georgia Colony, and were sorely needed in shipbuilding. George decided to give this shipment to the *Roanoke*, and loading began at once, even as a thunderstorm broke over the port.

It was during the height of the storm that a rider from Tybee Island came into the Custom House with word that a badly damaged, shot-up brigantine lay off the coast, waiting for the tide to come in. Captain George and his crew had been helping with the loading of the *Roanoke*, but all had retired when the storm did not abate. The Custom House sent word of the damaged ship and wondered if George and his crew could go to assist her?

As the tide was running out to sea, George left at once, and the

*Edisto* was soon passing Tybee to look for the wounded ship. Thankfully the storm passed, leaving a beautiful, cloud-free sky, a starry, moonlit night. When they came upon the wounded ship, they saw it was indeed shot to pieces, with only one mast still able to hold any sail at all.

George came alongside, sending out a friendly "Ahoy! What can we do to help? This is Capt. George Wolloston of the *Edisto* out of Massachusetts."

The riddled ship's master stepped to the gunnel on the portside, cupped his hands, and yelled, "This is the brigantine *Golden Eagle*, recently of His Majesty's Royal Navy, now in much better hands."

"And who is the master of this good ship now?" George bellowed.

Rob had come on deck and was standing next to him when his unbelieving ears heard the reply. "Capt. Jonathan Loxley and first officer, Lt. Robert Glynne!" Rob nearly fell in shock at first, and George had to restrain him from jumping overboard to swim to the other ship, as Rob shouted repeatedly, "Father! Uncle Jonathan!"

George finally managed to regain some order, and soon Dr. Maury Kensly was en route to help with some wounded aboard the *Golden Eagle*. Rob and his father spoke across the water jubilantly. They decided to wait to reunite once they were safely in port, but Rob's father couldn't wait to share the greatest news young Rob dared hope for: "We have your mother and sister on board too! We've been to England! And your Aunt Mary too." Aunt Mary was Uncle Jonathan's wife.

Rob was beside himself with happiness, and it was difficult being patient until he could see them. Finally, the wounded were comforted, the ship was patched up temporarily, a decent meal was eaten by those on board . . . and the tide had turned.

Soon the *Golden Eagle* was tied up safely along the riverfront and the excess military stores were unloaded. Rob had at once gathered George, Verdin, and Twig to go on board with him. His excitement was catching, as all the men smiled for the reunion.

They jumped down onto the deck of the *Golden Eagle* and at once were met by Rob's father and uncle. There were tears of relief, joy, and gratitude for the good fortune shared by all. Rob introduced them to George and Twig, and Verdin renewed his acquaintance with the seamen, whom he'd known when they were together on the HMS *Hawke*.

Then Robert and Jonathan turned to three beautiful women standing back a bit, waiting. Rob at once recognized his mother, his aunt, and his sister, Hope Ellen. More embracing, more tears as the womenfolk were drawn into the happy circle. Rob could not believe how beautiful his sister was, grown up and radiant, glowing as he was from being reunited as a family. He quickly introduced them as well, and they were received properly with hats off, bows, and smiles.

Out of the corner of his eye, Rob noticed George and Hope looking at one another in a prolonged series of gazes, trying not to be obvious, though obvious they were. Rob knew that look. He had seen it before on Twig's face when he looked at his betrothed, Louisa Medford.

*Well, I'll be—* he thought, and shook his head, smiling.

Just as he turned to his mother and father, he saw . . . a mirage? An angel? Dressed in white and dazzling, there she stood with a slight quizzical smile on her lips, eyebrows raised with a curious look. Rob's mind reeled with the possibility. *Can it be? How can she be here? Is it really her? Why, yes, it is her! No one else could possibly be her equal.*

Indeed, Hannah Lysbeth Burntthorne was there, standing not six feet away from him!

He dropped his hat, which he'd been holding in his hand, to the deck, unnoticed. As he took a step forward, he squashed it beneath his shoe, still unnoticed. He looked into Hannah's eyes, which were openly smiling now in her radiant face. Reaching out with his hand, he touched her hand, which she'd slowly extended. Her hand trembled as he brought it to his lips, and he bowed at the waist, heels touching, just like a gentleman. His eyes never left her face. He was totally mesmerized. As was she, it seemed!

Off to the side, Verdin watched the meeting and grinned. Rob's face held the same look that they'd witnessed on Twig, and then moments ago, George. The look of unabashed love. He shook his head, wondering when his day might come.

After a moment, Rob rose and said, "Welcome to Savannah, Miss Burntthorne. I am very pleased you are here and were able to overcome the extreme difficulties of your voyage." He spoke as a mature gentleman, and this caught him off guard a bit. He thought to himself, *Was that me speaking just now?*

Hannah smiled pleasantly and said, sounding like a grown lady, "Why thank you, Mr. Glynne, for your kind welcome and thoughtful expression of concern."

For a few moments, they simply looked at each other without a word. Someone coughed politely behind them, and Rob snapped out of it, saying, "Miss Burntthorne, I—"

Hannah broke in with a slight tilt of her head. "Rob, just call me Hannah. No more Miss Burntthorne for you. I've been talking with your family about you for weeks now. You know, we've been on board this ship together for quite a while, and I've heard so much about you . . . it seems as though I've always known you. No need for formalities between us. Please." She wore an impish smile with laughter in her beautiful eyes.

Rob had been holding her hand all this time until his sister Hope jostled Hannah. Then, putting an arm out to lead Hannah away, she said, "Come now, you two. You can catch up later. Right now, we have much to do."

# Chapter Twelve
## PIRATES

George Wolloston had informed Elisha Seagate of the identity of the new arrivals, and he at once sought accommodations for all. It didn't take too long. Just a few doors down from the Seagate's house was a home belonging to Mrs. Anne Brosia. An attractive, proper lady, Mrs. Brosia had been widowed some two years earlier by a man several years her senior. They had been married fifteen years when the elderly gentleman passed away. She was a young thirty-four years old now.

Mr. Brosia had been a successful merchant and farmer. He owned the modest Savannah home, which had been added onto until it was quite roomy. The structure was made entirely of brick with a clay tile roof, built upon a large city lot. A brick wall completely enclosed the lot with a double gate at the front. A brick carriage house, with apartments over it, was behind the house along with some other brick outbuildings.

Mrs. Brosia had also inherited a nice farm on the outskirts of town. A more modest version of the city home had been built on the farm, which Mr. Brosia called *Annefield*. They had divided their time between the two homes, raising and educating a young boy they had adopted. Details of how they came to adopt the boy were sketchy, but it was known that Mr. and Mrs. Brosia, not long after their marriage had gone to Charleston and then farther inland near Cherokee territory. When they returned to

Savannah by ship several days later, they had the infant boy with them. They never had children of their own but were completely devoted to their Indian half-breed son. The child greatly preferred life on the farm and seldom came into Savannah. Even now, he remained on the farm, which he was currently managing, and if he came into the city, it was a clandestine affair, where he would visit with his mother for only a few hours, or days at the most. Even so, it was well known that he was an equally devoted son.

Mr. Seagate had contacted the widow Brosia and asked about temporary quarters for the Glynnes and Loxleys. When she heard a Burntthorne was in the entourage, she balked at first. After some further explanations, she relented and graciously accepted them all to her home.

Anne Brosia had learned well from her shrewd, successful, businessman husband. She ran a tight ship and managed her money and properties frugally and wisely. Her home in Savannah was cared for by Lottie and Clovis Free, a free black family who lived in the nice carriage house apartments. They were middle-aged with two young children. Anne provided them food and board as well as a modest salary. They, in turn, cooked, cleaned house, managed the grounds, and maintained the house and outbuildings. The Frees had been slaves in South Carolina. The Brosias had bought them from their owner, brought them to Savannah, and made them free persons. Clovis and Lottie had been young, in their late teens, when they became free and accepted the job offer to work for the Brosias, adding "Free" as their last name. They had married and moved into their new home, positions, and life—and had been more than content with their good fortune and lot over the years.

They took a lot of pride in their work and their lives. It showed in the appearance of the Brosia house and grounds. Also evident was the mutual love and respect that Anne and the Frees held for one another.

Anne agreed to rent at least a portion of her home to the families, charging a modest fee for the space plus whatever Clovis and Lottie wanted for their increase in duties. Satisfactory terms were reached, and the move to new quarters was soon underway.

Eventually they found a draft horse and dray, and the menfolk busily engaged in moving trunks, crates, and other belongings from the *Golden Eagle*. The number of belongings for each person was modest but, in the aggregate, enough to be a manageable chore for the willing young men.

As they worked, they talked of the tale of how Jonathan and Robert had come to be on the *Golden Eagle* and how they had gone to England to retrieve their families and Hannah. Rob and Verdin had last seen Jonathan and Robert in Nassau just before the two men had departed on the HMS *Crescent*, bound for Savannah.

Jonathan told most of the story. The HMS *Crescent* never made it to Savannah. About halfway there, they were approached by a ship flying the British flag. She looked like a merchantman at first, a well-armed one with forty guns, but as it drew nearer, the true colors of the strange ship were revealed—namely, the black flag with skull and crossbones.

They were hopelessly outgunned and outnumbered. Surrender was the only choice, and their loud, rowdy, profane, half-drunk captors threw the crew in the brig in chains. First, Rob, Jonathan, and the others were made to watch as the British naval officers were stripped of their clothing, made to stand on the gunwales, and hacked at with cutlasses until bleeding and half-dead, and then kicked overboard for the sharks. Apparently, the captain of these pirates had received rough handling or some sort of insult at the hands of some British officers. He hated them with a passion.

The pirates liked the little *Crescent*. She would make a fine, fast pirate craft. They manned her with a makeshift crew after removing everything they wanted from her. Then they headed for the North Carolina islands that pirates had used as their bases for years.

Jonathan and Robert were stuck in the hold with other sailors for two days without food and water. The air was exceedingly foul there in the hold, and two sailors died. Finally, some of the more humane members of the pirate crew braved the stench and brought them fish stew and water. They also removed the dead bodies and overflowing buckets of human excrement, returning them empty and cleaned.

The two ships had dropped anchor in a little bay of an island off the southern coast of North Carolina. The prisoners were brought ashore and allowed to lie about in the sand of the beach. There was nowhere for them to go even if they tried to escape.

There had been other prisoners in the brig that the pirates had captured several days earlier. Some of them had been on an American merchant vessel, which was also at anchor in the bay. Jonathan and Robert got to talking with these prisoners and exchanging stories. They discovered they had something in common: they hated the British, and they hated pirates. Among their little group, they all agreed they would stick together in the event an opportunity presented itself for an escape. Power in numbers.

Over the next several days, the pirates removed goods from the ships, mainly looking for gold or silver items and strong drink. They found much more of the latter than the former. They also found cloth and household goods that had been bound for market, which they just threw onto the beach.

Then the pirates decided to load it all again to sail to Jamaica or New Orleans and sell the ship and cargo. Amidst much grumbling and drinking, the pirates reloaded most of it back onto the ship.

Two factions of the pirates got into a squabble over where to take the merchant ship and who would sail it there. Finally, one of the captain's lieutenants challenged the captain to a duel. The lieutenant won by shooting the captain in the left shoulder. The captain had been so drunk, his shot had gone wild. His loyal followers immediately picked him up, carried him to his ship, and set sail.

The victorious lieutenant hardly knew he had won, but his handful of followers got him aboard the merchant ship. Then somebody remembered the prisoners on shore, and they were brought aboard and told to help get her ready to sail.

Finally, the big, slow, lumbering merchant vessel was underway, headed out of the narrow mouth of the bay. The captain and his ship apparently had just gone far enough to get out of sight of the bay, when suddenly the pirates reappeared from around the spit of land to the northwest and came bearing down on the merchant ship.

At first, everyone on board thought the captain was just rejoining them. Several of the crew waved at the approaching ship. Suddenly, as soon as she was within range, the captain unleashed a broadside at the disloyal lieutenant and his followers. That first well-timed, well-aimed broadside did indescribable damage to the crewmembers and the vessel.

Chunks of wood, splinters, sails, spars, rigging, heads, arms, legs, torsos, blood, guts, teeth, skin, hair, fingers—it all went flying through the air. The merchantman was dead in the water. The crew of pirates and their prisoners suffered grievously. The crew grabbed their firearms they had brought with them and started firing back. Small arms fire was coming from the captain's ship as well.

Jonathan, Robert, and some other prisoners looked about for weapons. They were surprised to see there were eight cannons on deck that the pirates had somehow overlooked, as well as shot and powder in the hold.

They somehow managed to escape bodily harm as another broadside sent solid shot crashing clear through the ship. Using relays of men, the prisoners finally got ammo to the guns and opened fire with the 16-pounders. They were able to cause some damage and confusion, as well as casualties, but the broadsides kept coming. Smoke and flames were billowing up from the merchant ship. She began to list, bow down. Still they slugged it out. The unfaithful pirate lieutenant went down, shot through the head.

Jonathan motioned to Robert to look at something on the captain's ship. A man with long black hair, white shirt, and knee breeches had climbed part way in the rigging on the portside toward them.

Holding to a rope, he swung out over the water as close to the merchantman as possible. He sailed through the air, let go the rope, and dove into the water. He stayed under for a good ways to avoid being shot. Finally, he swam around the stern, and Jonathan and Robert dropped him a line and helped him aboard.

He was a Yankee sailor who had slipped aboard, posing as one of the captain's loyal crewmembers. He quietly warned them, "Get ready! She's gonna blow!"

He had set a hot fire to the bulkhead in the hold of the captain's ship, next to the magazine. He had made sure there was ventilation from above, then closed the door after fixing the latch to lock it from the inside.

Only seconds after he finished telling them what he had done, the pirate ship blew up in a huge fireball explosion that blew everyone on board the merchantman off their feet. It literally disintegrated into millions of small fragments.

Everyone on the surviving ship slowly rose to their feet to look through the smoke at the place where the ship had been only seconds ago. While they looked, the upper half of the former ship's main mast came hurtling straight down out of the sky to imbed in the main deck of the merchant ship just a little aft of the main mast.

Jonathan said, "Let's man the pumps and get back into the bay! Maybe we can run her aground then." Pumping away, the thirty or so prisoners and three or four remaining pirates turned her around and got her slowly underway, back toward their anchorage. She was still heavy in the bow. One of the prisoner sailors had gone below to assess the damage and reported to Jonathan that the ship was shot to pieces. She would have to be run aground in order to salvage anything from her at all.

Inside the little bay, quite unforgotten by the drunken pirates, was the little *Crescent*. Not a soul was aboard her.

They ran the merchantman upon the white sand as close to the *Crescent* as possible. For the next several hours, the former prisoners of the pirates found decent clothes and goods, bathed, and then transferred everything possible to the *Crescent*.

The officers of the Yankee merchantman had been shot by the pirate captain. Leadership had somehow naturally evolved to Jonathan and Robert, as the crew recognized their experience and abilities. Thanks to Jonathan and Robert's efforts and quick thinking, a good eighty-five percent of the cargo was salvaged.

The former prisoners of the pirates now had four pirates as their prisoners. An informal inquiry was done. Every last one of them had been involved in the drunken killing of officers, not just of the *Crescent* but the merchant ship as well. Every former prisoner was asked to vote life or death upon each pirate. Unanimously, the vote was death by hanging. The verdict was given to Jonathan, and he asked the former prisoners when they wanted sentence to be carried out on the pirates. They all cried, "Now!"

Jonathan also wanted to know the crew's desire about what to do with the cargo. They all agreed that it should be returned to the owners in Connecticut. With that settled, they got underway. As soon as they were away from the bay, out to sea, watches established, and the ship's operation organized and manned, Jonathan had the pirates brought on deck.

He asked them if they had any last words or requests. They did. Each pirate requested to be shot and his body thrown overboard. None wanted to be hanged. Jonathan asked the crewmen if they approved, and they did, with no dissenters.

Jonathan had Robert write down each name of the pirates, as well as the name and location of any kin. Then one by one, Jonathan stood them on the gunnel of the stern. Four members of the crew acted as a firing squad, and the pirates were quickly shot into eternity, their bodies falling into the briny deep.

The *Crescent*'s voyage to Connecticut was uneventful except for periods of foul and stormy weather. Once there, the owners of the ship and cargo were grateful for the efforts of the crew, and of Jonathan and Robert.

They had formed a board of inquiry, and when the meeting was over, they awarded the *Crescent* to Jonathan and Robert to keep since, as it turned out, the ship did not belong to the Connecticut group anyway. They also rewarded them a modest sum for recovering most of their cargo.

As joint owners of a brigantine and a little money now, Jonathan and

Robert thought about what to do. First on their mind was rescuing their families in England. But should they risk such a maneuver? Ultimately, they decided it was worth the risk, and they pulled together a fairly good crew of seasoned seamen for the eighteen-gun brigantine. Using most of their reward money, they re-provisioned her and replenished some naval stores, then got underway.

They had a good northerly crossing and anchored in Morecambe Bay in the dead of night, showing British colors anyway. Robert had taken eight men and had gone to Burntthorne. As it turned out, Lord Burson and the younger son Oden were in the colonies, in Savannah. The oldest son, James, who was Hannah's father, remained in England. He did not approve of nor participate in most of the schemes of his father and mean-spirited little brother.

He was mainly involved in trying to maintain the Burntthorne's holdings and level of wealth in England. He had agreed to Robert taking his wife and daughter at once. He even sent for Jonathan's wife, transporting her and her belongings to Preston for embarkation with Robert's family. He warned them of discretion in the matter, as he did not wish to unduly incur the wrath of his father.

Just as they were about to cast off, a young lady driving a carriage arrived with a small assortment of boxes and traveling trunks. She insisted the crew load her things as well, because Hannah Burntthorne was going too! And so, she was welcomed into the fold.

With women on board, Jonathan and Robert were reluctant to use their ship in battle or for raiding commerce. But they soon came upon a slow-moving British ship, slightly armed, headed for Nassau or somewhere in the Americas with preserved foodstuffs, uniforms, small arms, and gunpowder and shot for their military.

They had forced her to surrender, transferred a goodly portion of the cargo to the *Crescent*, then set out for Connecticut with the captured ship. Slowly and wearily, through bad weather and sickness and fever, they made it.

They presented the ship and its supplies to General Washington, the war, and the cause. Connecticut accepted the ship and paid the whole crew for the ship and its contents. They were now officially commerce raiders or privateers for Connecticut, and thus, for the whole cause against England.

They had dallied a while there in Connecticut, unsure of where to go. Where would Rob and Verdin be now? What had happened to them?

During this time, Hannah had grown dear to them. She told them some of the details about meeting Rob, though not all. She said she was drawn to young Rob and when his mother and sister had been forced to come to Burntthorne and work there, she became acquainted with them and soon grew close to them. They had taken her into their confidence finally and told her what had happened. Appalled that her family would do such a thing, she went to her father, James. He, of course, knew nothing about the travesty, but did say it was possible. He knew Oden was capable of it, and that his own father was easily duped by Oden.

Hannah had insisted on going with them, of course, so she had prevailed at the last minute. Her uncle Oden and grandfather had operations there. Maybe Rob would be there. She was drawn to Savannah, she said. Jonathan quietly listened to her story.

They had headed down the coast in time to run into an escort of Sir Peter Parker's fleet as it limped away from Fort Moultrie. Not wanting to take on an engagement with the families all on board, the *Crescent* had vainly tried to outrun the escort vessel. Heavily loaded as she was, Jonathan could tell she was losing ground. Finally, turning around so as to let the wind be in his favor, Jonathan and Robert cleared for action and prepared for battle.

And battle they did . . . for three hours! In the classic style of wooden sailing ships doing battle, they slugged it out. Finally, with her crew greatly decimated and her captain and most of the other officers dead, and with their ship riddled with shot, the British ship slinked away.

The gallant *Crescent* was badly shot up, but fortunately not below the waterline. She floated grandly, though limping, under cover of a storm on toward Charleston.

Jonathan looked around him and took a deep breath. His family and friends were wide-eyed, astonished by the story of how they all came to be together again. He laughed and slapped his thigh.

"Snap out of it, folks. Now, we're here and you're here. An ever-kind providence has certainly smiled upon us.

# Chapter Thirteen
## TO THE INTERIOR

The hot early days of August in Savannah brought news of the founding of the new nation and the determination to be free of British rule. The Declaration of Independence signed in Philadelphia was read aloud, and the Patriots rejoiced loudly and openly.

But bad news also came. In early July, the Cherokee and some Creeks, greatly influenced and supplied by British agents, had attacked all along the western frontier of Virginia, the Carolinas, and Georgia.

Jonathan and Robert settled their families in the Brosia home, along with Hannah. Capt. George Wolloston began visiting there quite often, getting to know young Rob's family better, especially his sister Hope. Young Rob often joined him to visit his mother, sister, aunt, and of course, to spend time with Hannah as well.

It was a happy time, and the families were feeling blessed and pleased to have a modest amount of financial security not known by them before. There was talk of purchasing land or a home somewhere. But there was a war to be considered as well, and with the strong British navy, coastal centers of commerce such as Savannah or Charleston were subject to attack and seizure. So they needed to locate near the coast since their source of income was from their seagoing vessel at the moment.

It was also a busy time as commerce continued. Elisha Seagate and others had cargoes for George to ship. Jonathan and Robert went to work with their crew repairing the *Crescent*. There was a lot to do but nothing structural, as the ship was sound and well built, originally in New England for the Royal Navy.

Rob, Verdin, and Twig joined in the repairs, and the intense physical work agreed with them. They became tanned by the sun, sweating and laughing as they labored together. Sometimes they would dive into the river to cool off. This astonished, and even petrified many of the sailors. It was an irony of the time that most men who spent their lives on the sea, who loved the sea, could not swim and were fearful of being in the water themselves.

With the help of Jonathan, Robert, and the trio, several sailors overcame their fears and became swimmers—even great lovers of the water—including shedding all their clothes, which were a hindrance under the water. In no time, it was not unusual to see naked men swimming in the river.

Twig once again proved to be a genius of sorts in repairing and creating ordnance. He also devised metal supports and bracing to help repair the ship. He worked at a blacksmith shop near the waterfront that was operated by a black man from Jamaica. He had come there of his own free will and had never been a slave. With his successful business on the waterfront, he was protected by the ship owners and merchants, who greatly appreciated his skills and service. Quiet and humble, he worked his neat shop day after day and slowly amassed a small fortune in gold. Though wealthy, he lived with his wife and teenage daughter in a small bungalow right next to his shop. His wife and daughter had an awning attached to that of the blacksmith shop, with small tables and chairs beneath. Using the fires from the forge and an oven especially built to utilize the heat of the forge, they cooked and served Jamaican food and bread. Unpretentious and welcoming, their outdoor café was a widely known place to get great-tasting food at reasonable prices. Sailors ate there frequently, and his wife and daughter quietly amassed another small fortune in gold.

Twig began going to the shop and became acquainted with the Jamaican family. They soon became good friends, and Twig taught the blacksmith many new things he knew, and vice versa. So it came about that they worked together often, and Twig had full, unlimited use of the shop. This became a good source of additional income for Twig, as the Jamaican shared his increased revenues.

On the surface, Twig was busy and happy, but on the inside, he was a bubbling cauldron of loneliness. He missed Louisa Medford. He posted letters to her at the farm. So far, he hadn't received a reply, and he hoped it was just due to the long distance and slowness of the postal service. Twig brooded as he worked on guns and inventions.

The *Roanoke* had returned finally with a cargo for Elisha. George Wolloston soon had the *Edisto* and *Roanoke* loaded for a voyage to Philadelphia, and in spite of not wanting to leave and thus not be able to see Hope, he finally sailed. This time, he went without the help of Rob, Verdin, and Twig, who stayed behind to help Jonathan and Robert on the *Crescent*.

The *Crescent's* transformation to a beautiful, glistening work of ship's art was slow but sure. She now stood tall, proud . . . and deadly as a ship of war. She also had a new name, rechristened the USS *Warrior* just before completion of the repairs.

The exact purpose of the ship and its new mission was the subject of much discussion. It could be used as a merchant vessel, but she was designed and armed as a vessel of war. Jonathan and Robert tried not to think of her warship worthiness, and instead, focused on her as a merchant vessel.

One evening during a family discussion of many topics—the Indian attacks, recent news of battles, and Congress addressing the need for a navy and calling for volunteers to raid the commerce of the enemy—the potential of the *Warrior* was readdressed. Washington and Congress both realized that their new country could not hope to build a large navy to compete against the Royal Navy in a short time. But individuals or companies with merchant ships could be outfitted as privateers or commerce raiders and severely hamper the war effort of the enemy. So the call had gone out for volunteers to do just that.

It was then that Jonathan and Robert understood it was their duty to use this captured warship of the enemy against them.

Then Rob's Aunt Mary, Jonathan's wife, made the statement that although they hated war, the women of this family were of the opinion that their menfolk owed it to their families and children to fight for freedom in the best way they could. Since they were seamen, what better way to fight the enemy than in a warship taken from the enemy? A look around the table and the affirmative nods of the other ladies confirmed the statement of this patriotic woman.

And that warship was now sitting in the harbor, refitted, repaired, resupplied, and ready for war.

Jonathan and Robert admitted their own unvoiced convictions on the matter and soon the whole family was talking about it. The women were sad yet enthusiastic and supportive. But they had further suggestions.

This time the talk died away to allow Rob's mother, Faith, to speak. The women did not wish to remain in the coastal area while their menfolk were gone. Young Rob would be charged with finding a suitable location for the families to settle, only if temporary, away from Savannah, yet not in range of Cherokee raids along the frontier.

After further talk and debate, everyone was finally convinced of the soundness of the plans. Rob was surprised he hadn't thought of it before. He asked for and got everyone's approval that it would be the responsibility of Twig, Verdin, and himself to take care of the ladies. Hannah's bright smile and twinkling eyes showed her approval, as she hoped this would lead to her and Rob spending more time together. That would be a very welcome set of affairs to him as well.

Soon, everyone had finished talking and helped clean up after the evening meal. The husbands and wives had drifted off to their sleeping quarters, and Rob stayed at the dining table, speaking with Hannah.

Twig had gone to get Ambro from the Jamaican family. The big, good-natured cat stayed there sometimes because he was accustomed to being there with Twig when he was working. Twig said he would sleep on board the *Warrior* tonight, and said goodbye to the group.

Verdin felt lonely as well, so he wandered down to the back door of the house. A chair sometimes used by the cook sat near the door of the kitchen in the shadows. Verdin sat there for a while, looking up at the lights in the rear windows of the handsome house and at the stars in the huge, black sky. He thought about how everyone seemed to have a girl now. Twig had finally fallen for Louisa. Hannah had come all the way from England for Rob, though she barely knew him. "Will I ever find someone?" he wondered aloud.

Shaking his head, he rose, heading toward the privy farther back in the yard. He went around the side of the kitchen, following the brick path to the outdoor toilet. Afterward, he slowly ambled back toward the house along the same path, intent on going to his quarters at Seagate's for sleep. As he neared the kitchen again, he heard a noise, muffled voices of a man and a woman. He couldn't make out the words but they seemed to be purposely quiet or muffled. It made him feel even lonelier.

The next several days went by quickly with all the last minute preparations. At last, the ship was ready to leave the next morning with the tide. All the goodbyes had been said the night before because the vessel was leaving before sunup.

Rob, Verdin, and Twig had decided to sleep on board that night, sprawling out on deck where it was cooler, under a piece of sailcloth at the stern to keep the heavy dew from soaking them. Ambro, the big kitten, was curled up next to Twig. One last night aboard the ship they knew so well.

About an hour after the witching hour, the three were awakened by a loud scream and an inhuman snarling. The sounds then stopped, followed by loud breathing and what sounded like sobbing. Springing up, they ran amidships where the sound came from.

The big cat was standing over a figure sprawled on the deck. The cat had the back of a man's neck in his mouth, holding the man face down.

Every time the man wiggled, the cat would growl in his throat and clamp down a little harder. Finally, Twig reached out and got hold of the man, urging Ambro to let go. The cat unclamped his bloody teeth, backed up, and sat down, his little short tail twitching. Then he started licking and cleaning his paws and his face.

As Twig held the man, Rob and Verdin investigated their surroundings and found a small trail of gunpowder leading from the magazine . . . and an open keg of gunpowder. The trail led up the side runner to the main deck. A piece of flint was found nearby with a striker. This man was going to blow them all to glory after he had made his escape. The big cat had spoiled his attempt and captured him to boot!

The crewmen who were on watch were questioned, and as it turned out, one of the seaman on guard was found dead, stuffed behind some kegs in the magazine. The others had seen a figure amidships but had assumed it was the guard.

Jonathan turned his fury upon the prisoner who had murdered one of his crew and had nearly blown his ship out of the water. He hit the man two or three blows in the face before he regained control. The man stood unfettered on the deck, surrounded by the crew. He didn't make a move to defend himself, only fell sobbing to the deck.

Robert seized the man by the hair and told him, "We'll turn the cat loose on you again if you don't tell us who put you up to this!" Then turning to his crew, he said, "Search this man!"

His belongings included a tomahawk and a few pieces of gold coin. Robert again demanded, "Who sent you to do this devilment, you black dog scoundrel? Bring the cat!"

At that, the prisoner bellowed, "McGrivin!" and fell to his knees. Twig and Verdin looked at one another. McGrivin? Reaching out this far? Just for a personal vendetta . . . or was there more to it?

The man talked loudly in between his sobbing, "They know this ship is going to be used against His Majesty's Royal Navy!" He whined and cried some more, then, "They also know Burntthorne's granddaughter is here and that you took their servants and brought them here unlawfully. McGrivin has sworn she will kill you all!"

Verdin looked at the man and said, "She?"

The man nodded. "Mrs. McGrivin, yes! Her husband is away fighting with his people, the Cherokee. She will kill you, and now she will kill me too."

Jonathan ordered the dead body of their guard brought on deck and sewed into a canvas bag. The magazine was cleared and the powder collected and put away. The prisoner was put in chains.

Jonathan then said to Rob, Verdin, and Twig. "Go ahead and go, and take this man with you. Get him to our military authorities. He should be hanged or shot at the very least. We'll try to leave now if the current is favorable . . . and you three, please look after our loved ones."

Goodbyes and good lucks and "Go with God" were said all around, and the three took their cowed prisoner and left, followed by a big kitten still licking the blood from his lips.

They locked the prisoner in Seagate's warehouse, leaving him chained to a huge support post. Then they sped away to check on the safety of their loved ones. Twig and Rob were surprised to see Verdin head for Anne Brosia's quarters. Was he going to make sure she was safe?

Twig and Rob looked at one another. They had noticed a difference in Verdin, now that they thought about it. A change in his expression, a little more cheerful demeanor, a little more spring in his step. Love was in the air! Of course, that was why he went to see about her.

The rest of the night they spent on vigil. Nothing was out of the ordinary. The ship had left, apparently with no further sabotage attempts. Seagate was told of everything that took place. When he sent the militia captain to get the prisoner, the captain found he was gone, chains and all.

Seagate said later in the day that the Tories were getting bolder and would put the royal governor back in the city, given the chance. They would probably deal very roughly with those who had helped the Rebels and their cause, such as himself and even Mrs. Anne Brosia and numerous others.

Rob, Twig, and Verdin put their heads together. What should they do? Should all of them leave the city at once? Or should one or two go scout out a destination first? They decided to ask those in their charge for help in the decision.

It became clear that the entire group firmly believed in strength in numbers and unity. But there was a good case to be made for having someone going ahead to determine the best place to go.

Seagate suggested going upriver to Augusta, the head of navigable waters on the Savannah. From there, the chosen scout could seek out the best location. But who would go?

The solution came from an unexpected source. The following morning, a man who hired himself out to haul goods in his wagon to the waterfront came to Seagate's office. He said he had a message for the man with the cat, and his friend. Seagate at once sent a messenger boy to fetch Twig. Rob and Verdin came along. The man said someone came to his dwelling the previous night by the name of Ambro. Ambro obviously knew the freight hauler and that he could deliver a message to Elisha Seagate. Ambro wanted Twig and his friends to meet him that night, about five or six miles outside of the city.

Just before dark, the three young men left on horseback for the place described by the wagoner. Ambro the cat rode across the pommel in front of Twig, as he usually did. The feline seemed to be content wherever he was, as long as it was with Twig. They reached the little path that turned off the main road, as per their instructions, to the tabby ruins of some old Spanish building. As they quietly approached, Ambro himself stepped out to raise a hand in greeting.

The trio stepped down from their horses to greet Ambro and introduce Rob. Ambro walked over to the big cat sitting up on the saddle and said, "So you were named Ambro too, big fella?" He reached up to rub the big cat's head and scratch behind its ears, as if it were a normal housecat. The cat lowered its head for more petting and began to purr.

The men then sat on the low, crumbling walls of the ruins and talked. Ambro told them of the arrival of Lord Burntthorne and his son Oden, not long after Verdin and Twig had left Thornewell. Oden was furious about Hannah's traitorous actions in turning to people in open rebellion against the king. Not only that, but she was denouncing her own family. He was determined to bring her back into the fold at once and to get her mind back on the right path.

Lord Burntthorne had suggested to his son that perhaps she had not done this of her own free will. Perhaps these Rebels were guilty of coercing her into her wretched behavior. Perhaps she was really being held prisoner and had no choice in the matter. This became the official stance of the old man and his son, and it was agreed to embark at once upon a rescue effort. Oden was given a free rein to use the family's resources to extract Hannah from her captors.

Of course, that was what Lord Burntthorne "officially" agreed to. He suspected the real truth was that Oden was furious Hannah was not with him, that he had been unsuccessful in seducing or subduing his beautiful, headstrong cousin so far.

Oden swore to kill her captors and anyone trying to prevent her escape. Meanwhile, though his father suspected the underlying reason for his son's desiring the return of Hannah, he did not realize the depth of Oden's rage and jealousy. He did not know how truly black, deceitful, and evil Oden's mind was—in fact, a blossoming insanity lurked in the deep, dark waters of Oden's mind and soul, so much so that their Indian allies secretly called him "The Black Smoke."

Ambro related that Oden had contacted Tory spies in the city. Their every move had been watched. Oden had paid the man who tried to blow up the *Warrior* before she sailed.

Oden knew that all of the ships—the *Edisto*, the *Roanoke*, and the other ships containing supplies, foodstuffs, mail, etc. were gone, and that the people with Hannah now were more vulnerable and open to attack. Ambro said he did not know what Oden's exact plans were, but he urged them to remain vigilant, as Oden sought not only to capture Hannah but also to kill the rest of them.

They discussed with Ambro their fear of being trapped in the city, a very real threat should the British decide to take the city with the help of their larger, superior navy. The British could do the same with Augusta, as the river was navigable to there. Where could they go that would be far enough away from the western frontier and Cherokee attacks?

Ambro thought for a moment, then said, "Cedar Shoals, Georgia. It's about a hundred miles northwest of Augusta on the Oconee. There are enough people there to provide protection should the Cherokee or the Creeks attack. There are more settlements to the west of there, maybe fifty, sixty miles away." He thought a minute then nodded his head emphatically. "Yes," he said, "that should fit your needs well, at least for now."

While they considered Ambro's suggestion, he added quietly, "If you would like to have my help, and if my family would be welcome into your fold, then I will join you. I no longer wish to be at Thornewell or to have my family there. Oden Burntthorne is a cruel, evil man, and I want my family out of his reach."

With that, the young men accepted Ambro's offer with gratitude. Then they began to discuss the *how* and *when* of the exodus. Ambro stopped them with his hand up. Motioning for them to stay put, he got up and disappeared into the shadows. He was gone for several minutes, then emerged from the darkness surrounding the tabby walls with a grin on his face. "Checking for spies," he said. "We're safe to continue the discussion."

And so they planned, with occasional checks by Ambro for any unwelcome eyes and ears.

***

Finally, it was decided that the three would return to Savannah and immediately get everyone ready to move via the river. They would go to Augusta then arrange for a wagon train to Cedar Shoals.

At first they considered having Ambro and his family—traveling on horses with pack horses to carry their belongings—to follow along the west side of the river, as a screen for any trouble that might come from that direction. The danger to Ambro's family, however, was considered too great, and it was finally decided that he would bring his family to a spot on the river, a little way out of Savannah. There, they could safely join the rest of the travelers aboard ship, and Twig and Ambro would travel by horseback, serving as guardian angels to their loved ones traveling up the river.

When they adjourned, Ambro left immediately for Thornewell, while the others returned to inform the rest of their group of the plans. There was much to do . . . and quickly.

Seagate once again proved to be an invaluable ally by locating two transports with crews to take them upriver. Their belongings were packed and carried to the transports by the menfolk.

When Verdin shared the agenda with Anne, he was disappointed to learn she would not agree to join the group. He begged and pleaded with her, to no avail. His heart was devastated. They had become increasingly closer and were insatiable lovers. She told him that while she was delighted in the time they had together, she would not leave her home. Verdin had asked her to marry him several times, but she kept postponing an answer. She did not overtly reject his offer, instead just wanted to wait until after the war was over. After all, she reminded him, they were already married in their hearts. She had no designs on any other lovers.

She was truthful in that, at least. She had for the first time in her life fallen in love and felt devoted to the most wonderful man she had ever met or ever hoped to meet. But there was more to her refusal to marry than she let on. She knew she was Verdin's first love. She didn't want to stifle him from possibly falling in love with a woman closer to his age. She also knew she couldn't have children, and she didn't want to deprive Verdin of being a father. Yes, she was in love with young Verdin, but she was unselfish. She put him first.

The case was different for Rob and Hannah. When he told her the whole story, she assured him she would be a willing participant. When she said the words, "Most definitely," she moved closer to him, looking up with a serious yet tender look in her eyes. So Rob did what to him was the most natural thing in the world to do at that moment. He slipped his arms around her waist and softly placed his lips on hers. At first, their kiss was gentle, but quickly progressed in its passion. They held each other tightly, as they lingered in a long embrace. Finally, they stopped kissing, and he took her sweet face between his hands and gently kissed her eyelids, nose, forehead, and then her cheeks. As he did so, she fixed him with a gaze that made his heart race. She finally closed her eyes and snuggled against his chest and shoulder. He stroked her hair and murmured words of love in her ears. They snuggled together and swayed on their feet, enjoying the closeness of this time together. Then one more heated kiss before they pulled apart, ready to face the world, together.

As the appointed time for departure drew near, last minute purchases of foodstuff and cooking utensils were made, including a supply of powder and shot. Twig had been carefully working on rifles and pistols, which he boxed up and placed on the river transports. He and Rob worked together making arrows and steel points for them, as well as an English longbow. These primitive bows and arrows were good second weapons for close-range fire, quicker to reload than rifles.

They presented the longbow to Verdin, who practiced determinedly with sharp wooden practice bolts until he became proficient with it.

Twig showed the boys two pistols he had made for himself. They were his own design and years ahead of their time. These became the prototypes of additional pistols he would make later for others. Simple in design, they were made with a hinged stock that broke the barrel down and forward to allow for loading of pre-made cartridges. They were smaller caliber than other pistols of the day, and the projectiles they fired were another of Twig's inventions. Instead of lead balls, Twig devised a mold to make a pointed, conical projectile that was much longer than a musket ball. This long projectile was hollow, which Twig filled with powder. The powder was held in place by a piece of paper wadding. When the barrel was closed and the hammer cocked, a small piece of metal moved forward from the thick stationary end of the barrel, compressing the powder and piercing the paper. The spark from the flint touched off the powder by means of a small hole in the tip of the compressor.

The pistols could be fired and reloaded many more times than a muzzleloader in the same space of time. The only downside to these weapons were that they had to be cleaned more often, and the projectiles were more difficult and time-consuming to make—a small price to pay for a finer weapon overall.

Twig wore these pistols in leather holsters on his sides. On his packhorse, he also placed two long rifles, also of his own design. They had longer, thicker barrels than normal, and fired a conical projectile similar to that of the pistol. The caliber was only .45, but a lot of powder could be packed behind the shot. The barrels of the rifles were so heavy that they had to be set up on a tripod, another item Twig made, or supported by a tree limb or other type structure to hold their weight.

Another innovation by Twig was the telescopes he attached to each rifle, aligned with sights. He, Rob, and Verdin test-fired these multiple times down on the river; they were exceedingly accurate for two hundred fifty yards, probably more if targets were larger.

# Chapter Fourteen
## EAST OF THE ETOHO RIVER

The first of September 1777 found everyone packed and on board river transport ships. Elisha Seagate was there to see them off. Ann Brosia had said her goodbyes the night before, including spending most of the night saying goodbye to Verdin. The transports soon pulled away, manned by their crews: Rob in the lead boat, Verdin in the rear.

They arrived in Savannah just after dark, where they hoped to rendezvous with Twig, as well as Ambro and his family, as planned. Ambro was of mixed race: red, black, and white. Technically, he was a slave of the Burntthorne's. So was his family. He had mentioned his family but not in detail.

Not long after they tied up for the night on the west bank of the river, Ambro appeared on foot, rifle in hand. He confirmed that his family was waiting in a grove of trees by a spring; they would come to the river and join the transports after daylight tomorrow.

Rob, Verdin, and Twig were thrilled when Ambro said everything had gone smoother than expected. Lord Burntthorne had headed back down river to where the Oconamaha entered the sea below Savannah. There, his ship awaited to take him to England, along with a cargo of Jamaican rum.

Oden and both the McGrivins had received instructions from the British agent in Pensacola to convince the Creek Nation to go to war.

They also needed to stir up more of the Cherokees. Only a few of the young hotheads had been fighting, and without sanction of the tribe....so far only warriors from the Cherokee towns in South Carolina, and a very few of the warriors of the Overhill towns, and towns along the Chattahoochee and Hatawwah rivers.

So the Burntthornes had left Thornewell just before Ambro had, and their attention was thus diverted momentarily away from Hannah. Of course, the Burntthorne's agents, spies—possibly paid killers— were still a real and present danger.

The next morning, Ambro brought his wife, Little Chicken, or "Chick" as she was called, and his two sons: Matthew, age six, and Luke, age four. Their belongings were transferred from the packhorses to the transport.

Although Chick was half black and half Creek Indian, the white women welcomed her to their circle as family. After all, they would all suffer the same hardships in the future. She was a happy, smiling person with dark red skin and straight, coal-black hair. She spoke perfect English and could read and write, though no one was certain how this came to be. She was also fluent in Creek, Cherokee, and Spanish, and had a bright mind and a calm, assuring, sweet demeanor. She dressed in the simple cloth clothing of the Creek women and wore beaded wristbands and matching headbands. She wore beaded, high top moccasins on her feet. She became a very welcome addition to the Cedar Haven family. On top of everything else, she was a Christian convert and great cook. She was openly in love with her husband and devoted to him and their children. Ambro was clearly proud of his wife, whom he loved so deeply. His devotion and kind caring ways to her and their children were obvious and absolute. They were without a doubt a match made in heaven—two soul mates forever.

In testament to her name, Chick brought with her two handmade chicken coops full of chickens. She knew that if a person had chickens and a place for them to scratch and eat bugs, worms, and seeds, then that person would always have something to eat. With eggs and maybe an occasional chicken, there would be enough to keep starvation at bay.

Twig loaded his packhorse with his weapons the next morning, and he and Ambro faded out of sight of the river. The riverboat crews soon had the transports moving toward Augusta. The weather during the morning was sunny and bright, and the passengers enjoyed the beauty of the river and the country on each side. They passed small cabins as well as larger, fancier homes. Sometimes the people along the shore would wave in greeting to them, and those on board would do the same in return.

That same late afternoon, Ambro and Twig were walking their horses along a trail that had head-high grass on either side. There were no trees along there. Ambro suddenly stopped his horse and listened. Then, holding his reins in his teeth, he stood up on the saddle. Looking over the tall grass, he saw nothing out of the ordinary. Then they noticed the big cat had stood up as well and was looking back down the trail. The cat's back was arched and his fur was fluffed while his little bobbed tail twitched as though in anger.

Ambro maintained his position standing on the saddle. Very faintly, he could see above the trail a faint hint of dust in the air. The kind of light dusting that hard-running horses might throw up on a sandy trail.

These horses and riders were well back but coming strong, whoever they were. Looking ahead, Ambro saw an outcropping of trees perhaps a half mile distant. There were no houses along this isolated stretch of the river. He suggested to Twig that they make haste to the trees to see if they could determine who they were. Ambro the cat had jumped down from his perch and trotted on ahead as though he knew the plan.

Once there, Ambro and Twig concealed themselves and their horses where they could observe the trail. There was no sign of the young bobcat. They waited for what seemed like hours before they heard the horses. Ambro and Twig still sat on their horses, reaching forward to pet their necks and muzzles to soothe them into being quiet.

The riders had slowed their mounts to a trot as they neared the trees, and they were clearly not at ease. There were four of them with their rifles slung across their backs. The front rider was a heavyset white man in shirtsleeves only, a wide-brimmed hat on his head, red-faced and perspiring as he trotted into the trees looking around warily.

The second and third riders were in shirtsleeves, dressed as white men, but they had red skin, long black hair, and headbands. They were young men, probably young, hot-blooded Creek warriors. The fourth man gave Twig a start. He was the one caught trying to blow up the *Warrior* and had disappeared from the warehouse where he had been chained.

Suddenly, from the other side of the trail, a big cat leaped from the limbs of a tree onto the fourth rider. This time, the big cat's teeth found the soft front of the man's throat and jugular vein. His claws ripped the soft flesh of the man's belly and chest. Not a sound was uttered—there had been no time. The man was dead before he hit the ground, his eyes wide with terror from the momentary glimpse he had of the pouncing cat of death. The first three riders had only seen a fleeting shadow and heard the uneven gait of a startled horse. They all three glanced behind them to check on the fourth rider, when they saw the wild-eyed, riderless horse now running pell-mell toward them, stirrups flapping crazily.

They instantly pulled up to investigate further. The big white man spurred his horse back around and hurried between his two companions to stare down at the body of their companion beside the trail. The terrified look in the fixed, staring eyes and the ripped, bloody throat and chest caused the man to gasp, then emit a stream of profanity.

He spun his horse around, looking about in terror and rage. He pulled a short sword or long knife from its scabbard on his side. He bellowed something unintelligible and started in the direction of Ambro and Twig, glaring and looking for something or someone to kill.

The roar of Ambro's rifle and its deadly messenger of death knocked the big man into a backward flip off his horse. He landed in a sitting position in the sandy trail with a bullet hole in his forehead, his sword still in his right hand. His horse shied to the right, became tangled in the reins, and stood stock-still, blowing and quivering.

The other two riders whirled around in confusion and, as they realized their leader was dead, broke into a run back down the trail. Twig fired first one pistol then the other just as the riders broke into a run, crouched low over their horses. The first shot hit the front rider in the right arm; the second shot hit the other rider in the side of the stomach. Though both had cried out in pain, they stayed astride their horses and kept moving.

Twig quickly reloaded the pistols, snapped them shut, and spurred his horse in pursuit. They were too far gone by the time he regained the trail to follow. He pulled up and returned to the battle site.

Meanwhile, Ambro had gathered the weapons of the dead men, along with their wallets and ammunition. He untangled the big man's horse from its reins and led him back to the body, which remained in a sitting position on the trail. Twig approached, and Ambro said, "That there was a good deed, very good indeed. If a man ever needed killing, that there is one. Man's name is Bolton Aker. Everybody called him Bolt Aker to his face, Bloody Bolt Aker behind his back. He would kill anybody anytime for the right money. He would kill 'em fast or slow, depending on what the person who was paying wanted. He sometimes killed just for the cruelty . . . especially killing people slow. It's a real pity he got to leave this world so quickly."

With that, Ambro spat on the dead man, then swung himself into the saddle of his own horse, leading the dead man's horse by the reins. They took the trail at a lope to get to the landing spot for the night. Once there, Rob, Verdin, Twig, and Ambro went through the personal effects of the dead men. They found quite a bit of British gold coins, mostly from the saddlebags of Bolton Aker. The same thought of relief was on everyone's mind—maybe it would be a while before they were pursued again.

The rest of the journey to Augusta was uneventful, except for some rain. Once they arrived, they wasted no time in procuring five wagons and teams, and heading west. Rob only purchased the absolute necessities for the next leg of their journey. They didn't linger in Augusta.

Ambro and Twig rode point for the procession, staying one to two miles ahead. They would scout out campsites for their followers—wooded sites with water preferably. Since others had come this way before them, the spots were easily identifiable, every eight to twelve miles, with trails that carried them to the best fords across the streams.

They passed a few dwellings along the trail and passed or met people coming and going. Most of the settlers were up or down the streams they crossed and away from the main trail. Twice they came to a little cluster of buildings and cabins with a trading post. These small settlements were at the intersection of old Indian trading paths that crossed the trail to Cedar Shoals.

Purposely moving slowly and deliberately, Rob led the procession across a hundred miles or so in fourteen days. He took advantage of the best campsites and watering places, making sure they were settling in by nightfall.

They crossed the small river called the Etoho, east of the small settlement of Cedar Shoals. The community was located between the Etoho and Ithlobee rivers, north of their joining together at the Big Shoals. After scouting around for a place to hang their hats, they learned of a man who owned some property but had basically abandoned it. Hoping to secure that land at a reasonable price for themselves, Rob and his group sought him out, discovering that he lived on a farm a bit farther north. After some discussion and negotiation, the man finally agreed to sell them his old farmland for very reasonable terms. The property included five hundred acres, a barn, and one partially finished log cabin, as well as plenty of good grass and water, including two springs and two small creeks running through it.

It only took another day and a half for their wagons to reach their new home just west of the Ithlobee River. The log cabin was poorly built and poorly sited, so they decided to tear it down and use it for firewood. The barn would serve its purpose for now.

They drew the wagons into a semicircle on a grass-covered area near one of the springs, staying close together for protection.

The spring for their drinking water was just a short walk away, up a slightly wooded rise. There were plenty of trees and firewood on either side of their little clearing. Using saplings cut from nearby, poles were fashioned to support a canvas awning attached to the canvas roof on the wagons. Firewood from the old cabin was stacked in the center of the semicircle for one common campfire.

Soon the camp setup was suitable for a semi-permanent arrangement. Clothes washed in the nearby stream hung on lines stretched from wagon top to wagon top. A big cast iron pot was full of stew, the meat coming from a big buck deer killed by Ambro. His wife had the chickens set up with nests in the coops, and began collecting eggs. The chickens roamed the campsite, eating bugs and larvae, never venturing far away, in fear of predators.

The horses were kept in the barn and a stock pen, which the menfolk made from poles and saplings cut from the nearby woods. They purchased a male and two female goats, along with a milk cow from the previous owner of the property.

Ambro rode over the farm and the surrounding country, scouting out the lay of the land and where the nearest neighbors were located. Due to the large tracts of land held by the area farmers, most neighbors, including the former owner of their property, lived about five miles away. Cedar Shoals was about fifteen miles away.

When Ambro returned from his roundabout reconnaissance, he reported signs of hogs that he suspected were domestic hogs just gone wild. He'd also found a herd of about fifteen abandoned cattle. In time, the men would build a fence around some of the pastureland and drive the cattle inside the fences, thereby protecting them and their young from predators.

With their camp established, comfortable and secure, thoughts turned to building a log house or houses. A planning session was held around a large dining table built by Twig, which was situated under a large tarp.

Finally, it was decided to build one large cabin, big enough for all. There would be one large stone fireplace at one end and a great common room for cooking, eating, and congregating. Down a long hallway would be rooms for sleeping quarters for the women and families. Single men would sleep in the loft area, which could also be used for storage.

Work began on the big house right away. Cold winter months were just around the corner and the beautiful bright colors of the fall foliage were all around to remind them. The men began cutting the big pines nearby and dragging them to the house site.

Using plans drawn up by Twig, piles of large stones were placed at the four corners of the rectangle. Other piles were placed at needed locations to support the outside walls and beams down the center. This home would have no dirt floor. It was decided to build the house on rock pillars about four feet off the ground. Crossmembers were run from the outside beams to the center beam. Then long, straight logs were split and laid across the supports with rounded side down. These were notched to the right depth at each support to make the top of the flat sides as uniform as possible. This achieved a rough but relatively flat wooden plank floor secured with pegs.

Using the horses, the logs for the exterior walls were snaked into place. Ambro and Twig fashioned a device—using big pieces of rope they'd brought from the ships—to hoist the long, heavy logs to the top spots. In no time, they were able to build nine-foot-high exterior walls. Door and window openings were cut and framed with hand-hewn boards, painstakingly shaped out of logs into two to three inch thick slabs.

The interior walls for the hallway and sleeping quarters were built the same as the exterior walls, only with smaller logs. Their corners were notched to make the logs fit together as closely as possible, just like the exterior walls. Smaller door openings were cut and framed.

Another plank floor was laid across the top of the lower rooms and hallway, fashioned in the same manner as the main floor. The area over the great common room was to be left open to the rafters. The rafters were straight poplar logs, hand-shaped to provide as much uniformity as possible. Small poles cut from the tops of the trees were used for the log walls and rafters. Saplings were laid across the rafters. Handmade cedar shingles were then placed on top of them to keep out the rain.

The women helped with the lighter work, handing up poles and shingles. They also gathered large stones for the fireplace, which would take up nearly the whole end of the dwelling. The women also began chinking the logs with clay and grasses that were mixed together by hand. Ambro had found a good source of clay just along the stream not far away. It was a dark gray color. Using water to make it more pliable and thus easier to mix with the grass, the women were able to make buckets and buckets of the durable, chink-like material.

Twig and Ambro were clearly leading the way in the building tasks. Twig had studied books on architecture and construction methods somewhere in his mysterious past. Ambro had more experience in buildings made of logs and applying materials and techniques developed through using what nature provided at hand. Ambro's wife was also a big asset in the construction process. Chick was a tireless, cheerful contributor and was able to teach the women many things that were necessary to survive and thrive in this environment. To everyone's surprise, Hannah took to Chick's teachings and examples like a duck to water. Chick was her mentor of choice, and the two became inseparable.

One thing they shared an interest in was bathing and skinny-dipping in the river. Only Chick knew that sometimes Hannah stayed longer or went by herself to meet with someone who shared this interest. After all, Rob and Hannah had shared this common interest since they first met!

Chick would sometimes linger in the shadows of the trees to watch the two frolic in the water. One day, she turned to find her husband smiling and waiting on her. She literally skipped to jump into his strong arms, and they went downstream to their own place to do a little skinny-dipping of their own.

As soon as the roof to the cabin was secured, Ambro and Twig went to work on the huge hearth and the central core of the fireplace. They experimented with the clays and sand to make a type of mortar that would be able to withstand the heat and not just crumble away. They began their experiments long before time to build the chimney but were unable to make anything work. Finally they decided to use only the best selection of rocks that would fit snugly together when stacked. Then using the mortar away from the direct heat to hold rocks in place supporting and surrounding the central chimney and firebox, they built a very strong, well-sealed fireplace. They embedded two cast-iron pot hangers that they'd brought from Savannah into the back of the fireplace wall. These hangers allowed the big black pots to be swung back and forth over the fire or out over the hearth.

Verdin and Rob used their carpentry skills learned on shipboard to fashion planks into doors and window shutters. They had no glass for the windows at present, so shutters would have to do. For these, Twig fashioned hinges made of wood, held together with long, wooden pegs.

Everyone seemed to take a good deal of satisfaction from their efforts; the sweating, the little hurts and cuts, the sore muscles, and the sunburn all were worth it in the end. As they worked to put the finishing touches on the big house, everyone was cheerful and healthy, for which all were grateful. Some relationships were indeed missed dearly—Twig pined for Louisa Medford something fierce, and Verdin would blush at the mere mention of Ann Brosia's name. Rob's sister, Hope, seemed to be the only one who never quite achieved a feeling of contentment; she missed George Wolloston more than she could sometimes bear.

Rob sent word to Elisha Seagate and Anne Brosia that they arrived safely. They were just getting ready to celebrate Christmas when a man appeared on horseback at the edge of the grassy clearing. He had ridden up from Cedar Shoals to bring them letters that had been brought to his store from Augusta.

He introduced himself as Henry Etton, and Rob recognized him from the main trading post in Cedar Shoals. They invited him to the campfire and to join them for Christmas dinner. He accepted their invitation, but first wanted to give them their letters.

He produced letters from Seagate, one to Verdin from Anne, three or four from Louisa for Twig, and one from George for Hope. The letter from Elisha Seagate was for the whole group, and included news of the latest war events. Apparently, the Indian agents sent by the British to stir up more of the Cherokees had been successful. Serious fighting with them had taken place near Seneca, South Carolina, and along the Tugaloo River. In August, Colonel Pickens had burned Tamnsey Town of the Cherokee. The Cherokee then struck at Colonel Williamson's Patriot force on the Coweecho River in North Carolina in September. Farther away, but important in the scope of the impact it could have on all the colonies, was the British capture and occupation of New York City.

# Chapter Fifteen
## TWO MEN AND A LADY

I n spite of all the disturbing war news, Verdin, Twig, and Hope could not have received better Christmas gifts in the form of these letters. Verdin was beaming and blushing from what Anne had written him. Twig had written Louisa Medford before leaving Savannah, telling her of the move and his desire to have her with him. Her return letters only stoked the fires of love and passion as she tenderly revealed her desire to be with him, expressing her love.

The letter that Hope received from George lifted her spirits so much that she became almost like another person—all bubbly with bright, cheerful eyes. He clearly expressed his love for her and was very impatient to be with her. This letter had come to Seagate from Charleston and was dated in mid-October. It contained nothing but personal and romantic content. There was a last letter from Seagate, which Rob opened and read in privacy, containing more up-to-date news. The letter dated the first of November came from Charleston.

George Wolloston's ships had gone on to Boston with supplies for the army. From there, they had gone to New York to pick up a cargo of war supplies the city fathers donated to the war effort. They successfully delivered that cargo to Boston, and while there, George had gone to the family farm to visit his mother and other family members and friends nearby. He also arranged to retrieve some of his money, which he had sealed in a heavy chest and taken aboard the *Edisto*.

According to Seagate's letter, George had received a note from Louisa Medford, who heard from a mutual friend that he was there. So, he paid a visit to Wilbraham Medford's farm, happy to see the dear friends once again. That visit resulted in Louisa and JenAnne begging him to take them to Georgia. At first, he adamantly refused, but finally relented. The Medford parents were unhappy that the young women wanted to leave the farm, but as they were both adult women, it was their decision to make for themselves.

With the help of the ship's doctor, Maury Kensly, they were able to transport the ladies to the *Edisto* and get them settled aboard. They set sail from Boston, unaware that the British had embarked upon taking the city of New York. Using every ruse known by Captain Wolloston and his officers, the *Edisto* and *Roanoke* had somehow eluded battle or capture. British ships were popping up everywhere, escorting their main fleet and controlling the approaches to New York.

Finally, their luck had run out. They were cornered and forced to fight it out with three ships larger and more heavily armed. A British shell hulled the *Roanoke* and struck the magazine. She blew up with all her crew. Gone were Ellis Rofford and Norwin Chaddham, both Patriots to the end and good friends to them all.

The *Edisto* was shot up but was able to escape under cover of darkness and a storm. They had inflicted enough damage on the enemy ships to discourage serious effort to stop them, so they barely limped away. The ship was badly damaged and many of the crew wounded and killed.

The saddest news from those casualties aboard the *Edisto* was the death of JenAnne Medford. Amazingly, she and Louisa had stood at George's side during most of the battle. He suddenly missed them both and looking around, located them helping a gun crew that had been decimated by enemy fire. Amidst the blood, brains, guts, and gore, they followed the example and instructions of those remaining to man the guns. Side by side, they helped fire and reload, tears running down their smoke-grimed faces, their feet and skirts bloody.

Suddenly, a shell struck JenAnne, fired from a ship on the opposite side. It literally blew her nearly in half as it hit her in the small of the back and went clear through her. Louisa reached to grab JenAnne as her dead body was knocked forward to the gunwale, where it paused before toppling forward into the sea.

George had seen it all and heard Louisa's screams. He roared in horror and rage, frustration overwhelming him, until he witnessed, in awe, Louisa turning back to the task at hand, firing and reloading. A few seconds later, a shot took George's left arm off just above the elbow. He crumpled to the deck in shock, watching blood spray out of his arm. Dr. Kensly knelt over him, stopping the bleeding and covering him with pieces of torn sails and clothing to keep him warm.

Not only did the doctor tend the downed captain, but he also orchestrated their disengagement and escape. Louisa then joined him in caring for the other wounded and dying. They barely had enough men to keep the *Edisto* afloat and underway, but they managed. They were afraid of stopping in a port anywhere nearby for fear of being trapped. Not knowing the true destination of the British at the time was New York, they just continued on down the coast to Charleston.

The letter had taken two months to reach the group, and Rob wondered, *Where are they now?* So many questions remained unanswered. He debated briefly about whether to tell the rest of the group this latest information, finally concluding that he should. There was no way the facts could be hidden forever; best to get it out in the open now.

When Hope learned of George being wounded, she began crying hysterically. Rob and their mom tried to console her, finally prevailing by reminding her that after all it was just an arm, not his life, that was gone.

Just as the winter cold of 1778 arrived, the log cabin welcomed its new residents. The fireplace was soon holding a hot, blazing fire, which in turn heated the stones. The stones held and radiated heat, too, helping make the large cabin warm and cozy.

The big eating table was brought inside, and Twig fashioned

sideboards, shelves, and food preparation tables along the back north wall. Verdin and Rob built a shed roof porch on the front and rear of the cabin, extending from one side of the home to the other, as well as a small one over a side door on the east side. They used stacked rocks and mortar to create the steps.

Meanwhile, Ambro shot two hogs and another buck. A few days later, he shot one of the young bulls, which was bound to cause trouble with the older bull come spring anyway. Chick had located some chestnut trees to the southwest of their house, and the womenfolk went there with baskets and two horses with canvas bags made to fit on each side of the horse. They harvested the abundant, tasty nuts from the huge chestnut trees before the hogs and deer and other creatures could eat them.

During the cold winter months, the family members, which numbered twelve in all, remained busy. The women did most of the cooking, food preparation, and preserving of the meat. Ambro helped in this as well; he had a special talent for it, which he enjoyed. As they had no furniture, Twig made bunks and shelving for each person's quarters. Rob and Verdin helped in cutting down trees and handcrafting planks and bracing for the furniture Twig then made.

Rob and Verdin learned to make stools and benches by adding legs to slit tree trunks, by burning holes in which to fit the round legs. They made these benches for the front porch and back porch as well as a few on the inside. After the house was completely finished, the trio worked on improving the barn, building a shed roof on each side, repairing the roof and shoring it up so hay could be stored next year for the livestock. Chinking was put between the logs, and the stalls were repaired and improved. On the southeast side of the barn, under the shed roof, Verdin started a woodshop area. In time, this could become a blacksmith shop, too, if he could find the tools and bellows.

As the days became noticeably longer and winter started to lose its grip, the menfolk began clearing the land on either side of the little creek between the grassy clearing and the Etoho River. They hoped to have enough land cleared to plant corn along the creek bottom by spring.

It was nearly April 1777, and the dogwoods and wild azaleas were beginning to bloom, when one morning, their isolation was interrupted by a shout from the front yard.

Twig, in a rare moment of relaxation, had been sitting idly in front of the fire in a large rocking chair of his own design and make. It was not graceful or pretty, just sturdy, practical, and comfortable. He had just stood up and ambled over to peer out the open front door when he heard the shout. Looking out, he beheld two gentlemen and a lady sitting on their horses at the edge of the clearing.

Twig tore out the front door, jumped off the porch, and ran across the grassy area toward the lady on horseback. At the same time, she vaulted out of the sidesaddle and ran to meet him. He held out his arms, and she floated into them, arms around his neck. He started slowly swinging her around as she laughed and cried at the same time. He, too, was laughing and kept calling her name, "Louisa! Louisa!"

By this time, the rest of the group had gathered to watch the reunion. They were astounded to see Twig transformed into an animated character so much unlike his usual business-like, methodical approach to everyday life. When he kissed his Louisa fiercely and passionately on the lips and she kissed him in matching measure, the curious group watched unabashedly. So this beautiful young woman was Louisa Medford, all the way from Boston.

Rob led the way to the two riders, recognizing them now as Capt. George Wolloston and Dr. Maury Kensly. The joy between old friends could not be contained, as they shared hugs and slaps on the backs, warm greetings. Hope had been standing back watching and waiting for the right moment. The good captain saw her immediately, kept glancing in her direction. Finally, his dear friends parted to open the path between the two lovebirds. Hope ran to George, arms outstretched.

They eagerly embraced and boldly kissed—a long, passionate, fiercely intense kiss. Finally they turned, walking toward the house, George holding her with his right arm around her waist, his left sleeve empty from the elbow down. Hope couldn't take her eyes from his face, and she smiled easily as they chatted and walked, like they had never been apart.

Dr. Kensly was surrounded by the others, and he was soon led into the house with Faith on one arm and Mary on the other. Rob and Verdin saw to their horses, taking them to the barn and removing their saddles. After rubbing them down, they gave the horses plenty of hay to eat. They returned to the house carrying the saddlebags for their guests and the weapons that had been strapped to the saddles.

Ambro, Chick, and their sons were introduced to the guests, and soon everyone was gathered around the big eating table. Rob, his mother Faith, and Aunt Mary took charge of feeding everyone. The fare wasn't fancy, but it was good; when it was all said and done, everyone was content, full, and warm.

George and Maury wanted to hear Ambro and Chick tell their stories, how they got to know Rob, Twig, and Verdin. They eventually met the big cat named after Ambro and how it had come to be with them. Ambro told of his capturing the Tory who attempted to blow up the *Warrior,* and how he would later kill him on the trail to Augusta.

Then George and Maury in turn shared details of their own recent histories, including how Louisa and JenAnne had come to be with them. In a vivid retelling of Seagate's letter, the men spoke of the horrible battle of the ships, the explosion of the *Roanoke,* and JenAnne's death. Louisa began sobbing and holding on to Twig as the grisly details were told. Twig pulled her close, comforting her.

Later, George and Maury told Twig that Louisa had not been able to cry about it since the battle. They told him she had been unable to come to grips with her sister's death and somehow blamed herself. She had been in a serious depressed state for days at a time, hardly able to function. But once George was well enough to travel and the weather began to be more cooperative, she had begun to be more like herself. She really became much more cheerful once they began to make actual preparations to leave Charleston.

Maury also related later that somehow George had lost interest in the

*Edisto* after that horrible, bloody battle. The loss of the *Roanoke* and its crew, including good friends Ellis Rofford and Norwin Chaddham, then seeing JenAnne die, and losing his left arm had taken a lot out of him. He had already lost his father in this war. Maury believed his ardor, his zeal for the cause was as great as ever. He believed it was simply that Captain Wolloston needed time to heal and to get over the great losses he had suffered. Spending time with Hope was sure to quicken that process; in fact, perhaps that was the medicine George needed most of all.

While he recovered in Charleston, Captain Wolloston had charged Dr. Kensly with overseeing the repairs of the *Edisto*. She had been repaired and refitted to perfection again, and before they left Charleston, George placed a long-time crewmember, officer, and trusted friend as captain. Capt. Zachary Jackson, known as Jack Jackson, was to take the *Edisto* to Savannah and report to Elisha Seagate for instructions. Captain Wolloston would semi-retire at the ripe old age of thirty.

They also brought news of the war. In spite of two brilliant strokes by Washington at Trenton and Princeton, the rest of the war effort was going badly. The British had tightened its grip on New York City and had also captured Philadelphia.

The spring rains and warmth soon brought planting and calving season. Several of the men on horseback went out on a cattle roundup and were able to bring most of the longhorn Spanish breed of cattle into the grassy clearing. There they rode guard over the herd, keeping predators away from the young ones.

Chick and Ambro had been taking scraps to feed a couple of young sows they had discovered down near the river. Chick especially was accepted by the two sows, coming close enough to almost let her scratch their prickly hides.

After a couple of close calls with their mean old boar and his tusks, Chick speeded up the process by trapping the two expecting sows with ropes. She soon had the two so completely rope broke and enamored with her, they followed her to the house. They lived under the back porch like two faithful dogs. They had their litters there, totally unaware that many of their offspring would eventually wind up on the table of their beloved master.

The goats had little ones, and the chickens had little ones, and the wild creatures had little ones. And Chick had a little one! They named her Lily, after Chick's mother.

Rob and the others had been going down to Henry Etton's trading post in Cedar Shoals as things were needed from time to time. They were there enough to consider him a friend, and they also got to know some of their neighbors and visited and talked with them at Henry's store.

A few days after the birth of Lily, Verdin and Dr. Kensly went into Cedar Shoals to pay a visit to Henry's store. Verdin had brought measurements of the windows to see if Henry could have the glass ordered.

But there was another, more important request they had of Henry. Did he know of a minister who was qualified to marry folks?

There were no churches as such in Cedar Shoals in those days. But they had heard of preachers conducting services in brush arbors from time to time, and in people's homes. But what was needed now was a preacher who could marry three couples right away!

Rob and Hannah had been discussing marriage. George had officially proposed to Hope the day after his arrival, and she had readily agreed. Twig and Louisa could hardly wait for the weather to get warmer so they could have their own "skinny dipping" experience; they wanted to get married soon.

Henry knew of just such a minister who would be glad to perform the triple ceremony, and for the small fee of having something to eat from the wedding feast table. Henry sent for Rev. Jesse Tattnall, who was all of five feet four inches tall, and looked like he had never had a full meal in his entire forty years.

Reverend Tattnall wore deerskin boots, deerskin breeches, and a deerskin vest over a white shirt. His hat was of deerskin but shaped like a gentleman's tricorn hat. It was said that he had taught himself to read and write from the large leather-bound Bible he carried in a deerskin pouch on his side. As a result, he talked and wrote like a Quaker, but he never claimed to be one.

The reverend agreed to perform the ceremony on the third Sunday of June, and he would bring along his wife and ten children, who ranged in age from one to nineteen. Invitations were sent by word of mouth to all the neighbors thereabouts to come to the triple ceremony and big cookout that day. So the day of the big event saw people coming by horseback and wagon to the farm. They came from all directions, bearing all manner of wedding presents. They brought peach, pear, and apple trees and grapevines. There were gifts of beehives and small crocks of honey. Small bundles of rich pine kindling were given, as well as willow withes for weaving chair bottoms. Some women brought flowers to plant, and men brought seeds for corn and beans. One family brought a cured ham, and another brought three small pigs.

They all gathered in the grassy field where the five wagons had been pulled together in a tight semicircle with their canvas awnings out. This produced a covered outdoor altar where the ceremony would be held. A large fire had been built for cooking a whole beef and, next to it, another for a whole hog. Planks were laid across sawhorses to form a long table covered in white linen sheets. The table soon held countless pies and cakes and a wide variety of dishes of food to eat.

Rev. Jesse Tattnall conducted a church service complete with prayers and a sermon. The sermon was delivered in the fiery fashion of country preachers but was not too long. It was charged with heartfelt emotion and moved many to tears of joy and happiness in Christ.

Capt. George Wolloston looked splendid in his almost new clothes. White shirt with buff-colored breeches, matching waistcoat, and a navy blue coat with matching hat. Rob and Twig wore matching sets of new clothing that they had scrambled to put together—white knee breeches, white stockings, white shirts with baby blue waistcoats and coats to match. Their low crown tricorn hats were navy blue wool as well. The three grooms looked handsome and suave as they waited for their brides to appear.

Verdin, Ambro, and Dr. Kensly agreed to serve as best men and to bear the rings for all six of them to be wear. Twig had taken coins and painstakingly fashioned by hand matching sets of wedding rings.

Fresh straw had been thickly strewn under the awnings, and in front of them for those in attendance to stand upon. The awnings had been decorated with flowers and bright-colored ribbons and streamers. Those in attendance were clad in bright colors and wearing hats of spring and early summer, which created a lively, festive atmosphere—perfect for the weddings and the blossoming of new love. The weather cooperated fully with sunshine, pleasant temperatures, and a slight breeze. Again, perfect.

Chick, Faith, and Mary had agreed to be the brides' attendants. They were simply attired in white blouses and dark blue long skirts. They walked beside each bride as they came from the house down to the wedding altar. With the help of Henry Etton from the trading post, the brides were all dressed in full, flowing white cotton skirts and blouses, with matching white bonnets.

Each bride-to-be was simply beautiful, and whispers of "they look like angels" went through the crowd as they passed. Hannah, Louisa, and Hope all wore shy smiles with bright eyes, their faces glowing and radiant as only brides can be on their wedding day. They had eyes only for their own handsome groom as they neared the altar. They soon joined hands and faced the minister.

The ceremony was brief with the exchange of rings and vows all done in unison. The grooms all said their parts together, and then the brides, and the couples were pronounced man and wife, all kissing their betrothed at the same time. A beautiful service, performed impeccably by Reverend Tattnall.

The guests then joined in congratulating the couples, and the wedding feast began. There was no music, as out there on the edge of the wilderness there was a distinct shortage of musical instruments. But a fun time was had by all, with the children romping and playing games, and the grownups laughing, talking, and visiting with friends and neighbors seldom seen.

By late afternoon and early evening, people were beginning to say their goodbyes and drift on back toward their own homes. What a beautiful, happy, and fulfilling day it had been.

Over the next few days, the decorations were taken down, and the newlywed couples slowly emerged from their own little worlds back to the real world. The ongoing farm chores and routines soon re-emerged. The trees, grapevines, and seeds brought as gifts were planted. The residents of the farm worked hard, yet found time to gather in the evenings to socialize and plan for their futures.

Rev. Tattnall was invited to return on Sunday mornings and hold church services for the residents of Cedar Haven, their neighbors, and anyone he would like to bring with him. They would meet in the same area where the weddings were held.

Captain Wolloston and his new wife announced their intentions to leave right away, to return to his home and be with his mother, build a life together there. Dr. Maury Kensly announced that he would like to stay there at the farm, for a while longer at least. Verdin Girard informed his friends that he wished to visit Anne in Savannah for a while. It was agreed then that Verdin would travel to Charleston with George and Hope. He then would find his way to Savannah by ship.

After all this sharing had gone on for a while, Ambro made a blunt statement to the group: he hated to put a damper on everyone's plans and sully the mood, but something was afoot. He had been scouting around the day before, just following his head, and had been drawn south toward Cedar Shoals. Slowly going down the trail, he suddenly saw Twig's big cat sitting on the side of the trail, as if waiting for him.

"When I got to the cat, he turned into the grass and trees to the left of the trail. He looked back to let me know I should follow, and led me to where someone had built a campfire a few nights before. Looked like two on horseback—two white men from the tracks, by the way they walked and what they had on their feet."

The others waited breathlessly for what was to come. Ambro looked around the table briefly and then continued. "I tracked their trail out of there. They went south back to the main trail. I could only guess they went on through Cedar Shoals because of so many having used the trail. But I picked up their trail again south of the settlement.

"They met some people who had been waiting for them at the Big Shoals. It was a man and woman . . . and I'm very sure it was Mangus McGrivin and his wife—your sister, Verdin."

Everyone was still, eyes wide, as he finished the story. "The big cat was there already. It somehow skirted the trail and the buildings of Cedar Shoals. It crossed the river and picked up their trail heading west. I soon called the cat back, and we crossed back over the river and came home."

Silence filled the room as minds brooded over this information. Finally, Rob said, "Well, it's clear that McGrivin and Burntthorne know we're here. They've been scouting us out and spying on us. It's just a matter of time before they move against us."

Ambro said, "We can prepare for what is to come, just be careful and watch ourselves, or we could try to find out their plans and move against them . . . wipe them out first." He shrugged, looking at the group for opinions.

At this, Chick spoke up. "I think it unwise to send anyone against them. We should remain vigilant here and post guards, even during the day. Keep someone on patrol, asking our neighbors to report strangers."

Ultimately, the group agreed to follow Chick's counsel, and immediately the men began alternating riding patrol and standing guard duty at night. George and Hope hated to leave at this time of possible attack, but everyone urged them to go on with their plans. They also insisted that Verdin continue his plans to see Anne.

Verdin was especially saddened to leave his friends, but he felt strongly about visiting with Anne. Preparations to leave got underway. With Rob and Verdin's help, Twig converted one of the wagons into a one-horse, two-wheeled cart for the travelers. The canvas top was cut down to fit the cart, with ample material left to completely seal the front and back openings. The cart would serve to transport their personal items and to provide sleeping quarters for the newlyweds.

Faith and Rob were terribly saddened to see Hope leave. They promised to visit as soon as the war situation was over. Hope cried at the prospect of leaving her mother and brother, but her husband was obviously her main focus now. She would follow him to the ends of the earth if need be.

Rob and Verdin spoke quietly before the departure. Rob expressed his complete understanding of his friend's need to go. Besides, who better to help look after his sister and George on their trip back to Charleston? Verdin slapped his friend lightly on the shoulder and said, "Well, brother, we're still like two strong trees. There for a while we had been knocked over—two bent young saplings. But now we've sprung back up with deeper roots to hold us in place, deeper than ever." Rob pursed his lips to contain his emotion at the sentimental words of his dear friend. He would be missed.

Twig presented George with a going away present. It was a perfect replica of a left hand, forearm, and elbow. Carved from cedar, it had a hinged elbow that allowed the arm to be pushed into various positions by George's good right hand. The hinge was tight, so the arm wouldn't just flop but would hold at whatever position it moved to. A leather cuff attached to the wooden arm above the elbow made a snug, secure fit to George's stump. It was held in place by a leather harness that George could wear beneath his clothing.

The captain was overcome by Twig's thoughtfulness and impressive craftsmanship. The fingers even had fingernail indentions!

George immediately took his shirt off and, with the boys' help, soon had his new arm strapped securely to his stump. He put his shirt back on and began practicing moving it around, bending the elbow. He would soon get to where he could quickly manipulate the position of his left with his right, and no one could tell it was an artificial arm. His new wife was just astounded and delighted at how natural it looked, and she was deeply moved by her husband's enthusiasm about it. It seemed to put confidence back into George—something he'd lost along with his arm. She sensed the device made him feel almost complete . . . a whole man again.

They left early in the morning about a month after the wedding. Those staying behind watched sadly as the three went out of sight down the trail. George drove the cart sitting beside Hope, his horse tied to the back. Verdin rode a little ahead on his dapple gray mare.

# Chapter Sixteen
## THE CAVERN TAVERN AND ROCK HILL SPRING

For some time, Ambro and Chick had been talking with the others about having their own cabin. They were much more accustomed to living by themselves after all, and it would give more room in the main house. It would also provide a second place of defense, which Rob had admittedly been pondering for some time.

Nearly due east of the main house just above the Etoho River was a small steep hill. It was nearly flat on top with an outcropping of rocks on the summit. One of the rocks was very large and flat, protruding over the east side of the hill with a large opening under it. The cavern was about twelve feet high and about thirty by forty feet inside. This had been known to the Indians centuries ago because the ceiling had been smoked by many campfires. Stones and ashes were still in the cavern from old fires. Spear points and arrowheads of stone were scattered about.

Across the floor of the cavern was a long narrow stone, about three and a half feet high, one-third of the way into the cavern. It looked like a bar in a tavern, so they began calling it the Cavern Tavern. The opening was on the east side toward the river. It was a thirty-foot sheer drop down to the riverbank. The steep sides were the east and north sides, but a shoulder more gently descending ran to the west from the summit. Just below the summit on the southwest side was a small spring. The stream from it ran south down the hill before curving east and then northeast to run into the river. Overall, it was a beautiful and unique setting of nature.

This would make a great place to rendezvous as a second refuge in case it became necessary. Ambro and Chick wanted to build a small cabin near the spring, but on the south side of the summit overlooking the new cornfield.

Everyone enthusiastically agreed, and by setting aside two days a week and arranging it where they could all work at one time, the new home progressed rapidly—a humble, one-family cabin. Twig, Ambro, and Chick agreed on a twenty-by-twelve-foot structure with a gable roof, a big main room, two small sleeping rooms, and a roofed front and rear porch. There would be a front and rear door, a rock fireplace, two windows in front, two in back, eight-foot walls, and a sleeping loft.

By the middle of December, every shingle had been placed, every rock had been laid, every peg had been driven. The neat, perfectly proportioned, solidly built little log house stood tall and proud among the oaks that grew along the sides of Rock Hill. Ambro, Chick, and their little ones all glowed with pride as they moved their scant belongings inside.

Rob presented Ambro and his family a deed for the home and surrounding acres. The families had all agreed to do it and had sent the deed to be recorded through Henry Etton. They had also written a letter to the new Georgia government declaring that: "Ambro and his family had belonged to British subjects as slaves, and as a consequence of Ambro fleeing from them with his family to gain his freedom and to fight for the Patriot cause, for which he had already yielded invaluable service and was continuing to do so, he should and of right ought to be declared a free man, along with his wife and children." They had further declared that they were sponsors of Ambro McGrivin and his family, and would remain their guardians and custodians as long as any of them should live. Everyone had signed in testimony. In early 1778, Ambro received a letter from the state, and a certificate declaring him and his family all free and therefore able to own land. A receipt for the recorded deed was also enclosed. As long as the British didn't win the war, Ambro and his family were free landowners.

In late May 1777, news came to the farm of the treaty struck with the Cherokee at DeWitt's Corner in South Carolina. The war against the Rebels in that part of the country had gone badly for the Cherokee. As a result, they lost most of their land east of the mountains. The Cherokee in that region began to trickle south and west, joining their brethren along the west side of the Chattahoochee and along the Hatawwah farther west. More and more would come, swelling the size of the towns already there, and even pushing the Creeks farther south to build new towns of their own.

Then as Christmas hovered just a few weeks away, the good news of General Burgoyne's surrender to American forces up north in late October reached their part of the world. Everyone was pleased by this news, in spite of the news of Washington's tough going against the other British army.

What the year 1778 would bring remained to be seen. Hopefully, good news would reach them from the Wollostons and from Verdin in Savannah. What they did know for now was that things were going well at the farm, which they now called Cedar Haven Farm. They remained on guard, but so far no attack. Ambro and his family were finally settled in their new home. Rob and Hannah were expecting a baby, as were Twig and Louisa. Then four days after Christmas, just before the New Year, Uncle Jonathan's wife, Mary, passed away. Aunt Mary had become sick and feverish, dying after ten days of nursing and caring that couldn't deter the march of death.

From the front porch of Ambro and Chick's house, the big house could be seen about three hundred yards to the west. Rob and Twig spent a little time there each week firing the two huge rifles that Twig had crafted and outfitted with telescopes. The two guns were impressive. They set up targets consisting of boards, chunks of logs, gourds, and pumpkins. They both became rather good at hitting the targets sitting to the left of the big house. Rob could hit a gourd on top of a log eight out of ten times.

But they limited their firing now. The ammunition was not easy to make, so they conserved it. There may well be a time soon when they could be called into service, and there was no reason to waste the carefully made projectiles. Rob and Twig were enthusiastic about the rifle's effectiveness. They could hit targets accurately that only artillery could hope to reach. What a weapon!

Mornings were cold, and thick frost sparkled in the sunlight on the big grassy field. In a little clearing southwest of Ambro's house, on a little shoulder of the hill just above the trail, was Aunt Mary Loxley's grave. The white cross Twig and Ambro made could be seen standing at the head of her rock-covered grave.

There still had been no word from Verdin or Capt. George Wolloston and Hope, or from Uncle Jonathan and Rob's father. Meanwhile, the folks at Cedar Haven Farm maintained their vigil, as they were sure the Burntthornes and McGrivins were gathering for an attack.

The winter days seemed to drag by, though they were filled with farm activities: caring for the animals, killing and curing hogs, beef, and deer, cutting, gathering, and hauling firewood, milking the goats and cows, spinning, weaving, sewing, churning, pounding corn into meal, cooking, cleaning, clearing more ground, cleaning and repairing the barn.

Twig had discovered the spring west of the house was actually higher than the ground on which the big house stood. Using some huge bamboo canes, he devised a way to burn out the sections inside the cane poles. He then slid the smaller ends into the larger ends and thus connected the hollowed-out bamboo poles into water carrying pipes. This brought fresh spring water to the end of the pipe right at the bottom of the steps behind the house. The water for cooking, drinking, and bathing could be caught in containers right at the end of the bamboo pipe. The excess water was caught in a wooden trough, which then had a bamboo pipe to take the runoff into the little South Creek below the house.

A similar system was found to work at the north spring above the barn. Twig installed the bamboo pipes to run into a trough from which the penned livestock could drink.

February brought snow and cold, but it also brought two new precious babies. Rob and Hannah's firstborn was a little girl, and Twig and Louisa's little girl soon followed. Both couples were overjoyed with the new babies, both deciding to turn to the Good Book for names. Rob and Hannah's little girl was named Esther Lysbeth Glynne, and Twig and Louisa chose Junia Anne Hayven, after both her mother and sister. Over time, Esther's nickname became Esbeth, and Junia came to be called JuneAnne, which sounded much like her dead Aunt's name, JenAnne. Louisa often remarked how much the baby reminded her of her late sister.

In spite of the happiness and contentment felt by the families, there was underlying tension in the air. The war news was not disastrous nor was it uplifting. Washington's army was hanging on. Still, the British were capable of landing troops anywhere to seize cities up and down the coast. It was like waiting for a hammer blow to come but not being sure where or when.

There were stories of small raids and attacks by the Cherokees and renegade Creeks. A feeling that spring might bring more serious raids and attacks from that quarter permeated the thoughts of the settlers.

Still trying to remain on the alert, Rob and one other man sometimes rode patrol on the trails and paths around the Cedar Shoals area. So far, nothing was out of the ordinary—at least that had been noticed either by them or by any neighbors.

# Chapter Seventeen
## THE BATTLE AT CEDAR HAVEN FARM

T he tension soon lit up with frightening rapidity. Rob had been on self-imposed patrol and guard duty one night in late March. He usually stayed mostly focused on potential threat out of the west, which was reasonable, since enemy territory lay mostly in that direction. But for some reason on this particular night, he decided to cross the Etoho River a little south of their land and scout toward some farms that lay to the east.

He had taken to wearing long deerskin breeches, over which he drew on knee-high moccasin boots. They looked like moccasins laced up the front, but they had hard soles. He and Twig had made several pairs, even some for the womenfolk. He wore a long sleeve linen shirt, laced up to the throat, over which he wore a deerskin waistcoat tied with deerskin thongs down the front. Over this, he wore a knee-length deerskin coat. This coat was buttoned to the waist only, so it could be worn while on horseback. Over this, he wore his shot pouch, powder horn, and a wide leather strap, from which his leather scabbard knife was suspended. His head was covered with a simple deerskin hat, the brim curled up on the sides to form a point in the front, and curled up in the back as well.

Rob had his rifle butt propped on his right thigh, and his right hand gripped the barrel up high, pointing into the air. His trusty longbow and quiver of arrows were across his back.

Walking his horse in the pale light across the shallow river, he followed a faint path made by cow or deer, which went east, away from the river. He could see quite well in the muted darkness, something he noticed was much more pronounced after the head wound at Breed's Hill.

It was cold enough this evening that he could easily see his own breath and that of his horse. He slowly skirted around the residence of one farm, where everything looked fine. Smoke curled lazily from the chimney and he could hear the horses clomping their feet in the barn. The dogs were asleep under the porch, and he was far enough away to not disturb them.

He passed quietly on to the east with the thoughts of going on to the next farm about two miles away. About halfway there, he sensed a change in the air. A feeling of danger, evil, and death came upon him, making him shiver as the hair stood up on his neck. His senses went on high alert; he thought he could smell blood in the air.

Fighting the urge to turn around and flee, he decided to further investigate, to see if this feeling of dread was justified or not. He checked his rifle, softly put his heels to his horse, whose manner had changed as well. Apparently, the animal sensed the change in his rider, and the animal seemed to glide quietly and cautiously along now, ears standing up.

Approaching the next farmhouse, Rob moved from the path into the trees to the left of the path and up the slight rise. Approaching from the north, he steered his horse into the small stream that ran down the gentle slope toward the house. The stream had trees on each side, most of which were pine, and their limbs overhung the stream. Stooping low over his horse's neck, Rob could clearly see the back and sides of the house and the surrounding area. In a few seconds, he saw dark figures moving silently around the house, and then he heard screams and muffled voices from inside the house.

There were no gunshots, no fires. Rob couldn't see any more movement around the sides or back of the house. Everyone seemed to be in front of the house, out of his line of sight. Moving slowly and quietly to his left, Rob changed his position to the slight rise to the left of the house.

Once there, he could plainly hear the sounds coming from the front— people being beaten with rifle butts, muffled screams. Finally, he reached a point where he could see through the trees to the front of the house. What he saw filled him with rage and trembling. The farmer and his sons had been stripped and were being beaten with gun butts, sticks, and fists. The attackers were being careful to inflict painful, torturing blows, but making sure their victims were not knocked unconscious. The farmer's wife and teenage daughter had their hands tied around the posts of the front porch, and they were screaming and flailing about. Finally, the men were thrown out into the yard, blood streaming from hideous wounds all over their bodies, and strung up by ropes to tree limbs, where they hung by their ankles. While still alive, they were scalped and their bodies mutilated. Then their killers began throwing knives, tomahawks, and spears at their bodies, until they hung still, dead and soaked with blood.

The renegades then turned their attention to the two women. They were thrown into the yard near where the men hung, where they were scalped and killed in the same manner as the men. The bloody frenzy of stabbing and jabbing continued long after all of them were dead.

The killers then quietly regained their horses and weapons and stood over their victims for a few minutes. Rob sensed these weren't a few drunken warriors on a killing frenzy. These were sober, cold-blooded, methodical killers . . . on a mission.

Slipping away undetected, Rob made it back to the trail and headed west, riding hard. When he got to the next farmhouse, he flew into the yard, tied his horse to the rail, and started pounding on the door. In a matter of seconds, the farmer yelled a challenge from inside the door. Rob identified himself and told the farmer what he had seen. At once, the door was opened, and the farmer began shouting frenzied questions at Rob. Rob stopped him with a firm instruction: "Get your family to my house NOW! You've got no time to bring anything! Get your horses and run to my place. Hurry!"

Rob then sprang back into the saddle and was off for Ambro's. He crossed the river and sprinted across the new cornfield, which was waiting for the next crop. Up the curving steep trail, he galloped to the house, yelling for Ambro and Chick all the way.

Ambro met him on the porch, rifle in hand.

Out of breath, Rob managed, "Come on, Ambro. We've got no time to lose."

Ambro held up his hand, urging him to calm down and explain in detail what he had seen.

Ambro listened to the horrific news, then said, "Did you see Oden or McGrivin?"

Rob closed his eyes to concentrate. He shook his head, saying, "No! No, they were not there!"

"That means they are with another part of their whole war party. They may be waiting to ambush you at the big house." Ambro's voice was low and trembling.

Rob shivered at the words. The thought of those bloodthirsty savages being at Cedar Haven already made his blood run cold. And the farm family he had just warned . . . they might get there and be ambushed before he could do anything to prevent it!

As if in answer to his thoughts, shots rang out in the river bottom just south of the new cornfield. The collective sounds of galloping horses, screams, thuds, and gunfire filled his ears. Chick came to the door then, and she suddenly gasped, looking back across the river. Flames could be seen leaping up in the darkness where the farmer's house stood. Other smaller flames also appeared as the outbuildings were torched.

Rob started off the porch to get back on his horse, but Ambro stopped him. "No good that way!" he said. Turning inside to Chick, he ordered, "Get the little'uns to the Tavern Cavern, quietly, and take the guns and ammunition we've talked about."

He ran inside for the rest of his clothing. When he came back out, he shouted to Rob, "Follow me!" He ran on foot to the spring above his house, out the ridge of the hill, and west above the north creek. Rob followed like a shadow.

They ran over a mile in the woods without stopping. The eastern sky was getting a slight rosiness as they neared the spring above the barn. They had been running as quietly as possible but apparently not quietly enough. Someone fired at them from the barn, and they hit the ground, unharmed but shaken. Suddenly, war shouts and muzzle flashes erupted around the house on the west and south sides.

Rifle fire immediately answered from the house windows, and the night was alive with gun flashes from the house, the woods, and the field to their left. Ambro and Rob counted the flashes from the ensuing firefight and estimated there were only about ten of the enemy there.

*** 

Twig had been uneasy that night himself. He finally went to sleep but woke up about an hour before daylight when the big cat suddenly growled and sprang for the door. He stood at the front door of the cabin listening. Checking the bars on the doors, Twig awakened everybody with quiet instructions to take their weapons to their assigned windows. Quickly slipping into his clothes, he went to the front door and uncorked the peephole. Making sure no one was there to poke him in the eye, he looked out but saw no one. He let the big cat out the door and then slipped out himself to lie behind the railing. He then noticed figures moving in the shadows, taking up positions around the front of the house. One figure began moving toward the barn.

Twig watched the shadowy figure of the man disappear into the barn. Then he saw briefly the profile of a bobtailed cat slipping through the grass.

All was quiet for several minutes, except the beating of Twig's heart. Suddenly, the sound of gunfire toward the river broke the momentary stillness. For several minutes sporadic shots were heard, then silence again. Twig rolled to the door of the house and, once inside, he bolted the door and tried to think. He guessed that the gunfire to the east may have had something to do with Rob. After all, he was out there somewhere on patrol. One thing was certain, this was finally the attack everyone had been fearing and dreading.

Those inside the house peered through the cross-shaped firing holes in each of the thick board shutters covering the windows. Twig moved from each person inside the house, checking rifles, whispering words of encouragement.

Another single rifle shot coming from the direction of the barn rang out. A short silence, then shots came from the front and west side of the house. Shots from the big house answered back.

Meanwhile, Rob and Ambro decided to eliminate the attacker in the barn because he was obviously the only one there, isolated from the others. Suddenly they heard a loud snarling from the big cat, and a man screamed, but it was only a half-scream. The terror-filled sound died midway. Rob looked at Ambro, and they knew. Never mind the lone attacker in the barn, thanks to Ambro the big cat.

Slipping quickly through the trees, they gained the back porch and started yelling for Twig to let them in. He heard them and opened the rear door, quickly closing and bolting it behind them. Rob quickly told everyone what had been happening, then gave firm instructions. "There's twenty more of these murdering devils on the way, so watch your powder and lead. Don't fire just to be firing. Shoot to kill when you have a target!"

The sound of galloping horses came to their ears just then, and the sound of gunfire from outside increased, the bullets thudding into the thick walls, doors, and windows harmlessly.

Ambro, Rob, and Twig conferred in the great room. They had to eliminate the enemy one by one if they had any chance at all. Outnumbered with no outside help to come, they had to somehow kill enough of the enemy to cause them to withdraw.

Hannah suddenly yelled, "They're burning the barn!"

Flames shot through the roof of the barn, illuminating the grassy field and the big house. "Now they're burning all the wagons," she yelled. And looking through the firing slots, everyone could see all five of the canvas-covered wagons engulfed in flames, livestock running away toward the river.

Those attackers on horseback, fresh from their killing frenzy at the river, charged the house. They were almost to the porch when five gunshots rang out from inside the house. Instructed by Rob on how to choose targets so they wouldn't shoot the same one, those in the house fired on his command.

The volley stunned the attackers, and as they turned to seek cover, two more shots rang out from Twig's pistols. Two more fell off their horses, and just like that, the enemy had lost seven men.

The sun was shedding more and more light on the scene as dawn broke finally. The burning barn and wagons lit up the surrounding area, more to the defenders' advantage. Rob was at the window in the great room facing south, and he noticed three figures huddled together, almost out of gunshot range, next to the path leading up to the house. He yelled at Ambro to take a look. "Do you see them?"

Ambro nodded, hollering over the din of rifle fire, "The one in the British army uniform is Oden Burntthorne. The other two are the McGrivins: Mangus, my cousin, and his wife, Sylvia . . . Verdin's sister!"

They looked at each other in shocked sadness. To think Verdin's own sister was actually here taking part in this . . . it would break his heart.

Even as they watched, the three figures moved a little closer to the house and fired shots at the front door and windows, trying to hit the firing slots. Ambro quickly took aim and fired at Oden, but the devil was on the move just in the nick of time, and the shot missed.

Oden yelled at some of the others in front, and they began moving to the west end of the house, which was dominated by the huge rock fireplace. There were no doors or windows with firing slots there.

Twig at once bounded to the big fireplace, holding two pistols, and yelled, "Throw a blanket over the fire!" The fire's coals were low, being banked for the night. Hannah was quick to respond, grabbing a blanket off the bed and throwing it over the coals. This temporarily stopped most of the heat and smoke, and Twig's skinny frame soon disappeared into the chimney.

Twig suspected the intention of the enemy was to gain access to the roof by climbing the stair-stepped shoulders of the chimney. One of the renegade Creeks was halfway up when Twig raised up out of the chimney and fired point blank at his face. Another one was just starting up the other side when he heard the report of Twig's pistol. Thinking he had the advantage of an adversary with an empty gun, the warrior kept coming, only to be shot in the top of the head by Twig's other pistol. Though he didn't fall off the rocks, he slumped, face down, dead and unmoving.

Twig ducked back down into the chimney as shots were leveled at him. One sent his hat flying and parted his hair. The others bounced harmlessly off the rocks.

Quickly changing tactics, Oden had his followers move on around behind the house. Now the house was encircled by approximately twenty-three of the enemy.

Faith, Rob's mother, suddenly screamed as one of the murderers grabbed her rifle barrel, trying to yank it through the narrow firing slot, but it wouldn't go.

Twig had slid back down the chimney, and when he heard Faith scream, he ran down the hallway where she was frantically trying to maintain control of the rifle. He stuck his loaded pistol into the firing slot and fired. Immediately, the hold on her rifle was released, and she pulled its barrel back inside. Looking out, they saw a Creek clawing at his throat, which was gushing blood, his eyes bulging in horror. He fell backward, sprawled over the steps. A moment later he stopped clawing, and his body twitched a few times until he lay still, staring upward, bloody hands at his gory throat.

According to Rob and Ambro's count, that left twenty-two murdering savages. The enemy all seemed frustrated at not being able to breach the defense of the house and were disgusted at the number of their casualties. They were firing spasmodically from all around the house now, but more cautiously, being careful to not expose themselves.

Oden Burntthorne and the McGrivins were behind the little roofed area that was Twig's workshop. They added more lead to the attack, firing at a door or window and trying to hit the firing slot and defender behind it. The shop and smokehouse were about a hundred yards away from the big house.

Louisa, Hannah, and Faith defended the front, back and end wall of the eastern portion of the house. Twig, Rob, and Ambro defended the other end of the house in the great room, running from side to side, checking on the women from time to time.

Meanwhile, back at Tavern Cavern, Chick was beside herself with anxiety. She had quickly carried the young children to the hideout, trying to leave no tracks. Then she hurried back to their house and watched from the porch as the drama unfolded below her.

She saw the flames from the barn and wagons and heard the firing and gun flashes. She opened one of the boxes containing one of Twig's big rifles with the telescope attached. Propping the rifle on the porch railing, she looked through it as the sun began creeping up the eastern sky. She counted the number of enemy attackers and stomped her feet in frustration. She had to do something! She couldn't fire the big rifle from here. That might send a contingent of the enemy, against which she had no hopes of defending herself. But maybe she could get help.

She ran back to the cavern and told the kids where she was going. The older ones nodded bravely as little Lily, less than a year old, slept soundly at their feet. Matthew, who was nearly eight, sprang up as his mother turned to leave. "Ma, you can't go," he shouted. "It's me that has to go because Luke and Lily need you, and you can shoot and load better than me!" He blurted this out with his eyes glowing as he stood in a serious stance, shoulders erect, feet apart, hands on hips.

His mother considered this, then nodded. He was right. Besides, he could ride better and faster than she. It broke her heart to send him on such a grown-up errand, and she cried as she watched him run to the cabin to jump astride Rob's big horse and start down the trail.

Matthew took it slowly at first until the horse got to the bottom of the hill. Then he cut through the trees to the river. Once in the shallow water, he turned south until well past South Creek. Then he turned southwest through the woods for a mile and a half until he came to the road to Cedar Shoals. Then he turned the horse toward the settlement and let it open up while he hung on for dear life. The horse ran in an all-out sprint for a few hundred yards then settled back into a long-distance canter.

***

In the meantime, Verdin Girard was on his last leg of the journey home. His letter informing everyone back at the farm that he had seen George and Hope safely to Charleston never reached them, unbeknownst to him. His letter telling them of his visit with Anne and his pending departure from Savannah never reached them either.

He had camped at the Big Shoals before arriving in Cedar Shoals the next morning on horseback with a packhorse behind him. It was about an hour after sunset when he approached Henry Etton's trading post. Henry was already up bustling around and whistling softly under his breath. He noticed Verdin riding up to the front door and stepped out onto the porch to greet him. They spoke cordially for a bit, Verdin telling him a little about his trip to Charleston and Savannah. Henry asked about the latest news and commented that he hadn't seen anyone from Savannah for nearly six weeks and hadn't got any letters either.

Just then, a horse could be heard approaching in a lope from the north. Looking up, they saw little Matthew waving at them frantically. They stood spellbound until he pulled the horse up and started yelling, "The farm is attacked! People are shooting at the house, and they burned the barn and wagons! Ma says get help and hurry!" With that, he turned the horse and was gone.

Grim-faced, Verdin looked at Henry and said, "See what you can do to get some folks rounded up. I'm going to hurry on up to the farm." He sprang into the saddle and pounded up the road after Matthew. He heard Henry yelling to rouse his sons as he rode off.

Rob's horse began to show signs of fatigue after nearly fifteen miles of cantering to the trading post, but the eight-year-old on his back refused to let up with just fifteen miles to go. Thankfully, the horse obliged, though Matthew was aware not to push too hard. He sensed Verdin would not be far behind.

Verdin urged his horse harder and soon had the little boy in sight. He eased up on his own mount as he noticed the boy was not pushing hard. When Matthew turned off into the woods to skirt the big grassy field, he turned and gestured for Verdin to follow. They slipped through the woods and up the river in no time and soon were racing up to Ambro's house on the hill. They could hear gunfire to their left.

Chick was jubilant over seeing Verdin and her boy. She tried to explain to Verdin what she knew so far, while hugging him and jumping up and down. Matthew went scurrying back to the cavern to look after the other two little ones and to tell them about his ride. Verdin listened to Chick while he grabbed the rifle and looked through the scope. She told him her fear about firing from here and Verdin nodded. "You were right not to, but now I'm here. Maybe together we can make a difference. Help should be on the way soon as well!" He told her about Henry hopefully gathering up some reinforcements.

They loaded the big rifles and took up positions to survey the scene below through the telescopes mounted on the long barrels. "All right, Chick, let's give it a go. You pick out a target, and I'll choose another. The wind is in our face, so no need to adjust for wind."

Chick squinted through the scope, then said, "I'm trying to hit the big fellow by that lone tree right in front of the house."

Verdin looked to the other side of the house and saw one figure firing and reloading from behind the smokehouse. He said, "I've got one behind the house. Don't forget to aim a little high and squeeze the trigger. You count to three, and we'll fire."

"All right," she said, then, "One, two, three!" They fired together, and the roar of the guns was terrific in their ears. The smoke blew back in their faces as they kept their eyes on their targets. Chick's victim had been standing, pointing his rifle alongside the tree toward the house. The bullet struck him in the right torso, knocking him to the left and to the ground, as if kicked by an angry horse.

Verdin's target had been propped up against the back of the smokehouse, loading his rifle. The huge bullet hit him in the head, which blew up like a watermelon. Red gore and bone fragments flew everywhere, and the man's body and rifle fell immediately to the ground.

Verdin didn't know it, but that left twenty murderers still to be dealt with. Luckily, none of the other attackers had seen the shots from over two hundred yards away or had seen their targets fall. He and Chick pulled their weapons back and started reloading.

Back in Cedar Shoals, Henry and his sons soon had ten people armed, mounted, and pounding their horses up the road toward the farm. If the defenders could hold out, the odds would be more even.

Verdin and Chick once again sighted through the scopes searching for good targets. As they looked, one painted warrior ran around the house from the front, keeping next to the wall and stepping up on the stoop next to the door in the east wall. This was where Faith was stationed; the dead body of the savage that had grabbed her rifle earlier was still sprawled on the steps.

Faith had stepped back to load her rifle, leaving the firing slot uncovered. The red man jammed his rifle in the slot and looked in. Faith immediately dropped to the floor when she saw the barrel. The painted face could not see her, but he could see another woman standing in the back corner bedroom with her back to him. He swiveled his gun barrel to the right and pulled the trigger.

It was the last thing he did on this earth. Verdin's bullet hit him in the chest, tearing into his heart. The impact of the bullet knocked him hard left into the door, and his dead body ricocheted onto the steps across the dead body already lying there.

Nineteen to go.

Chick's new target was an Indian firing from one knee at the house. She let loose the bullet, and it hit just in front of the Indian's eyes, into the oak tree. The bark and bits of oak splinters blasted his face and knocked him backward. Though dazed and bloody, the savage was still in the fight. He quickly looked around for the source of the shot, focusing to his right toward the grassy clearing and the trees on the right side of it, but not up the hill.

Verdin's last shot had been a second too late to save the victim of the red man's last bullet. The bullet entered Hannah's back, passing clear through her heart and that of her nursing baby. She had stooped down to pick up the hungry, fretting little girl and was standing there a moment, her loaded rifle in her right hand, as she held the nursing baby in the crook of her left. When the bullet struck, she slowly sank to her knees, carefully keeling over on her left side as if to keep from falling on the infant. Hannah's rifle fell against the wall, butt on the floor, still loaded, ready to fire.

Faith didn't know why the attacker had gone away from the door. She ran to the firing slot and peeped out to see two bodies now lying on the steps. She quickly pulled the block of wood down to cover the firing slot and looked to her rifle to reload it. In the melee, she didn't notice Hannah and the baby on the floor. In fact, it was a few minutes before they were discovered.

Louisa was firing from the window in the front room when a bullet came through the firing slot. It gouged a groove in the left side of her neck and sent her staggering backward. She cried out in pain, and Faith rushed to her side. She reassured the dazed young lady it was nothing serious while she grabbed some strips of cloth to bandage the superficial wound.

Faith's rifle was leaning against the wall, loaded, and suddenly Louisa grabbed it and fired. A painted face was peering at them through the slot, and the man was just getting ready to stick his rifle in when Louisa's shot tore through his eye and out the back of his head.

Eighteen attackers left.

Oden Burntthorne was furious. The surprise attack in the dark with so many men should have worked quickly. Instead, it had turned into a long, drawn-out gun battle. Something needed to be done quickly. He had no way of knowing that the true object for this whole affair lay dead with her infant child inside.

Oden motioned for Mangus, who crawled to his side. Oden spat, "Burn the house, Mangus!" Nodding his head in confirmation, Mangus returned to where Sylvia was firing and reloading and told her what Oden wished. She pointed at the barn to their left, which was still burning, the roof caved in.

Staying among the trees behind the smokehouse and around the spring, Mangus ran to the barn. He was able to snatch some burning pieces of wood from the hot, flaming wreck of the barn. Faith saw him from her position at the east door and fired at him. He was moving rapidly so as to get what he needed quickly and retreat from the heat. The bullet hissed harmlessly by.

Faith dodged into the room to her left to keep her eye on the running figure. She was going to yell at Hannah to shoot him when she noticed Hannah and the baby lying on the floor. Immediately, she knew they were dead. She screamed in anguish, flinging herself down by their side. "Rob!" she shouted repeatedly, her voice cracking.

Rob came running at once, and as he entered the door, he saw his mother kneeling over his loved ones. Grief overcame him, and he crumpled to the floor by his sweet wife and precious little girl. Sobs of grief and pain rose from his heart and soul as he tried to pull the two loved ones to him. He could not believe that they had been taken from him after such a short time together. His body shook in agony and despair.

Verdin had spotted the figure running to the barn through the scope. Watching him grab up the burning firebrands, he knew what the man was up to. It would be next to impossible to hit the target moving from left to right, but if the man turned to run in a direction nearly straight away, it might be done. He kept him in the sights.

He yelled at Chick to watch the man at the barn. She had just reloaded and propped the long gun barrel on the porch railing. She got the figure in her scope and muttered aloud, "Mangus McGrivin!"

Verdin's skin prickled at the name—his sister's husband! As he watched, Mangus reached the North Creek and turned toward the spring.

The recoil of the rifle was nearly as bad as the bullet that ripped through Mangus's back, but Verdin didn't mind. The man stumbled and fell face forward, landing on the burning sticks. He thrashed about a few seconds, as though trying to escape the burning, and then lay still.

Verdin pulled back and began to reload. Chick continued to look through the scope, trying to find a target, when she saw movement in the vicinity of the spring near where Mangus had fallen. As she watched, Sylvia appeared clearly in the scope, looking for her now dead husband. Chick saw her continue on toward the spot where he lay and saw the look of horror and grief come across her face when she saw him. The dead man's hair and clothing were beginning to smolder.

As though in a trance, Sylvia walked slowly toward the smoking body, her rifle still held at the ready, and stood over the body. Chick fired. The bullet went through Sylvia's body, entering just below her sternum and severing her backbone. Sylvia staggered backward, dropping her rifle. Her knees buckled, and her back hit the ground. She stared at the sky for several minutes while she bled to death, unable to move. Chick shook her head sadly. Such a sweet, pretty girl gone so horribly wrong. Why did it have to be?

She laid her head over on the rifle and said quietly to Verdin, "I just killed your sister."

For a moment, there was a terrible silence. She raised her head to look at Verdin, who was just sitting there with his head bowed. Without looking up, he said in a soft voice, "Don't worry 'bout it. It had to be done. She took up with some very bad people and turned against her own. She sold her soul to the devil. She's better off dead."

He shook his head slowly, filled with remorse for what could have been. Then grimly he took up the rifle and the business at hand. Chick tried to gulp back her tears as she reloaded her rifle.

The firing continued at the house, but the painted warriors seemed to be losing steam. This was a far cry from the easy killing spree of last night.

Oden was feeling this, too, and his patience was really growing thin with Mangus and Sylvia, who were supposed to burn the house. He got up from his concealed position and ran in the direction of the spring to look for them. "Can't follow simple instructions," he muttered between gritted teeth.

Chick and Verdin watched through their scopes as Oden pulled up short at the sight of the dead bodies. His expression was a mixture of horror and dismay, then realization as he looked around him. He stooped down in alarm, looking about just as Verdin squeezed the trigger. The bullet shattered his left forearm and glanced downward to lodge in his upper left thigh. Chick fired, too, but a little late. He had been spun to his left by Verdin's bullet, and her bullet exploded his rifle stock. This sent little splinters flying into his right arm and side. They could almost imagine him screaming in pain as he grabbed his mangled left arm and began hobbling back toward the smokehouse and his horse.

Just as Oden pulled himself into the saddle, he heard the sound of pounding horses approaching on the trail. He held the reins in his bloody right hand, screaming at his men to flee with him. More than ready to oblige, they began rushing toward him.

A group of hard-riding horsemen could be seen crossing the Little South Creek. As they neared the house, the new men began firing at the fleeing attackers. Some of the warriors were able to find their horses and escape on horseback, pulling some of their comrades up behind them, following Oden in the direction of the Ithlobee River to the west as fast as they could.

In the ensuing pursuit, four more of the painted murderers were shot down before they reached the river. Oden Burntthorne escaped with well less than half of his original band. He was shot up to boot. But he still didn't know that the person he had come to snatch from Rob's grasp—Hannah Burntthorne Glynne—was dead.

The group of settlers who had come to the rescue eventually gave up the chase. There were still enough of the fleeing men to be deadly to a pursuing force of equal or even less strength. So they returned to help clean up the slaughter.

The stripped and mutilated bodies of the farm family who had been warned by Rob at the start of the massacre were found below the new cornfield at the river. They had been caught there and slaughtered as they tried to make it to the Rob's big log house. Their farmhouse and barns had been burned to the ground.

The survivors of the fight at Cedar Haven buried their dead just below Aunt Mary's grave, along the trail to Ambro's cabin farther down the hill. Hannah and her baby were buried close to Aunt Mary's grave. Rob would spend long periods of time there, sobbing, remembering the short time they all had together. Hannah's death made a noticeably changed man out of him. He was more serious and grim as he assumed a new kind of leadership role within their group. He became their war chief with a definite goal in mind: track down and kill those murderers.

The cattle, goats, and hogs were all eventually rounded up, and the burned wagons and barn cleared away. The menfolk soon were cutting the timber for a new, bigger and better barn. The neighbors had suggested a barn raising and big dinner to celebrate their survival. Had the raiders not been held up at Cedar Haven and cut to pieces attacking the big house, they might have scoured the countryside murdering and burning out all the homesteads thereabout.

Rob was not much interested in the socializing. He was interested in getting the barn up and then hitting the trail to track down Oden Burntthorne. He intended to put the murderer in the ground if it was the last thing he did. Ambro, Verdin, and Twig understood his feelings, so they began discussing the upcoming pursuit openly with him. The plans began to take shape as the barn was raised and the spring planting was done. It was June 1778, and Rob had grown impatient to leave for his mission, though he knew the work around the homestead had to be completed first.

Finally, the time had come for his departure to Thornewell, for starters. Ambro and Verdin would accompany him, and Twig would remain with Louisa and the others at the farm while the three went to Thornewell.

Rob spent some time at the graves of Hannah and their baby before he left. Then he, Verdin, and Ambro said goodbye to their friends and loved ones. It was a grim and sad farewell. They were going on deadly business. Some or all of the three might not return, but the risk had to be taken. Oden Burntthorne was an animal who needed to be stopped. The trio mounted their horses and headed south, with two packhorses trailing behind. It was three days before the second anniversary of the Declaration of Independence.

# Chapter Eighteen
## MANY THINGS TO CONSIDER

Ambro returned to where Rob and Verdin were waiting for him in the trees, just south of Thornewell. He had suggested he go alone to the slave quarters to garner information, if possible, about Oden Burntthorne's whereabouts.

He learned that Oden had been there up until a week ago with six Creek warriors. His shot-up left arm had been set and healed, although it was mangled and useless. The Creek warriors who remained with him were loyal followers as survivors of the raid. The rest of the Creeks were hostile toward Oden Burntthorne for leading so many warriors to their deaths on the disastrous raid. He had fled north to be among the Cherokee, where most of them were still under the influence of the British and still venturing out on raids against the lone settlers along the frontier. He reportedly had gone to Frogtown on the Hatawwah River.

A lone overseer was all that was left at Thornewell to keep the farm going with the slave labor. Apparently, Oden had no fear of his home being raided and burned. But that was exactly what happened.

Sweeping in immediately after gathering that intelligence, the trio set fire to the house and the big barns. The overseer was out with some slaves and didn't realize what was going on until the smoke and flames were noticeable from afar. Instead of urging his horse toward the fires, he immediately turned tail to run. Ambro cut him off at gunpoint with a not-so-gentle reminder for him to leave with no intention of coming back, or he would be dealt with. The white man, probably in his early forties, left Thornewell forever, never to be heard from again.

They told the slaves they should flee and live their own lives. Oden Burntthorne would not be returning to this place ever again. As Ambro, Rob, and Verdin looked on, the slaves busily gathered foodstuff and their meager belongings. Many of them fled south to live among the Indians in Florida. Others fled to the west to find refuge with the Alabamas, a Choctaw tribe who lived in the Alabama.

Before they left, the three men burned the slave cabins, completing the utter devastation of the Thornewell property. It would never be rebuilt. As the men watched the last of the residents leave for hopefully better pursuits, they considered their options for pursuing Oden Burntthorne.

Ambro knew these trails well, having traveled them often, even as a boy. Those paths led to the heart of the Cherokee Nation, where Oden purportedly now hid. There were many things to consider before following their nemesis deep into enemy territory. Would it be better to wait and find him someday outside of the protection of large numbers of Cherokee warriors?

The men talked quietly among themselves, trying to decide the best thing to do on the whole. "Following Burntthorne into Cherokee territory will not be an easy thing to do," Rob said finally. "We need to go home and speak with the others and make better plans."

Verdin nodded slowly and leaned forward in the saddle to rest on his elbow. "Agreed, and we need to remember the war too." He paused a moment, a glean in his eye. "There might be better things we can do to whip the British than to follow one British officer into Cherokee country."

Rob lifted an eyebrow as Ambro nodded, a half-grin on his face. With that, the three turned their horses toward Cedar Haven with thoughts of the future, and victory, on their minds.

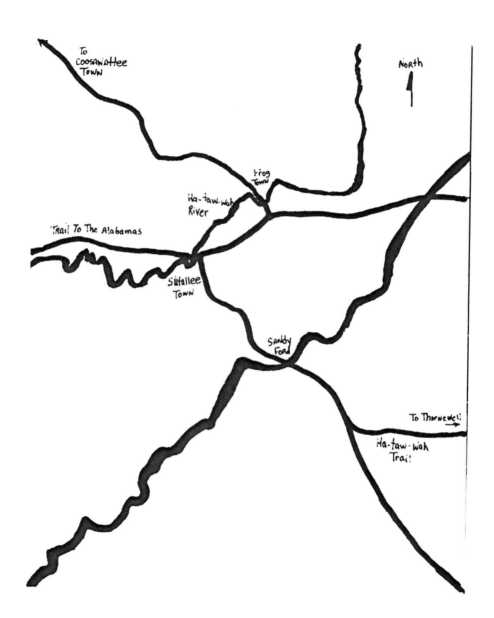

To
Coosawattee
Town

North

Frog
Town

Ha-taw-wah
River

Trail To The Alabamas

Sittallee
Town

Sandy
Ford

To Thornewell

Ha-taw-wah
Trail

# ABOUT THE AUTHOR

David lives in Canton, Georgia, in what was a part of the Cherokee Nation along a small tributary of the Etowah River near the site of Hickory Log Town. Many arrowheads and other Native American artifacts have been found on his land. Family has lived in this county since 1836, prior to the Cherokee removal in 1838.

Born in Atlanta, Georgia, David grew up and attended public schools in Cobb and Cherokee Counties. He is a graduate of Shorter University, Reinhardt University, and the American Institute of Banking.

He became a very enthusiastic student of history, particularly American history, while in elementary school. He has visited several Civil War, Revolutionary War, and War of 1812 battlefields and other historic sites and museums. An avid student of Cherokee Indian history, myths, and legends, he has visited a number of sites of Cherokee Towns.

He was formerly a radio announcer, entrepreneur, banker, and financial services company owner. He grew up riding horses, playing football, swimming, water skiing, singing and playing guitar, and reading. Favorite authors include Jack London, Jack O'Brien, Mark Twain, Louis L'Amour, Zane Grey, and many others.

Current projects include taking pictures of every historical marker pertaining to the Civil War Atlanta Campaign of 1864. He has plans for writing more novels, songs, and a book of short stories.

CPSIA information can be obtained
at www.ICGtesting.com
Printed in the USA
LVOW12*2154010416

481730LV00001B/1/P